REBIRTH

D MCCORMICK

ISBN: 978-1-0686799-0-2 (Ebook)
ISBN: 978-1-0686799-1-9 (Paperback)

CHAPTER 1

Do you ever find yourself wondering when your life will finally take a turn for the better? For what felt like an eternity, my days had been filled with nothing but monotony and disappointment. But today, as I gazed at my reflection in the bathroom mirror while getting ready for the day, something about myself caught my attention. The morning light danced across my features, highlighting the subtle changes that had taken place in me. My once lanky frame now held a sense of strength and vitality, muscles toned and defined beneath my skin. My hair cascaded down to my waist in soft waves of chestnut brown, each strand gleaming with health and radiance. With a faint feeling of uncertainty lingering in the back of my mind, I shrugged it off and finished getting dressed.

As I stepped out of my luxurious hotel room and made my way to meet my Dad at the reception area, I couldn't shake this strange sense that something unexpected was waiting for me just around the corner. The hotel lobby was a grandiose display of opulence and extravagance, with sparkling chandeliers hanging from high ceilings and plush velvet furnishings lining the walls. I spotted my father's familiar figure standing tall and proud amidst the lavish surroundings. A wave of relief and comfort washed over me as I made my way towards him.

He was my rock, my hero, and just the sight of him was enough to chase away any worries or fears that had been plaguing me. At 6 feet tall, he towered over my own 5 foot 5 frame, his broad shoulders exuding a sense of strength and protection. His salt-and-pepper hair was perfectly tousled in a way that only added to his rugged charm. My gaze drifted to the intricate designs covering his forearms - permanent reminders of his love for me and my late mother. Thoughts of her still brought a twinge of sadness, a sensitive topic between my father and I that we carefully avoided discussing. Losing her to cancer had nearly destroyed us both, but my Dad always tried to put on a brave face, even when he thought no one was looking. But I could see the weight of sorrow in his eyes, hidden behind his strong façade. Despite it all, he remained my pillar of support and the most important person in my life.

After enjoying a delectable breakfast at the hotel restaurant, our hearts filled with excitement, we eagerly set off on our journey through Ireland. We navigated through the winding paths, surrounded by emerald green hills and quaint cottages. My anticipation was palpable as I climbed aboard the tour bus, my heart racing like a child on Christmas morning. Surprisingly, it was the off-season for tours, so our group consisted only of my Father, myself, a knowledgeable guide, and an elderly driver. We settled onto the open-air double-decker bus, basking in the warm embrace of summer air as our adventure began. My father's eyes lit up with pure joy and delight, mirroring my own emotions. Our driver exuded positive energy and our enthusiastic guide was brimming with knowledge and passion. As we journeyed towards our destination, our guide enraptured us with enthralling tales of Irish lore. He seamlessly wove together ancient legends and fantastical fairy tales, transporting us to another world with her words.

I was completely and utterly enthralled by his voice. It was rich and velvety, like a warm blanket on a cold night. With each syllable that rolled off his tongue, I felt myself melting and swooning inside. His microphone amplified every note and inflection, drawing us in closer to the story he was about to tell.

"Now here is a tale that will stay with you until your dying days," he began, his voice laced with excitement. "Finn McCool, Son of Cumhull, leader of the Fianna. He stumbled upon all the knowledge in the world, entirely by accident. Can you imagine such a thing?"

He let out a husky laugh, pausing to let the wonder settle in before continuing.

"I suppose it would be like having Google running through your brain," he chuckled again, his laughter infectious as my own grin widened.

"As I was saying," he continued, "there was a magical salmon in the river Boyne that was said to hold all the knowledge of the earth. And our dear Finn was tasked with cooking it for the chief poet Finnegus." He went on to describe how Finn had burnt his fingers while preparing the fish and instinctively put them in his mouth to cool the pain. Little did he know that a small amount of the magic from the salmon had transferred onto his fingertips. A flash of light and suddenly Finn knew everything - past, present, and future.

Our guide paused, letting the story sink in before delving into Finn's thoughts and fears. How could someone go from being a simple village boy to possessing all-encompassing knowledge? Would people believe him? Accept him? Or would they shun him from society? What would it do to his worldview?

As I sat there listening to our guide, completely enamoured by his lilting brogue, I couldn't help but feel like I had found my soulmate at the young age of sixteen (although this feeling would change more than I care to admit). I could have listened to him speak for hours on end, my eyes full of both sorrow and wonder.

In a shaky, melancholic tone, I turned to my father and said, "Just think, if the salmon in the river was real, we might have been able to cure Mum."

Suddenly, a loud, explosive bang echoed through the air, jolting me from my dazed state. The tour bus swerved violently, throwing me against the side of the vehicle. Through blurry vision and head spinning with pain, I could make out our driver's panicked shouts as he struggled to regain control. The metal frame of the bus screeched in protest and seemed to bend in on itself as the two ends pulled in opposite directions. My eyes darted around the chaos, searching for my Dad for reassurance, but all I saw was fear and terror etched onto his face.

The bus tilted to one side and I reached out for my Dad's hand, but it was too late. We were suddenly thrown into a frenzy of motion as the bus flipped over, tossing us around like rag dolls. The impact of my body hitting the window panel knocked me unconscious before I could even comprehend what was happening.

When I finally came to, everything was a blur of pain and confusion. I found myself outside of the wreckage, badly injured and disoriented. As I stumbled towards the twisted remains of the bus, desperately hoping to find my Dad and the others alive and well, a strong hand grabbed my shoulder and held me back. But I hardly registered its presence, all my focus on the wreckage in front of me.

Then something caught my eye - my Dad's tattooed arm dangling from one of the shattered windows. Panic surged through my body as I turned to the person holding me back. They were dressed strangely, but at that moment it didn't matter. All that mattered was getting help for my Dad and the others.

"Please," I begged through tears streaming down my cheeks. "My Dad is in there. Can you help him and our guide and driver? They could be hurt."

But instead of offering assistance, the taller of the two sneered down at me with contempt. "Why the hell would I help them?" he spat. "They are of no use to me or my cause. I caused this wreckage so I could get to you, my pet. Now shut up and stay still while I deal with this."

My mind couldn't comprehend his words. What did he want from me? And why wouldn't he help the others in need? Fear and confusion flooded my thoughts.

Determined to save my Dad and the others, I tried to get up and make my way towards the bus. But before I could take a step, the shorter, shabbier figure grabbed me by the back of my neck and yanked me back down roughly, causing pain to shoot through my body.

"Master said to stay there, runt," he growled at me, the grip on my neck tightening.

Suddenly, a blinding light erupted from the taller man's hand - a ball of flame that seemed to float effortlessly above his palm. In shock and disbelief, I wondered if I had hit my head and was now hallucinating. This couldn't be real...could it?

With a lazy flick of his hand, the man in front of me sent a blazing inferno towards the bus, engulfing it in flames. My heart sank as I realised there were still people inside. Before I could process my thoughts, I turned to face him and screamed with all my might, "Why did you do that?! You monster!". My pleas fell on deaf ears as he simply stared at me with pure fury in his eyes. It was like looking into the depths of hell itself, flames dancing and swirling within his irises.

As I struggled against the larger man holding me by my hair, my body wracked with pain from the rough treatment. But even through the agony, I couldn't tear my gaze away from the taller man in front of me. He growled at me, his voice low and menacing as he spoke through gritted teeth, "I told you to shut up." His breath was hot against my face as he leaned down, his grip tightening around my throat. The threat of suffocation hung heavy in the air.

In that moment, another guttural growl erupted from him before he locked eyes with me once again. "You will learn to obey me or end up like your father," he spat out, his words dripping with malice. Suddenly, his other hand came flying towards me in a powerful backhanded slap, causing stars to explode behind my eyes. He dropped me to the ground like I was nothing more than garbage, disgust etched on his features as he glared down at me.

The force of the blow rattled my senses, sending me spiralling into unconsciousness once again. It was a crushing weight, made even heavier by the events that had led up to this moment. The world around me faded to black as I crumpled to the ground, my father's screams echoing in my mind.

When I came to, it was impossible to tell how much time had passed. My surroundings were blurred and distorted, my thoughts muddled and sluggish. The only thing that cut through the haze was the searing pain at the base of my scalp. Confused and disoriented, I reached up instinctively, only to be met with a rough, calloused hand tangled in my hair.

I jolted awake in terror. This couldn't be happening. It had to be a nightmare. With a desperate scream, I tried to will myself back to reality. But the hand in my hair only tightened its grip, and a low chuckle rumbled in the darkness around me. My captor sneered and pulled me closer, his gravelly voice sending shivers down my spine.

"Look who's finally awake," he taunted. "Master sleeping beauty has awoken from her slumber." His companion laughed along with him, his voice dripping with both excitement and disdain. "Shall I subdue her for you?"

But their glee turned to malice as they discussed their plans for me like I wasn't there. "No Mallory, the first man Said. "Just bring her along. I want her to see what we have in store for her." The other man nodded eagerly, relishing in the power he held over me.

With every ounce of strength I had left, I struggled against their grasp and begged for mercy. "Please! I won't tell anyone about this, I swear! Just let me go!" But the man in front of me merely smirked and shook his head. "I could say I'm sorry and that I'll release you," he said in a sickly sweet tone. "But that would be a lie." His smile widened as he continued, "You see, my dear, I have plans for you. Plans that my employers are eagerly waiting for me to fulfil. So, unfortunately for you, escape is not an option. Not now, not ever."

The horrifying realisation of my situation finally sunk in, causing a surge of panic to course through my body. I doubled my efforts to resist Mallory, thrashing and flailing against his monstrous grip as he held onto my hair with an unyielding grasp. Each time I tried to pull away, he only tightened his hold, causing me to cry out and whimper in pain. The sharp tugs on my scalp felt like he was tearing chunks of my hair out, but I didn't care. All I could think about was escaping from this nightmare. As I continued to scream and fight with all my might, I could feel the tears streaming down my face. My mind raced for a plan as I desperately searched for any way out. And then, a glimmer of hope - I felt Mallory's grip loosen ever so slightly. Without hesitation, I made a break for it in the direction we had just come from, but my legs were slow to respond. It felt like I was running through quicksand as fear and adrenaline coursed through my veins. But despite my efforts, Mallory's hand closed around my arm before I could get far, bringing me crashing to the ground with a painful thud. The frustration and terror inside me only grew stronger as I attempted to lash out at everything around me ...

CHAPTER 2

MALLORY'S HAND SHOT out, striking me with a force that sent me stumbling into a rough and damp wall. As I gathered my bearings, I realised that we were in some sort of tunnel or mine shaft, the air thick and musty. Mallory pinned me to the wall, his iron grip twisting into the fabric of my shirt. "Are you going to behave now, or do I have to hurt you even more?" he snarled, his eyes glinting with twisted satisfaction.

I met his gaze head on and spat the small amount of saliva in my mouth at him. "Go screw yourself, you scumbag!" It was a reckless move, but I couldn't help myself. Without hesitation, he raised his fist and drove it straight into my solar plexus, knocking the wind out of me. I gasped for air, struggling to breathe as tears welled up in my eyes.

Just as Mallory was preparing to strike again, a stern voice cut through the tension. "Enough." Both of us turned to see Mallory's master standing behind us, his presence intimidating and commanding. "Mallory, you know better than to let your anger get the best of you. We need our 'lab rats' healthy if we want this experiment to succeed. I hope you haven't caused too much damage."

"I'm sorry, master," Mallory replied meekly, like a scolded child seeking approval from his parent. If I wasn't so terrified for my life, I might have chuckled at the sight.

Still clutching me tightly in his grip, Mallory began dragging me along as his master led the way. We soon arrived at a solid-looking door that seemed to blend seamlessly into the wall itself. Mallory stopped abruptly, still holding onto me like a rag doll. His master traced something in the air with a glowing finger before muttering an incantation. The door suddenly swung open, revealing a pitch-black room beyond. My heart raced in fear as I was pulled towards the unknown.

As we entered the darkness, I heard the faint sound of metal on stone, like chains being dragged or machinery grinding. But I couldn't see anything in the darkness except for occasional flashes of light from Mallory's master muttering his spell. Suddenly, a deafening roar echoed through the room, causing me to freeze in terror. Mallory laughed at my reaction, taunting me. "Don't be scared of the creature, little one. Fear my master instead."

He dragged me further into the dark abyss, with his master leading the way and continuing his chanting under his breath. Then, in a split second, everything went silent and still. The only sound was the distant rumbling of the door slowly closing behind us. Panic set in as we were plunged into complete darkness, with only the ferocious roar of some beast to keep me company.

I couldn't take it anymore – the fear, the uncertainty, the pain. Tears streamed down my face as I realised that I was at the mercy of two madmen who had something terrible planned for me. Desperately, I tried to wake up from this nightmare, but it was all too real. This was my reality now, and there was no escaping it.

The room was suddenly engulfed in a blinding explosion of light, causing temporary blindness. As my vision slowly returned, I found myself bathed in the warm glow of a brilliant blue fire emanating from strategically placed torches around the room. My lead captor stood before me with an imposing stance, his figure silhouetted against the eerie blue flames.

From behind him, I could make out a chair that seemed to have been plucked straight out of the Middle Ages, resembling something out of a torture chamber. Intravenous poles surrounded the chair, each holding numerous bags filled with unknown fluids connected by tubes to various points on the contraption. Fear and dread filled me as I realised that I was about to become a part of this twisted experiment.

With rough hands, I was thrown into the ominous chair and held down by Mallory while his master cuffed my arms and wrists in metal restraints, rendering me practically immobile. Desperately, I struggled against their grip, determined to resist them even if it meant causing harm to myself. But their hold was too strong, and my efforts were futile. I even attempted to kick out at my captors, hoping to inflict some damage, but it was no use.

Within minutes, I was completely restrained with only my neck and head still able to move. But this small freedom didn't last long as leather restraints were quickly fastened over my forehead and neck, effectively silencing any further attempts at resistance. As I resigned myself to my fate, one last plea escaped me in a desperate attempt to appeal to their humanity: "Please, if you're going to kill me, just do it."

For the first time since being captured, Mallory's boss turned to look at me with genuine curiosity. He brushed stray hairs from my face as he spoke once again. "I have no intention of killing you...yet," he said calmly. "You see, my experiment is almost complete. Just a few more test subjects to survive and I will prove to our lord that his trust in me was not unfounded." Despite my fear and anger towards this man for using people as his guinea pigs in this dank and dark cave, I knew arguing or pleading would be pointless.

"What do you hope to achieve by bringing me here?" I asked, a mix of resentment and resignation evident in my voice. Mallory's boss turned and regarded me with genuine curiosity for the first time. "Very well," he said, brushing some stray hair from my eyes as he spoke again. "I don't want to kill you, well, at least not yet. You see, my experiment is very near completion. Just a few more test subjects to survive, and I will show the lord that his faith in me wasn't misplaced." My heart raced with both fear and disgust at the thought of being used as a mere pawn in this madman's twisted game. But I knew there was no use in fighting against it now. The only thing left to do was wait and see what horrors awaited me as a test subject in this dark and sinister place.

The overwhelming stench of chemicals and decay assaulted my senses as I lay strapped to this tourture device the room seemed to close in on me as I listened to my captors words. My body trembled with fear and anticipation as they prepared to inject me with an unknown concoction. The smell of disinfectant and chemicals filled my nostrils, making me want to gag.

"I am going to start by giving you an IV," he stated calmly, their voice devoid of any emotion. "Or several. The different compounds are going to force a change in your body over days and weeks."

I couldn't believe what I was hearing. This was all some twisted experiment, and I was just a mere subject.

"After every successful course of treatment, I will change the various drugs and compounds," he continued. "And monitor what these multiple things do to you. Most don't survive the first few days of the first treatment. But occasionally, I have subjects that live through several treatments."

My fate was sealed. There was nothing I could do but accept it.

"How long do you think you will last?" He asked, a hint of sadistic amusement in his voice.

But then came the final blow - "I forgot to mention that you will be a plaything for Mallory between your treatment and my other experiments.". It was too much to bear. They had destroyed my life and now reduced me to nothing more than an object for their sick games.

But before I could process this new information, the pain started. Needles pierced my skin in various areas - arms, legs, neck, chest - and fluids were pumped into my body. The burning and freezing sensations sent shockwaves through my veins and muscles, causing me to cry out in agony.

I tried to stifle my screams, not wanting these monsters to revel in my pain, but I couldn't help it. The intensity was unlike anything I had ever experienced before. Tears streamed down my face as I thrashed against the restraints holding me down.

Just when I thought it couldn't get any worse, his final words echoed in my mind. "I hope you survive. I really am looking forward to breaking you." And then they left, leaving me alone with the eerie blue fire of their torches and my own screams as my only company.

As my senses slowly faded, the pain overwhelmed me and dragged me into an abyss of darkness and oblivion. In the distance, I could hear the clinking of chains and the scratching of claws against the cold, rough ground. I struggled to hold onto consciousness, knowing that I was not alone in this place. There was a monster locked away here, just as I was.

But then a voice broke through my thoughts: "Please do not fear me, child." The words echoed in my mind, not spoken aloud but somehow familiar, like a memory or a dream. I tried to respond, but the drugs coursing through my body made it difficult to form coherent thoughts.

"Who... who are you?" I managed to mumble, hoping that whoever or whatever was communicating with me could understand.

"Just stay calm," the voice continued. "I know you're in immense pain, but it will be less agonising if you stay calm and don't panic."

I strained to turn my head and see who was speaking to me, but they remained hidden in the shadows. "I'll try..." I whispered hoarsely.

"My name is Lyn Saar," the voice replied. "And I swear on my blood that I will not leave your side during this ordeal. Your ancestors will give you strength as you endure this cruelty. We will watch over you, little one."

As Lyn finished speaking, I slipped back into unconsciousness, grateful for its temporary respite. But even in these brief moments of clarity, I couldn't escape the agony that consumed my being. My mind was a chaotic storm of suffering, anger, and desperate longing for death. Time became meaningless as I drifted in and out of consciousness; sometimes hours passed, other times it felt like only minutes before the pain returned.

But gradually, the periods of unconsciousness became shorter and less frequent. Each time I woke up to searing pain, my throat raw from screaming, I couldn't help but wonder if this would be the time that the man torturing me had finally let me die. But as each day passed, and I remained alive, it became clear that he enjoyed prolonging my suffering.

I lost track of how many times I woke up to agony, but eventually, there were moments when I awoke to blessed relief, and I wept with gratitude. My sobs echoed in the empty room, my voice hoarse and strained from the countless hours of screaming. And in those moments of peace, I clung to the hope that perhaps death had finally claimed me and that was the only reason why I wasn't strapped into that torturous chair anymore.

My body ached as I pushed myself up, struggling to stand on shaky legs. My surroundings were foreign and unfamiliar, the rough surface of the cave floor cutting into my exposed skin as I fell back down. Disregarding the pain, I desperately looked over my sensitive skin for any sign of injury. "I can't be dead," I muttered to myself. "I shouldn't still bleed if I was dead, and I wouldn't still be here...would I?" My eyes scanned the walls of the cave until they landed on a faint glimmer in the distance - a door. Without hesitation, I rushed towards it, driven by a need to escape this place. If I was alive, I needed to get out and find my father. And if there was even a chance that he was still alive, I had to save him at all costs. The adrenaline coursing through my veins drowned out the pain and fear as I focused on reaching that elusive door, desperate for a way out of this nightmare.

My mind flashed back to the harrowing image of my father's arm hanging limply from the shattered window of our tour bus. The memory fuelled me, pushing me to charge faster towards the door in front of me. I needed to escape this nightmare as quickly as possible. As I neared the door, a faint distortion in the air caught my attention, but I ignored it and continued my sprint. With all my might, I slammed my shoulder into the door, only to be thrown back by a blinding flash resembling the flares used by SWAT teams on TV. I flew through the air, landing roughly 30 feet away on the hard cave floor. The impact knocked the wind out of me, leaving me gasping for breath as I struggled onto my hands and knees. But even as I tried to recover, I couldn't help but scream in frustration, "WHAT THE FUCK? JUST LET ME OUT, YOU PRICKS! YOU'VE HAD YOUR FUN!" My words echoed off the walls, met only with eerie silence. Defeated for the moment, I collapsed onto the floor and curled up into a ball, allowing self-pity to consume me in that dark, desolate cave.

I lost track of time as I lay on the cold, hard floor, my tears drying against my cheeks. My gaze was fixed on the intricate patterns of cracks on the ceiling, but my mind was trapped in a cycle of self-pity and fear. Why did I have to be the one to survive? Why was I stuck in this horrifying place, with no hope of escape?

As I lay there, consumed by my thoughts, I heard the faint sound of claws scraping against the rough rock floor. A chill ran down my spine as I remembered that I was not alone in this dark, dank dungeon. And then I heard it - a voice, whispering into my mind.

"Hello again, little one. Do you remember me?"

My heart raced as panic and confusion set in. Who was this mysterious voice? And why wouldn't they come out so I could see them? Fear and curiosity warred within me as I searched for any sign of movement in the shadows.

With trembling legs, I slowly rose to my feet and strained my eyes to see through the darkness. attempting to pinpoint the source of the mysterious voice. "Enough with this game," I growled, frustration seeping into my words. "If you are indeed working for Mallory and his boss, then stop playing games and get on with your task." I was tired of being manipulated like a pawn on a chessboard. They may have had their own agenda, but I wasn't going to make things easy for them.

But then, as if in response to my anger, the darkness seemed to shift and swirl before me. A figure emerged from the shadows, slowly taking shape before my eyes.

"If it is proof you seek, then allow me to provide it," the figure spoke calmly, its voice deep and commanding. "But let it be known that I have no ties to Jeremiah or that spineless creature Mallory." The figure stepped closer, revealing itself to be a huge and imposing presence, cloaked in an air of mystery and authority. My heart raced as I awaited its next move.

As the sound of chains scraping against the rough cave floor grew louder and louder, accompanied by the crunch and scrape of heavy talons on stone, a chill ran down my spine. I strained to see through the darkness, until suddenly, a burst of eerie blue light from nearby torches revealed a massive dragon before me. Its scales gleamed in the light, reflecting back a sinister glow as it let out a deep, rumbling laughter. My mind reeled with disbelief. "This can't be real," I thought to myself. "Dragons don't exist." But there it was, in all its terrifying glory, speaking to me in my head. Panic set in as I tried to make sense of everything, my murdered father, being abducted and experimented on for who knows how long. Was this what finally pushed me over the edge? Was I having a complete mental breakdown? I huffed and collapsed onto the cave floor, unable to process anymore. And yet, there the dragon remained, watching me with those piercing eyes and speaking words that echoed in my mind

The dragon's voice in my head hissed with amusement, a deep rumbling sound that echoed through my mind. "That was quite the spectacular tantrum, little one," it chuckled, its voice laced with humour and condescension. Despite my fear and disbelief, I couldn't help but feel a slight sense of awe at the creature's powerful presence. And then, as if reading my thoughts, the dragon let out a low grumble that could only be interpreted as laughter. "The nerve," I muttered to myself, feeling foolish for believing this was all a hallucination. "I must be the only person in the world that has their imaginary dragon mocking them." The sound of its laughter filled my head, mixing with the flickering images of scales and fire that danced behind my closed eyes.

The deep rumbling grumble continued, its low growls reverberating through the air. "You can think of a hallucination if it helps you cope with your fear little one." As it spoke, I couldn't help but stare at the creature before me. Despite its intimidating appearance, there was a certain regal beauty to it. Its scales were a mesmerising shade of purple-grey, reminiscent of storm clouds, with a pearlescent shimmer that caught the light. However, upon closer inspection, I noticed that large patches of scales were missing all over its body, revealing raw and wounded flesh beneath. The creature held itself with pride and dignity, but it was clear that it was in poor shape; its claws and horns were chipped and broken, and streaks of dried blood marred its once-perfect hide. One of its eyes had a milky white film over it, giving it a haunting appearance. It was heartbreaking to see such a magnificent creature suffering so greatly. Who could have inflicted this kind of damage on something so beautiful?

Tears immediately sprang to my eyes as I gasped, taking in the sight of the chained dragon before me. Its once proud and majestic form was now marred by cruel mangles on its legs and a heavy chain around its neck. "What happened to you?" I cried out, unable to contain my sadness and shock.

"Little one, do not cry for me. I am but a prisoner," the dragon replied with a gentle voice that belied its massive size. It continued, "I have been held captive here for many years, my power suppressed by these maniacal chains. A hatchling could easily defeat me now."

Feeling helpless and defeated, I turned away from the dragon's sorrowful gaze. I couldn't bear for this magnificent creature to see me cry.

But the dragon spoke again, reassuring me, "No, little one. All hope is not lost. You have survived longer than any other human brought here. Your will to survive is incredible and necessary in this place."

Through sniffles and tears, I managed to introduce myself, "I'm Jessica, but you can call me Jess."

"It is an honour to meet you, Jess. I am Lyn Saar, mistress of the sky and storms," the dragon responded.

Gathering my courage, I asked her for more information about our situation. "Can you tell me how long I've been here and what he has planned for us?"

After a pause, Lyn Saar answered gravely, "You have been here for several weeks now. Most humans who are brought here last only a few days before succumbing to their fate. In all his years of doing this, you are the first to survive being released from the chair." Her words hung heavily in the air, emphasising just how dire our situation truly was.

"I think I know what he is attempting to achieve, but I can't be a curtain. please allow me to explain". I listened to her words, and images of a distant past flooded my mind. "A time when war raged among all the realms - humans, elves, vampires, shapeshifters, harpies, and all manner of fantasy creatures battled for dominance. Even the older species, like the watchers, the dragons, and the elementals, were not immune to the conflict. While some chose to stay neutral, others were forced to defend their borders against those who dared to challenge them.

To combat this constant threat, a solution was devised - the creation of soldiers who could be controlled. The process involved a powerful ritual that combined human soldiers with the blood of dragons and a significant amount of magic. The result was extraordinary - enhanced strength, speed, intelligence, dexterity, longer lifespans, and increased magical abilities. They even gained innate gifts from the Donner of the Blood.

At first, this solution brought peace and satisfaction to all parties involved. But then something went wrong. The details are hazy, but it is believed that a group known as the "blood worriers" rose up and attempted to seize control of all the realms. This led to an unprecedented war that left devastation in its wake.

in response to this chaos, the council was formed - representatives from each species came together to govern and maintain order. However, even they were answerable to a higher power - the watcher council. And in their first act as a united front, they issued an order for the extermination of all blood worriers and banned any further creation of their kind.

The memory of this dark period still lingers in the minds of all creatures, serving as a reminder of what can happen when power falls into the wrong hands.

Jess furrowed her brow, her thoughts fixed on the man who had kidnaped her. The man who may have given her abilities beyond human comprehension. "You think he made me into one of those thing's?" she asked, her voice laced with fear and uncertainty.

"I honestly don't know," Lyn replied, her eyes scanning the room for any sign of danger. "From what I've seen, he can't be doing that, but I can't think of what else it could be. I know he's trying to develop a weapon, but that's all I know for sure."

jess felt a rush of relief at Lyn's words, but it was quickly replaced by a surge of uncertainty. "Wait, you said these blood worriers are stronger than most other things, so I will get stronger too, right?" she asked, her mind racing with possibilities.

The corner of Lyn's mouth twitched into a small smile. "Not that straightforward, little one. Look at your ankle!"

Confused, Jess glanced down at her ankle and saw for the first time a thin silver band encircling it. The intricate markings etched onto its surface glinted in the dim light of the room. Panic rose in her chest as she turned to Lyn with wide eyes. "What's this?"

Lyn's expression darkened. "If I had to guess, it's something similar to what he has on me to stop me from escaping."

Jess took a step back as it dawned on her. She was trapped here, just like Lyn. But she refused to let fear take over. "Okay, that just means we need to be more creative with our escape attempt," she declared with determination in her voice.

A low, menacing growl rumbled from within Lyn as I watched her eyes flash with fury. In a voice that only I could hear, she warned me of Jeremiah's approach. The chains that bound her were pulling her back, preventing her from attacking.But she refused to be silenced, letting out a deafening roar that echoed off the stone walls.

As I turned towards the door, it creaked open slowly and in strode Jeremiah, followed closely by his sleazy lackey Mallory. Their presence made my skin crawl and fear spike through me.

"Oh, look, master sleeping. Beauty is awake," Mallory's voice was sickeningly sweet and full of malicious delight.

Jeremiah sneered at me, his cold eyes gleaming with arrogance. "So it would seem, Mallory."

Mallory giggled to himself, the sound sending shivers down my spine.

"So Jessica, are you ready to be a well-behaved little girl, or are you going to make me punish you?" Jeremiah asked with a sly grin.

I tried to hold onto my confidence and defiance. "Why don't you just let me go and leave us alone?" I blurted out, surprising even myself with my boldness. But Jeremiah recoiled at my words and quickly regained his composure. He took a step towards me, his hand raised threateningly. "You'll learn to watch your tongue," he spat before striking me with the back of his hand across the face.

I stumbled backwards and fell to the ground, pain radiating through my cheek where he had hit me. My vision blurred for a moment as tears welled up in response to both physical and emotional pain.

Meanwhile, Jeremiah formed a glowing ball of purple mist in his hand. With a silent command, he sent it flying towards Lyn who was still struggling against her chains. The mist washed over her body, causing her to let out an agonising roar that shook me to my core.

As the events played out before me, I could see Mallory's twisted joy and amusement in his sickening giggles and claps. My heart broke at the thought of what they were doing to Lyn, a powerful dragon reduced to this helpless state.

"Now Jessica, come with me quietly, or I will be forced to continue hurting your friend," Jeremiah threatened, forming another ball of mist in his hand.

My resolve shattered at the thought of Lyn suffering more, so I sobbed and tried to look obedient as I followed Jeremiah out of the room with Mallory close behind. But inside, I was seething with rage and determination. I would find a way to free Lyn and make them pay for their cruelty.

Just then, I heard Lyn's voice in my mind, urging me to be brave. "Please be strong, my little dragon," she whispered.

"The things I plan to learn from you will change the world," Jeremiah's excited voice brought me back to the present. "You're the first step to realising my dream. If I can unlock how you survived all these years, my research will finally be complete. Nothing in history has ever been as special as you will be."

He led me out of the room and into a different part of the cave, with Mallory following closely behind. With my head down and shoulders hunched in a show of submission, I still tried to take in my surroundings and create a mental map. One day, when we escaped from this place, it would help us get far away from these sadistic men and their experiments on creatures like Lyn and me.

CHAPTER 3

F EAR AND ADRENALINE coursed through my veins as I continued to follow, too afraid to speak up. My eyes darted around, taking note of the downward incline and the twists and turns we were making. As our path seemed to lead further and further into darkness

Desperately, I tried to commit the route to memory so I could make my escape later. But for now, I had no choice but to keep following, trying to appear weak and timid I kept my posture hunched and meek, hoping they would underestimate me. After what felt like an eternity, we finally reached a massive steel door. Its surface was etched with intricate symbols that seemed to glow in the faint light. My heart raced as I wondered what kind of horrors awaited me on the other side. Jeremiah typed in a code on the keypad, his fingers moving with practiced precision. With an unsettling grind, the door slid open, revealing a cloud of dust that momentarily obscured my vision.

I braced myself as we stepped inside, my mind racing with fear and anticipation. What did these psychos have in store for me? The unknown was terrifying, but I knew I couldn't give up without a fight. Steeling myself, I followed behind them into the unknown depths beyond the steel door.

Jeremiah strode into the chamber with a confidence that showed he was at ease in his surroundings. This was a place where he held all the power and control, and it made my skin crawl just being near him. Seeing him so comfortable here only added to my uneasiness, and I hesitated to follow. But Mallory, always eager to please his master, pushed me forward none too gently. "Hurry up, the master is waiting," he sneered. My feet dragged along the cold stone floor as I resisted his prompt to move forward. He grew impatient and shoved harder, causing me to I stumbled towards the centre of the room, my eyes widening as I took in my surroundings. My blood turned to ice as I realised that the operating table placed prominently in the middle of the room was not for traditional medical procedures. Instead, it was surrounded by a trolley filled with sharp scalpels, saws, and other ominous-looking tools I had only ever seen in horror movies.

The walls were lined with shelves upon shelves of specimen jars, each one holding a grotesque display of limbs and organs. Some were recognisable human body parts, while others were unidentifiable mutations. The walls of the chamber were lined with shelves upon shelves of specimen jars, each one holding a different body part or organ preserved in formaldehyde. Some were recognisable, while others were distorted beyond recognition. My stomach churned as I spotted jars containing claws, teeth, and even scales from unknown creatures.

But what horrified me most was the eye displayed front and centre on a pedestal. It could have belonged to anyone, perhaps even Lyn. My mind raced with gruesome possibilities as I fought back a wave of nausea and terror. This was no ordinary laboratory - it was a house of horrors controlled by a madman.

With a frustrated grunt, Mallory shoved me harder, his hands digging into my shoulders as he tried to force me onto the table. The cold stone of the chamber sent shivers down my spine as I resisted his push. "I said move," he growled, his face twisted in anger. "We don't keep the master waiting." I stumbled to the side as he pushed me further into the room, my heart racing with fear and adrenaline.

But then, in a moment of blind courage, I saw my chance and took it. Ignoring Mallory's threats, I bolted towards the back of the chamber where my fellow captive was being held. My feet pounded against the smooth stone floor as I desperately searched for a way out. I followed a narrow path that led upwards, praying that it would lead me to freedom. As I ran, I could feel Mallory's heavy footsteps behind me, but for some reason, he didn't seem to be giving chase.

My mind raced as I wondered why they weren't pursuing me more aggressively. Was it some kind of trap? Or were they simply overconfident in their ability to catch me? But there was no time to dwell on these thoughts; all that mattered was finding a way out.

Suddenly, the path split into two directions and without hesitation, I veered left. My instincts told me it was the right choice and I prayed silently that it would lead me closer to escape. And then, just like a beacon of hope, a bright light appeared at the end of the tunnel. A surge of relief washed over me as I realised that this could be my way out.

With renewed energy and determination, I picked up my pace and sprinted towards the light. But just when I thought I had made it, something struck me from behind with an intense burst of pain. The shackles around my leg glowed with an eerie light and I could feel searing heat spreading through my body. Before I knew it, I was on the ground, my body convulsing in uncontrollable spasms.

The pain was unbearable, and all I could do was scream as tears streamed down my face. I had no idea how long this went on for, but when it finally stopped, I was gasping for air and my whole body was trembling with exhaustion. My throat felt raw from screaming and my cheeks were wet with tears, but at least I had survived. For now.

Jeremiah knelt in front of me, gripping my face tightly between his hands. His eyes burned with a maniacal glint as he spoke to me. "I have allowed you to roam free in my facility, to indulge your desires and run wild. But do not be fooled, little one. You can never escape me. You are mine to control, a mere plaything for my pleasure. And when I am finished playing with you, I will dispose of you like trash." He stood up and dusted off his clothes, looking at me with disdain. "Now, enough wasting time on your foolish attempts at escape. It is time for me to begin my work," he sneered.

I remained still, knowing that resistance was futile. What was the point of struggling against this madman if death was inevitable? But Jeremiah wasn't satisfied with my compliance. "So you refuse to walk?

Very well then," he snapped his fingers and suddenly my limbs became stiff and frozen, locked in place by some unknown power.

With a wicked grin on his face, Jeremiah began to chant in a language I couldn't understand, but it sounded almost musical. Despite my anger and fear, I couldn't help but find it absurdly comical. After a few moments of chanting, he stopped and walked away, leaving me levitating in his wake. This was certainly an interesting way to force someone to follow.

As we made our way back to the cave where I had tried to escape from earlier, I saw Mallory sulking in the corner, his rage barely contained. Jeremiah gestured towards the operating setup and my body floated into place without any resistance from me. I couldn't move or fight back, which only served to infuriate me more. Jeremiah seemed to sense my thoughts and sneered at me. "Even if you could move, do you really think you stand a chance against me?"

As he secured restraints on my arms, legs, hands, feet, and even my neck, I noticed that holding whatever magic he used in place seemed to exhaust him. At least his power was not infinite, giving me a glimmer of hope. I tried to wriggle free from the restraints, but they were tight and unyielding, just like his hold over me.

The deep, rumbling voice of my captor filled the dimly lit chamber, his words echoing off the cold, stone walls. His eyes flickered with curiosity and malice as he pondered aloud, "Now we know the dragon can regenerate, but has it passed that ability on to you?" With a grim smile, he lifted a glinting scalpel and sliced through my filthy clothes, the sharp blade leaving trails of blood in its wake. Each cut sent waves of pain coursing through my body. Methodically, he peeled away the layers of fabric, revealing my wounds in all their rawness. His hands ran over them like a macabre artist examining their latest masterpiece, pressing into the torn skin and urging the wounds to bleed even more freely. I could feel my blood mingling with the grime and filth on the table, creating a sickening pool underneath me. The metallic scent of iron filled my nostrils and made me lightheaded. Every beat of my heart seemed to throb in time with each cut and gash on my body. But despite the agony pulsing through me, I refused to show any weakness in front of this man who seemed determined to push me to my limits.

Mallory's feet bounced eagerly, causing his entire body to shake with excitement. He couldn't contain his giggles as his master leaned in closer to inspect his own handy work, a mischievous twinkle in his eye. The air was tense with anticipation, as if the very ground they stood on held its breath. Mallory's hands twitched with eagerness, waiting to see what his master would do next.

Jeremiah's face was lit up with a frenzied joy as he gazed straight into my eyes. "Yes, they are already healing faster than anything I have seen before," he exclaimed. His voice trembled with excitement as he continued, "Oh, do you know what this means?" But he didn't wait for a reply, too consumed by his own thoughts. "I've done it," he declared triumphantly. "The superiors will be ecstatic. But now, it's time to collect more data." A predatory grin spread across his face as he stepped closer, wielding a scalpel in his hand.

As soon as the cold metal touched my skin, I let out a blood-curdling scream. Ignoring my cries of pain, Jeremiah began cutting deeper and deeper, carving chunks of flesh and muscle from my arms and legs. It felt like an eternity as he worked methodically and relentlessly, his focus solely on obtaining more data.

My screams turned into whimpers long before he was finished. My voice had abandoned me, leaving only the searing pain that engulfed every inch of my exposed injuries. Each passing gust of air felt like hot coals being pressed against my raw flesh. In that moment, all I could do was suffer in silence as Jeremiah completed his brutal experiment.

Excruciating pain wracked my body, reducing me to nothing but a quivering mess. I could do nothing but whimper and writhe in agony, my muscles contracting and spasming uncontrollably. In the dimly lit room, Jeremiah leaned close to my ear and whispered, his voice dripping with sadistic glee. "I hope you've enjoyed this as much as I have. Next time, we'll push the boundaries of your healing abilities even further. We'll see if it's just the flesh that can regenerate, or if you possess the power to heal organs as well," he chuckled darkly, relishing in my suffering. He turned to Mallory who was waiting eagerly in the corner "I'm finished for now.take her back to the holing area And make sure she receives the new solution," he said with a hint of excitement in his voice. "I've mixed in traits from multiple more paranormal specimens, more than what we used in the original batches. Let's see how her body responds to a higher concentration and dosage." With a final order, he strode out of the room, leaving me alone with my torment and thoughts. My body was on the verge of giving up, unable to handle the brutal treatment any longer. As darkness enveloped my mind, I heard Jeremiah's sinister laughter echoing through the room, serving as a cruel lullaby before I succumbed to unconsciousness.

As my consciousness returned, I found myself on the hard cot in the main cavern. Lyn's face hovered above me, her eyes locked onto mine with concern. I tried to sit up, but my body was heavy and sluggish. It was then that I noticed I was completely naked, covered in a thick layer of blood and filth. An IV dripped into my arm, connected to an empty fluids bag. Panic set in as I wondered what substances had been injected into my system. Every inch of my body throbbed and ached, as if I had been beaten with a metal bat.

"Hey Lyn," I croaked, struggling to form words. "How long have I been out?"

"He brought you back two days ago. Honestly, I didn't think you would survive. But I'm glad I was wrong. What he did to you...it's horrific, and I hate that you had to endure it."

"I tried to escape. I made it to the entrance, but I couldn't go any further. The cuffs on my legs triggers something the pain was so intense it dropped me to the floor when he came to retrieve me, He just laughed , like it was all just a game." The memory of my failed attempt at freedom filled me with anger and frustration. How could someone be so cruel and heartless?

Lyn's expression turned grim as she snarled her anger about what had happened was clear. "He enjoys playing with his prisoners. It's sickening." She replied

We sat in silence for a while pondering what our next move might be when lyn spoke in my mind again .the words fell from her like a boulder rolling down a mountainside, heavy and resigned. "Thank you for trying," her voice laced with exhaustion. "We will bide our time. Maybe they will slip up, and we will escape soon." I could hear the desperation in her voice, the hope that was slowly fading away.

"When he took me, he hit you with a spell," I said softly, trying to keep my voice steady. "He didn't hurt you too badly, did he?"

"No, I was fine within a few hours," she replied, but I could see the pain etched on her face. The bruises were still visible, faint but not yet healed.

"I'm assuming it was more of your blood in those bags," I pointed to the empty IV bag. Her blood that had been drained and used to heal me. The thought made my stomach churn.

"It was, but I don't think it was only mine". she said, her voice barely above a whisper. "But if it helped you recover, then I'm happy to give it."

A shudder ran through me at the memory of the place he had taken her to. It was a nightmare come to life. "When you said he was harvesting tissue from you, I did not know how bad it had been," I said quietly. "Lyn, I saw your eye in a jar; he had body parts and organ specimens. Is that what will end up happening to us? Are we just going to end up dissected and put on display for this psycho's pleasure?" My words hung heavy in the air as the gravity of our situation sank in. We were nothing but pawns in this twisted game of his; mere objects to be studied and used for his sick pleasures. And there seemed to be no escape from it all. At this realisation My tears began to flow freely, like a waterfall cascading down a rocky cliff. Gradually, they slowed and then stopped altogether, leaving behind a sense of relief and release. I took a deep breath, my chest rising and falling with each inhale and exhale. In that moment, I felt like I could finally move forward, no longer weighed down by the weight of unshed tears and bottled-up feelings.

"Jessica," the dragon began, her voice deep and resonant, carrying hints of wisdom and experience. "I am a dragon and have lived for centuries, enduring countless traumas and unspeakable horrors many of which have been forgotten by history it has been a long time since I was last among my people, until I met you I was unsure if I would ever get to walk the world again or if I would choose to take my last sleep just so I could escape this hell.

Pausing she glared at me with her one good eye and continued

"But meeting you in this place has given me hope, and has swayed my decision. I will venture out into the world once more, see the realms with fresh eyes."

Lyn's words brought me great comfort and strength. Together, we shall fight and we shall persevere." The dragon's powerful wings unfurled slightly as she looked into the eye's. "For now, let us focus on staying alive and finding a way to defeat our enemies." She growled

As the second day of the experiment dawned, I found myself rousing from a deep slumber brought on by my first treatment. The hours since had been a blur, but I could feel my strength returning. Only one visitor had come to see me, aside from Lyn. It was Mallory, a stern and imposing figure who strode into the room and threw a crusty loaf of bread at me before snatching the IV equipment away. "The master will continue his tests shortly," he grumbled before exiting with an air of authority.

CHAPTER 4

JEREMIAH'S VOICE WAS smooth and taunting as he spoke, "Are you looking forward to today's session, pet?" I refused to give him the satisfaction of a response and just lay on the cold metal table, my body already tensing in anticipation of being strapped down. "Oh, are you not feeling talkative today? That's okay, I'm sure you'll find your voice soon enough." His words dripped with malice as Mallory, his henchman, rushed over to me and quickly began securing my limbs to the table. I could feel his hot breath on my skin as he muttered about how excited his master was to harvest organs from me today. The thought sent shivers down my spine. I had known Jeremiah wanted to cut me open, but surely he was lying. I couldn't survive such a brutal procedure. "Now, Jessica," Jeremiah's voice lowered to a whisper as he leaned in closer, "since you're so brave, I'll let you in on what I have planned for you."

He was fidgeting from side to side, unable to contain his excitement. But before he could begin, he wanted to instil fear in me first. "Your cells have undergone incredible changes while you were recovering. We've been closely monitoring your healing process as your muscles and flesh knit themselves back together at a remarkable rate. However, there are beings out there that possess similar abilities, so I need to push your body to its limits and see just how much it can take before it stops recovering." He clapped his hands together eagerly.

"First, I'll make a Y-shaped incision," he explained as he pointed to where he would cut on my body, tracing his finger along the imaginary path his blade would take. "Then, I'll have to go through your ribs to access all the fascinating organs inside of you. And for that, I have this." He gestured towards a metal contraption that appeared straight out of a medieval torture chamber. After carefully placing it back on the table, he picked up an electrical saw.

My sense of horror deepened as I realised what was about to happen. But the man seemed oblivious to my distress. "Don't worry, Jessica," he said with a twisted smile. "I want you to survive this experiment so we can repeat it again and again. It's crucial for me to replicate my results, after all."

But that was only the beginning of his twisted plan. "You see, a normal human body cannot survive without lungs, kidneys, spleen, appendix or gall bladder," he continued nonchalantly. "And we already know that your body can withstand more than a regular human's. So now, I want to see just how strong your healing factor is. One by one, I'm going to remove these vital organs and time your recovery while you lay helplessly on this table with your insides exposed for me to observe." He paused, his eyes gleaming with excitement. "Isn't that going to be fun?"

The man was clearly insane. But I refused to give him the satisfaction of seeing me scared.

With a sickening squelch, the blade sliced into my skin and I felt the warm rush of blood soaking through my shirt. The metallic tang filled my nose and made me want to retch. But I couldn't scream, couldn't give him the satisfaction of hearing me in pain. Instead, I focused on the sound of my own harsh breathing, trying to drown out the wet scrape of the knife against my flesh. When he was done with the first round of cuts, I thought it was over, but then came the excruciating moment when he pulled back the flap of skin to expose my ribs. My sobs turned into desperate wails as I felt like every nerve ending in my body was on fire. How could anyone endure this? How much more could I take? "Such a beautiful reaction," he sneered, his eyes gleaming as he gazed at my exposed chest. A shiver ran down my spine as he reached for the rib shears, his excitement palpable as he brought them closer to my torn body. In that moment, I didn't care about anything except escaping this nightmare. If I blacked out, maybe I wouldn't have to feel anymore. Maybe I wouldn't have to suffer through his twisted pleasure. But even as I prayed for unconsciousness, part of me knew that there would be no escape from this hellish torture

After enduring countless experiments at the hands of Jeremiah, it turned out that my healing factor was strong enough to regrow organs no matter how many times or how roughly they were removed. Every time I lay on the cold metal table, waiting for the next round of torture to begin, I couldn't help but feel a sense of dread wash over me. But to my shock and surprise, each time Jeremiah attempted to use his rib shears to break through my rib cage or remove any organs, my mind would shut down and spare me from the excruciating pain. After each session, I would wake up a couple of days later, bruised and battered but with no lasting damage.

But with every experiment in which I passed out, it seemed to infuriate Jeremiah more and more. His once calm demeanour was replaced by one of madness and obsession. And then one day, maybe six or seven weeks after his first attempt at organ harvesting, he strolled into the cave with Malory at his heels. As he made his way over to me, I could see the crazed gleam in his eye and knew that whatever he had in store for me would be brutal.

"You haven't been proving to be the sort of test subject I was hoping for recently," he snarled, circling around me like a predator stalking its prey. "And I must confess, this has been putting me in a foul mood." He let out a chilling cackle as he continued, "You see, part of the fun in doing these tests is seeing your reactions and emotions. It's all important data that must be collected. But every time we start, you decide to blackout."

I tried not to shiver under his gaze as he towered over me, revealing in my fear. But I refused to give him the satisfaction. I knew that was what he got off on- my fear and pain. He leaned in closer, his hot breath fanning against my face as he whispered, "Don't worry, pet. You won't escape me today. I have lots of delicious treats in store for you." My heart raced with terror as I braced myself for what was to come.

I was dragged, trembling and terrified, to the room that haunted my nightmares. The walls still lined with specimen jars I was sure a few of which now held some of my organs. As soon as we enteredI was thrown onto a stiff, metal table, my body shivering in the cool air. In this place of fear and pain, I had become accustomed to being stripped of all clothing.I couldn't help but shiver as Mallory approached me. Without a single word, he began strapping me down, making sure I was completely immobile. His words slithered into my ear like snakes, sending goosebumps down my spine. "No escape for sleeping beauty today," he chuckled darkly. My heart raced as I realised what he meant - there would be no mercy this time. Dread filled my mind as I anticipated what horrors Jeremiah had planned for me. "I hope he will let me have a turn," Mallory sneered, his eyes glittering with sadistic pleasure. My worst fears were about to come true, and there was nothing I could do to stop it.

Mallory instinctively backed away as Jeremiah advanced, his eyes studying the shackles that bound jess to the table. She could see the wheels turning in his mind, his usually calm demeanour now replaced with a frenzied determination. He pulled a syringe from his pocket, filled with an eerie green liquid that glowed under the harsh lights of the laboratory.

The colour and consistency of the liquid reminded jess of dish soap, but she knew it was something much more sinister. "No more passing out for you," Jeremiah said in a singsong voice, before violently jabbing the needle into her upper arm.

jess cried out in pain and shock, unable to believe what was happening. "Ouch, that hurt asshole!" she screamed, immediately regretting her outburst when she saw the look of pure rage on Jeremiah's face.

The colour drained from her face as she realised the gravity of her mistake. "Well, aren't you a mouthy little lab rat today?" Jeremiah sneered, his voice dripping with malice. "I was going to wait till later, but I think I'll do it now. Yes, now will be good. Maybe it will teach you who's really in charge around here," he muttered to himself, almost as if he needed to convince himself that what he was about to do was justified. jess shuddered as she watched him discard the now empty needle, knowing that she was completely at his mercy.

Terror coursed through my veins, paralysing me as I braced for the inevitable. Every time he had inflicted his cruel ministrations upon me before, I had been fortunate enough to pass out and escape the pain. But not this time. This time, I would have to endure it all. "Now I'm going to show you just what a little slut does," he taunted, his words dripping with sadistic glee as he stripped off his clothes. My heart pounded in my chest as I realised what he had in store for me. Panic consumed me and I thrashed against my restraints, desperate to break free from the nightmare unfolding before me. To make matters worse, Mallory stood by watching with sick fascination, applauding and cheering like it was some kind of twisted game.

As I LAY there, broken and bruised, I couldn't remember how I had made it back to the cave where Lyn and I were imprisoned. But as I slowly regained consciousness, I felt her projecting a calmness to me, assuring me that we would be alright. It wasn't until I tried to move that I realised the true extent of my injuries - I was in worse shape than I could ever imagine. Another IV line pumped Lyn's blood into my veins, providing me with much-needed sustenance. By my side sat a bowl of stew and bread, but I could barely stomach anything through the excruciating pain coursing through my body.

"Stay still," Lyn cautioned as she saw me attempt to move. "Your bones need to set properly."

Bones...the word echoed in my mind as memories flooded back. Memories of him - the man who had raped me and then systematically broke my bones with careful precision. He started with my legs, shattering them into multiple pieces before carving away at the flesh to better observe their healing process. The sound of my own screams filled the room as he took pleasure in watching my bones fuse back together.

I thought I was going insane - the constant breaking and slicing was enough to drive anyone mad. But even when he grew bored with my legs, he moved on to my arm and fingers, dislocating each one before breaking them in different ways just for his own twisted curiosity. And all the while, I was forced to witness this torture, unable to do anything to save myself.

"How often do they change the IV bag?" I managed to ask through gritted teeth, determination filling every fibre of my being. I had a plan - escape or die trying.

Lyn's head was tilted to one side, her eyes fixed on me as if trying to decipher my thoughts. "I think the bag needs to be refilled every few hours," she said, nodding towards the IV bag hanging above us. I furrowed my brow in thought, realising that they must have given it to me to speed up my recovery for their experiments. "But how does that help us now?" Lyn asked, confusion evident in her voice. I turned to face her and asked, "Can your teeth or claws cut through a bone?" Her response was hesitant but certain, "Yes, but it will hurt. What are you planning? How do you expect us to get out of here?" My mind raced as I formulated a plan. "When Mallory comes to change the IV bag, I'll kill him," I stated coldly. The realisation hit me that these people were no longer humans in my eyes, they were ruthless and cruel individuals who deserved to be taken out of this world. My determination only grew stronger at the thought of ridding the world of their presence.

IT WAS FINALLY time. Lyn had successfully removed the silver band from my ankle, although it wasn't as easy as I had hoped. Luckily, the drug Jeremiah gave me to stay awake was still working. I gritted my teeth and endured the excruciating pain as the metal tore through my skin and muscle, knowing it would all be worth it soon. Once the process was complete, I made my way towards the cave entrance and waited for my prey to arrive, allowing my leg to heal in the meantime.As Mallory sauntered through the doorway, I could feel my injured leg throbbing beneath me. Despite this, I stood tall, bracing myself against the cold wall for support. My eyes never left his form as he entered the room, too consumed with his own mutterings to notice my presence. "Maybe next time," he muttered under his breath, a sickening grin spreading across his face. "Master will let me have a turn; I want to make her cry too." The thought of him causing any more harm made my skin crawl and I knew then that I had to put an end to this monster.

Summoning all the strength in my body, I swung the IV pole with all my might into the side of his head. The sound of impact rang out through the room, followed by a sickening thud as his body hit the floor. But even as I approached him, seeing the damage I had caused, I could still see he was breathing. With a primal rage burning inside me, I crawled towards him, dragging the pole along with me as I delivered blow after blow to his head until it was nothing but a pulpy mess.

Catching my breath, I looked down at his unrecognisable form and couldn't help but think how fitting it was for such an evil creature. Doubtful that he would survive such injuries, I turned towards the door and shouted to Lyn, "I will be back for you." My promise hung heavy in the air as I slowly made my way out of that nightmare and into the safety of the outside world.

My heart raced with fear as the warning echoed in my mind, "Go before it's too late." I scrambled to my feet and navigated the maze-like corridors of the dungeon, my memory guiding me towards the quickest route to freedom. My injured leg burned with each step, but I refused to let it slow me down. I repeated "I can endure this" like a mantra, pushing myself beyond what I thought possible. And then, finally, I was out. The bright blue sky stretched above me, the salty smell of the ocean filling my lungs. In that moment of relief and triumph, I heard a slow applause, like a mocking soundtrack to my escape. "Well done, Jessica," came Jeremiah's voice from behind me. "I never would have imagined you capable of such an act." He leaned casually against the rocky wall beside the exit, as if we were simply having a friendly chat instead of being mortal enemies. But then I noticed the ball of crackling energy hovering in his palm. "But don't worry," he continued nonchalantly. "I won't make that mistake again." With a flick of his wrist, he sent the ball hurtling towards me. The impact knocked me unconscious immediately.

Lyn and I then developed a daily routine, one that we clung to with all our might. Every morning, Jeremiah would stride into our makeshift prison, his eyes gleaming with malice as he decided which of us he would experiment on first. His cruel intentions were clear in the way he handled us - rough and forceful, trying to break our spirits and leave us broken. Once he was satisfied, he would leave, leaving us trembling and bruised.

But through it all, we held onto each other and our routine. Each day, I would receive We were given meagre rations - a bowl of thin stew and stale bread for me, and once a week, Lyn received two slaughtered cows for food .

In those moments, we would forget about our captivity and revel in the taste of our food.

But amidst the darkness and despair, there was a glimmer of hope in the form of Lyn's stories. She would tell me stories of the paranormal world - of other realms filled with creatures beyond my wildest imagination. Her words transported me from this hellish place and gave me hope for something more. I hung onto her every word, hungry for any escape from the darkness that consumed my days with Jeremiah

With each passing day, Jeremiah's behaviour became more erratic and cruel. As time went on, he delved deeper into his twisted experiments, even going so far as to remove my Limb's in a sick attempt to see if they would grow back. In the days that I would need to recover, I was forced to bear witness to the atrocities he inflicted on lyn while I was restrained in my cot within the dark, damp cave we called home. The days dragged on slowly, blending together until I no longer knew if it had been days or weeks since my captivity began.

But during this time, I could feel changes happening within myself. Was it because of the constant IV drip of unknown substances that Jeremiah forced into me? Or was it simply because I was growing older? My body was taller now, my figure changing and developing in ways I couldn't fully understand. But it wasn't just my appearance that was transforming; my once timid and submissive nature was fading away, replaced by a newfound sense of defiance and strength.

Jeremiah's punishments were always cruel and merciless, but they became even more extreme whenever I dared to talk back. Often, he would chain me to the unforgiving cave walls and floor, just as he had done with Lyn, to ensure that we could not interfere when he brought in his next test subject. As we watched, their bodies writhed in agony under the influence of his experimental drug. None were unable to endure for even 24 hours before succumbing to its effects. And when they finally succumb, with every dead test subject Jeremiah's rage grew. He would unleash his fury upon me, beating and violating my broken body until I was nothing but a shattered and battered mess, unable to even stand on my own two feet.

After a particularly brutal experience in the lab, I found myself seeking solace in Lyn's comforting presence. I leaned against her strong front legs, finding peace in her calming energy. She projected stunning images of soaring over snow-capped mountains, the beauty of nature momentarily distracting me from my ordeal. Suddenly, she spoke up.

"So what did you do to make him remove your fingers and break your toes?" Her voice was gentle but curious.

I couldn't help but laugh at the absurdity of it all, despite the pain still fresh in my mind. "Well," I began, "after he was finished with his sick enjoyment, I noticed one of my restraints had come loose. So, being the feisty person that I am, I may have thrown something at his crotch and given him the finger." A smirk tugged at my lips as I remembered his enraged expression. "Needless to say, he was not amused by my actions. And as punishment for damaging his precious manhood, he broke each of my toes with a hammer." My words were laced with bitterness and humour.

I chuckled again, remembering how I had goaded him even further by sarcastically asking if he was done with my pedicure and informing him that I was overdue for a manicure. The image of his bewildered stare was too much for me to handle, and I burst into uncontrollable laughter once more. "Maybe it wasn't the wisest decision," I gasped out between giggles, clutching my ribs with my stumpy hands. "Because then he decided I didn't need my fingers for a while."

As I recounted the ridiculousness of the situation to Lyn, her chest rumbled with laughter alongside mine. Despite the pain and trauma, we found some humour in my misfortune together.

I couldn't help but think that at least Lyn enjoyed my sense of humour, as she looked at me with a quizzical expression and asked, "What warranted such an outburst? You rarely lash out without reason." Taking a deep breath, I tried to compose myself. "While he was doing his business," I explained, my voice trembling, "he said just think how proud my mother would be that she raised a freak slut." The memory of those cruel words sent a wave of anger coursing through me. "After that, I just wanted to hurt him even though I knew he was going to punish me after." Before Lyn could say anything more, we felt a massive tremor reverberate through the cave. The walls shook and debris fell from the ceiling as we braced ourselves for whatever was causing the disturbance.

With lightning reflexes, Lyn threw her body in front of mine, shielding me from any potential debris that may have fallen from the crumbling ceiling. The sounds of chaos and destruction echoed outside, causing our hearts to race with fear and anticipation. I could hear screams and explosions, a cacophony of danger and uncertainty. My heart raced as I dared to hope that this was it - someone had finally found us. But deep down, I knew better than to get my hopes up too high. In this cruel world, anything was possible and nothing was certain.

With a resounding creak, the heavy door leading out of the damp cave swung open, revealing Jeremiah as he came charging in. Behind him, a group of people dressed in sleek, black tactical gear followed closely, each wielding their own unique weapon or power. The air crackled with sparks of energy as they made their way forward, determined and focused. Unlike most invading forces, there were no guns to be seen amongst them. Some carried swords and daggers while others held orbs of shimmering energy in their hands, much like Jeremiah.

As they entered the dimly lit cave, one figure stood out amongst the rest. His posture exuded confidence and his sharp gaze scanned the room with authority. In his hand, he held a pulsating orb of vibrant red energy that seemed to pulse with a life of its own. Without hesitation, he spoke in a commanding tone that left no room for question or disobedience.

The commanding officer made a swift gesture to his team, signalling for them to keep their distance from the impending confrontation.

Fear and caution were evident on their faces as they took several steps back, creating ample space for the two men to face off.

With a confident tone, the officer called out to Jeremiah,"Tell you what, if you can defeat me in battle, my team will release you as free as a bird." Without hesitation, Jeremiah charged forward with an explosive burst of energy, hurling balls of power towards his opponent. But the officer remained unfazed, gracefully dodging each blast with fluid movements that seemed almost otherworldly.

As Jeremiah attempted a physical attack aimed at the officer's solar plexus, the skilled fighter effortlessly evaded it with a mesmerising display of agility and grace. With one swift movement, he pivoted on one foot while whipping the other around, delivering a crushing blow to Jeremiah's rib cage. The sound of breaking bones filled the air, followed by a piercing scream of agony from Jeremiah.

"Restrain him!" the officer commanded as he calmly watched Jeremiah crumple to the ground in pain. "He won't be down for long." The rest of his team immediately sprang into action, swiftly restraining Jeremiah and neutralising his abilities with ease.

As the red orb of energy dissipated from his hand, the officer removed his helmet and face coverings to reveal a strikingly handsome face. A five o'clock shadow adorned his strong jawline, highlighting his piercing blue eyes. His nose showed signs of being broken multiple times, adding to his rugged appearance. But what caught my attention were the faint laughter lines etched in the corners of his eyes, hinting at a kind and humorous soul behind his tough exterior. He walked towards Lyn with slow and steady strides, exuding confidence and control in every step.

the officer appeared suddenly, his footsteps muffled by the damp rock of the cave. He greeted Lyn first, bowing slightly before addressing her as "Lady Saar." His voice was firm and confident, tinged with an air of authority that seemed to command respect.

"We will have you out of these shackles as soon as possible," he assured her. "We also have healers waiting on standby for you."

"Thank you, Commander," Lyn replied, grateful for his concern. "But I am more worried about my comrade. This is Jessica, and she requires urgent medical aid. She shouldn't be forced to walk as he broke all her toes earlier today, and she will not be questioned until I am with her. Do I make myself clear?"

The commander nodded quickly, already turning to leave the cave in search of healers. "Yes, ma'am. I will retrieve them immediately. And I will also get a team working on your restraints."

With that, he rushed out of the cave, barking orders at everyone he passed. Lyn turned to Jessica, who was now sitting up and watching the scene with wide eyes.

"Lyn, that wasn't very nice," Jessica scolded playfully.

"I didn't notice," Lyn shrugged nonchalantly. "That being said, he should have had better priorities. You are a human girl who has been held captive by a lunatic, but instead of focusing on you, he comes over trying to fawn over me like I'm some injured kitten. The nerve of some people." Her tone was laced with sarcasm and a touch of bitterness towards the commander's misplaced attention.

The commander's sharp tone and condescension had rubbed Lyn the wrong way, igniting a fierce sense of defiance within her. She stood tall and straight, asserting her dominance with every word and movement, determined to show that being a captive hadn't broken her spirit. "Anyway, I wanted to talk to you before they start asking questions about what has happened." Her words held a sense of urgency that caught me off guard. "I need you to trust me and let me handle everything. And do not leave my side unless I give you explicit permission."

I couldn't help but feel worried as I looked into Lyn's intense gaze. "Lyn, why are you acting like this? Aren't these people supposed to be the good guys?"

She gave me a small, reassuring smile. "You need not be concerned. We just have to tread carefully until we know what's going on and who is pulling the strings. Once we have all the information, we can decide how much to disclose."

I nodded, trusting in Lyn's judgment and leadership. But there was still one nagging thought on my mind. "Can you try to find out what happened to my father?"

Her expression softened as she placed a comforting hand on my shoulder. "Child, I will do everything in my power to find out the truth about your father and reunite you with him if they are still alive. But for now, we need to put our game faces on. He is coming back, and remember, let me do the talking."

I took a deep breath and braced myself for whatever was about to happen, grateful to have Lyn by my side in this uncertain situation.

Commander Robinson sprinted towards us, his face flushed with urgency as he led a team of equally harried individuals.

"Well, commander," Lyn called out, "are your people going to tend to my injured comrade? And while you're at it, perhaps this team can finally free us from these wretched chains."

She paced back and forth, her huge bulk causing the chains around her foreleg to clang together in a menacing rhythm. The metallic sound only added to her fierce determination to be freed from captivity.

CHAPTER 5

TIME FLEW BY in a blur, the hours melting into minutes as I was tended to and healed. The magic they used was astonishing, knitting together my broken fingers and bones with ease. As the healer's hands moved over my body, I could feel a sense of calm and rejuvenation wash over me. My restraint bracelet had been removed, freeing me from the heavy weight that had held me back for so long. With each step, I felt lighter and more alive, my toes no longer throbbing in pain but dancing across the ground. Adhering to Lyn's instructions, I kept my interactions minimal and brief, not wanting to cause any trouble or draw attention to myself. Once my healing was complete and I was released from the healer's care, I eagerly made my way back to Lyn's side. She was still struggling to remove the chains that bound her, but as I approached, I saw the final cuff clatter to the ground with a satisfying thud.

The relief was palpable as she let out a deep sigh, finally able to release the tension that had been building in her muscles. With fluid motions, she shook out her limbs and stretched her wings, arching her back like a graceful cat basking in the warmth of the sun. As she extended her talons, they left deep gouges in the solid rock beneath her, a testament to their strength and sharpness. I couldn't help but marvel at the raw power and flexibility displayed by this magnificent creature.

With Jeremiah detained and his magical bindings removed, Lyn felt her power rush back to her like a long-lost lover. It embraced her in an all-consuming, exhilarating embrace. The air in the chamber crackled with raw energy, the stillness shattered by bolts of lightning and gusts of wind that whipped around Lyn like a hurricane. She stood at the centre, shrouded in an otherworldly aura that obscured our view. But we caught glimpses of iridescent scales shimmering in the light and arcs of electricity dancing across her body.

As she transformed from dragon to human, time seemed to slow down, each second stretched out into an eternity. We watched in awe as her features shifted and changed, her form growing smaller and more beautiful. And then suddenly, there she stood before us - a powerful and regal young woman, radiating strength and authority.

Despite her physical appearance as a young woman in her late twenties or early thirties, it was clear that Lyn was ancient and wise beyond measure. In that moment, she commanded respect and held herself with a poised grace that demanded attention and reverence.

The woman's voice was like a gentle caress, soothing and comforting. "It's nice to be in my human form again now, child," she said, her eyes sparkling with joy. "Come here so I can hold you. I have dreamt of comforting you from the day I met you and I will be denied no longer." Her voice was like honey, sweet and alluring, drawing me closer with each word. As she enveloped me in her arms, a sense of safety and warmth washed over me, as if I had finally found my true home. And in that moment, I knew that she was right - I would no longer be denied the comfort and love that I had been longing for all this time.

As Lyn's strong arms wrapped around me, I felt a sense of safety and comfort wash over me. My worries and fears seemed to melt away as she held me tightly against her chest. In that moment, nothing else in the world mattered. All I could focus on was the warmth of her embrace and the sound of her steady heartbeat.

In the midst of this intimate moment, I heard Lyn speaking to the commander. Her tone was firm but respectful as she addressed him.

"Yes, commander, I understand your need for answers, but as I have told you before, we are leaving. We will accept an escort, but our destination is a hotel. We must bathe, eat, and perhaps find some new clothing suitable for this location," she stated confidently. It was then that I realised we were both completely naked.

Feeling my cheeks flush with embarrassment, I shifted slightly in Lyn's arms. She noticed my discomfort and casually added,

"Also, would you happen to have any spare clothing we could borrow for our stay at the hotel? It would be much appreciated.It would be preferable not to check into the hotel unclothed." The commander's shocked expression only made her request all the more amusing to me. It was clear that we were quite the strange sight in this unfamiliar place,

As the dust settled and all preparations were completed, we were given a change of clothes - basic combat gear that would protect us on our journey. We were then escorted to the Aurora lodges, a hidden oasis where the extraction team had established their command centre. The scent of freshly cut grass greeted us as we entered the lodge, its walls made of sturdy logs and its roof adorned with shingles. Inside, maps and charts covered every surface, while agents in tactical gear worked busily on computers and radios. It was clear that this was a serious operation.

As we arrived at the lodge, we were escorted to a breathtaking cabin that we insisted on sharing. The commander grumbled, clearly disappointed that his plans to interrogate me would be hindered by Lyn's presence. She was immediately on the phone, trying to reach anyone who could help us in our current situation. As she handled the logistics, I made my way to the bathroom, eager to wash away the memories of Jeremiah's touch. I was stunned by the luxuriousness of the bathing area - a shiny silver freestanding bathtub and a pile of fluffy white towels awaited me. The sight nearly brought me to tears, as it was a stark contrast to the fear and danger we had been facing. Taking a deep breath, I ran one of the hottest bubble baths I could remember and spent what felt like hours scrubbing every inch of my body in an effort to rid myself of any lingering contamination. Even after my skin turned pink from the scrubbing, I couldn't shake off the memories.

Desperate for some semblance of peace, I drained the tub and filled it again with fresh water, hoping it would soothe my troubled mind and allow me to contemplate my uncertain future.

As I lay submerged in the warm water, a dreamy aroma of lavender wafted through the air from the bubble bath concoction I had used. The soft bubbles tickled my skin and eased my tension as I contemplated what lay ahead. It was hard to fathom just how long I had been held captive, and the thought made my head spin with uncertainty. Had my father perished in the explosion? If so, where would I go? Where would I call home now? These unanswerable questions swirled around me, taunting me with their weight. And so, I let out a soft cry, tears mingling with the fragrant water as I wallowed in my grief. Eventually, I noticed the once-warm water had turned cold, and my body began to shiver. Slowly, I dragged myself out of the tub and wrapped myself in the softest towels imaginable. Taking a deep breath, trying to steel myself for what was to come, I reminded myself that I had already allowed myself this moment of breakdown - now it was time to put on a brave face and face whatever challenges awaited me. But first, a nap. Lyn had given me permission for some much-needed rest, and nothing was going to take that away from me. With determination fuelling my steps, I made my way to the bed and crawled under the comforting folds of the duvet. Oh, how I had missed duvets - how they cocooned you in warmth and protection. As exhaustion overtook me, I relished in the comfort of this momentary reprieve from reality.

My exhaustion caught up with me the instant my head hit the soft, downy pillows. Thankfully, it was a dreamless sleep, free from any worries or fears. When I woke, I saw the sun peeking through the window and could hear a heated conversation coming from the next room. The delicious smell of food cooking wafted into my room, causing my stomach to let out a demanding growl for sustenance. I chuckled to myself at my rumbling belly and took in my surroundings. A pile of clothes and boots sat neatly on a chair beside the bed, with a note on top that read "I hope these are to your liking." I eagerly dressed in the offered attire - stone-washed jeans, a long-sleeved black shirt, a pair of sleek timberland boots in black, and a flowing cardigan in matching black. As I glanced at myself in the mirror, I couldn't help but feel transformed - my new outfit fitting perfectly and giving me an air of sophistication. The only thing that didn't quite fit was my hair length, which now reached past my waist. It made me look older, not old per se, just more mature. My features seemed more pronounced and my eyes brighter than before. For a moment, I almost didn't recognise myself in the mirror. But before I could dwell on it too much, my grumbling stomach reminded me of my mission - to find some food. Without hesitation, I headed out of my room and towards the source of commotion and hopefully a warm meal.

As I stepped into the dimly lit cabin, my gaze was immediately drawn to Lyn. Dressed in a similar style to mine, she exuded an aura of confidence and power that demanded attention. Her posture was straight and her shoulders squared as she sat at the head of the long wooden table, her presence filling the room with energy.

Across from her sat Commander Robinson, his stern expression giving away nothing of his thoughts. Beside him was an official who appeared out of place and less than thrilled to be there. Next to Lyn sat a man with a friendly smile, his face radiating genuine interest and excitement.

But it was Lyn who commanded the room. Her voice carried through the air, vibrant and commanding, as she addressed the other official with a steely determination. "I am not saying you cannot speak to Jessica," she asserted, her gaze never wavering from them. "But I will not allow you to hold her accountable for something that was done against her will." The tension in the room thickened as she spoke, drawing everyone's focus towards her.

"I can personally testify that she shows no signs of dragon madness," Lyn continued, her voice unwavering and confident. "And as I have already informed you, she is under the protection of both the dragon and elf council."

Silence hung in the air as Lyn glared at the official beside Commander Robinson. Before anyone could say something that could make the situation worse, the gentleman beside Lyn cleared his throat subtly to shift the room's attention to him. Then, rather boldly, he said, "I, for one, would rather you not question Jessica. I feel she has been through enough trauma. Do you really think we should force her to relive it all just to satisfy our curiosity? There is enough evidence for all of us to be busy investigating for months. But if you insist, then get on with it." His words hung in the air, a clear order for the official to follow.

The official sat nervously, obviously out of his element, before he reluctantly relented. "Fine, have it your way. But I want to be kept in the loop on all relevant details of the investigation moving forward," he huffed with obvious resentment.

The gentleman beside Lyn clapped his hands together, the sound echoing in the room like a resounding symbol of his delight. His beaming smile lit up his face, revealing rows of perfectly white teeth. "That's wonderful!" he exclaimed, his voice filled with genuine enthusiasm. "Now, before we go any further, I'm famished." His eyes sparkling with anticipation.he asked "Will you both be joining us for breakfast, or do you have somewhere else to be?" The official that sat with Commander Robinson stood abruptly and excused himself, while Commander Robinson remained seated, his expression still serious and focused. After a tense few minutes, the commander spoke. "Well, that went better than expected," he said, a hint of relief evident in his tone. "So what? For breakfast," he added with a small chuckle, "the three of them broke down laughing." The tension in the room dissipated as they all shared a moment of lightheartedness amidst the serious situation at hand. Their laughter filled the air and echoed off the walls, bringing a brief sense of warmth and camaraderie to the otherwise austere atmosphere.

My throat felt tight as I cleared it, trying to announce my presence in the room. The group of people turned to look at me, their eyes curious and assessing. Lyn, the woman who had taken me in, spoke up with a warm smile. "Ah, there's my Little Dragon. I should explain everything over breakfast."

We all made our way to the dining table, but before we could sit down, a woman who appeared slightly older than me informed us that the food would take a little while longer. As she ushered us to make ourselves comfortable, I couldn't help feeling out of place and vulnerable. I sat as close to Lyn as possible, seeking her protection and guidance. The commander and another man, who seemed like a mystery gentleman, were kind enough not to comment on my behaviour as Lyn made introductions.

"These gentlemen," she began, gesturing to them, "are Commander Killian Robinson and Alexander Elric." Her voice held respect and admiration for both men. "Commander Robinson leads a joint task force between the paranormal military and the paranormal investigation agency. And Alexander here is the head of the paranormal investigation agency." She paused, then added with a hint of pride, "He is also an ancient friend of mine and a member of the elf's council." Lyn turned to me with a reassuring smile. "He has vouched for you."

I couldn't hold back my confusion any longer. "I'm sorry, but I don't understand why I need to be vouched for or what that other man was so angry about. Can someone please explain what's going on?"

There was a moment of silence before Lyn sighed and motioned for everyone to sit down at the table. "Before we get into that," she said calmly, "we should have some breakfast first." Her words were comforting, but I couldn't shake off the unease that lingered in the air. It felt like there were layers of secrets and mysteries in this group, and I was just beginning to scratch the surface.

A heavy, weighty sigh escaped my lips, filled with the despair and disappointment that settled heavily in my chest like a leaden stone. My gaze flickered between Alexander and Lyn, searching for answers that I feared I wouldn't receive. But before I could voice my thoughts, Alexander raised his hand to silence us all. His voice was low and solemn, tinged with regret and sorrow.

"I apologise for our previous attempt to pacify you like a child. We should have been more honest with you, Jess."

My heart clenched as I remembered Lyn's words about their histories being intertwined with mine. But it seemed that she had left out crucial information - as Alexander now revealed. He continued, his tone grave and serious.

"Our joint councils made a treaty long ago, when my grandparents were still young. This treaty decreed that any who dabbled in ancient blood magic or created a blood-born would be sentenced to life in Tartarus." The mere mention of this place sent shivers down my spine.

And then came the final blow - a clause in the treaty that stated all products of these experiments would also be destroyed. Fear and confusion raced through my mind as I looked at the three of them with wide eyes.

"So... does that mean you're going to kill me?" My voice trembled with terror as I finally managed to choke out the question, unable to hide the fear and vulnerability that consumed me.

Alexander's head shook slowly, the firelight from the cabin fireplace casting shadows across his face. "

Jess, we are not going to kill you. but we are concerned about the risk you represent," he said, his tone serious. "You see, the paranormal world has changed and evolved significantly since then, but we elves have always guarded the secret of how to create dragon blood warriors." He paused "I have examined Jeremiah's workspace in those caves while you slept, and I also spoke with him. I even took a look at your genetic makeup." My heart skipped a beat as he continued, "Don't worry, I did not touch you or cause any harm. But what he did to you is something that cannot be easily explained, his eyes scanning my face for any hint of understanding. "You see, what I found in those caves revealed that he has manipulated your DNA, giving you not just dragon blood but also genetic markers for multiple supernatural beings – feline shifters, mages, vampires and dragon to name a just few."

My mind reeled at this revelation. "So...what does that mean? What will happen to me?" I couldn't help but feel a twinge of fear creeping into my voice. "Are you going to lock me up and experiment on me like he did?"

In a flurry of movement, both Alexander and Lyn rushed to my side, their concern palpable. Lyn's grip on my hand was firm yet comforting, while Alexander's calming touch on my shoulder helped ground me. As I struggled to regain control of my breathing, a peculiar sensation washed over me. It was as if sparks of electricity were buzzing under my skin, disrupting any sense of calm I had left. My mind raced with thoughts and emotions, making it difficult to focus on anything else.

The sound of Lyn's voice was like a gentle breeze, cutting through the thick haze of fear and uncertainty. "Don't worry, Jess," she said, her voice soft and reassuring. "We won't let anyone harm you or use you for their own twisted experiments." Her words were like a shield, protecting Jess from the dangers that lurked in the shadows.

My gaze fell to my outstretched hand, and I was shocked to see tiny sparks of electricity dancing between my fingertips. In a panic, I attempted to wrench away from Lyn's grip on my other hand, but she held on with a fierce determination. The energy surged through me like a wild current, coursing up my arm and filling me with a buzzing, crackling sensation that was both frightening and strangely alluring. The air around us seemed to hum with the power of it all, as if the very atmosphere had been charged with electric energy.

My eyes were glued to the magnificent display of power in front of me as I pleaded with them. "How do I make it stop?" My voice was desperate, my heart racing with fear and confusion. "What is happening to me?" Every inch of my body felt like it was on fire, as if each individual cell was pulsing with an unknown energy. I could feel the weight of their gazes on me, their expressions a mixture of awe and apprehension. The air around us crackled with electricity, and I couldn't help but wonder if this was all just a dream or some kind of nightmare.

Alexander and Lyn exchanged a glance, their eyes filled with understanding. I could sense the tension building in their bodies as they turned to face me. "We can't say for certain, but it appears that removing the power nullifying cuff and you heightened emotional state has triggered your body to adapt to the changes forced upon it by Jeremiah," Alexander's voice was calm but his words held a hint of uncertainty. His brow furrowed in deep concentration as he explained the situation.

The light in Lyn's eyes became radiant and proud as she spoke, her voice soft yet full of conviction "You are on the brink of a powerful transformation are evolving into something entirely new, Jess. And though the journey ahead may be dangerous and uncertain, we will be by your side to help you navigate it."

Lyn squeezed my hand gently as she continued, her voice now barely above a whisper. "Just close your eyes and focus on your breathing. Imagine each breath is filling you with energy, becoming one with your being." I followed her instructions, inhaling deeply and feeling the warmth of energy coursing through my body like a river. The air around us seemed to vibrate with an otherworldly power, crackling with untapped potential. With each exhale, I let go of any doubts or fears letting the vibrant energy from the world around me. pulse through my veins, filling me with renewed strength and clarity

I slowly opened my eyes, taking in the curious gazes of those around me. Their expressions ranged from awe to admiration, and a sense of accomplishment washed over me.

The woman cooking breakfast stood at the stove, a wide grin on her face as she stirred a bubbling pot of scrambled eggs with one hand and flipped golden pancakes with the other. The sizzle and aroma of bacon wafted through the air, making our stomachs growl in anticipation. "That is impressive for your first time," she exclaimed, giving a hearty clap before announcing, "Breakfast is served." The table was filled to the brim with steaming dishes overflowing with fluffy eggs, crispy bacon, and perfectly browned pancakes. Each dish looked more tantalisingly scrumptious than the last, and we couldn't wait to dive in.

In that moment, all thoughts of anything else disappeared as we focused solely on the feast before us. I ate heartily, unable to remember a time when I had enjoyed a meal so much. Despite my apparent gluttony, no one seemed to care as conversation flowed easily between us.

As soon as every last bite had been savoured and every dish cleaned, the woman whom I had not yet met clapped her hands together and the table was magically cleared. In its place appeared steaming pots of tea and coffee, inviting us to sit back and relax after our hearty meal. Unable to contain my amazement any longer, I turned to her and exclaimed with a grin, "That was incredible! How did you do it?"

She laughed lightly, brushing off my praise. "Oh, it was nothing maybe I'll show you how it's done one day. I'm Mini by the way. It's nice to meet you."

"Hi Mini, I'm Jessica," I replied with a smile, still in awe of the incredible display.

Just as things were beginning to settle down again, Alexander cleared his throat to get everyone's attention. "Jessica, I have a proposal for you," he said earnestly. "I'd like to invite you to join The Agency's training program. It will not only help you adjust to your new worldview, but also provide a safe place for you to call home. And with our protection, you'll never have to worry about being attacked by anything again." He motioned towards Mini beside him. "I brought Mini along because she's currently in the training program herself, and I thought you might like to discuss the possibility with someone your own age." His offer filled me with a sense of relief and security, and I couldn't wait to learn more about this mysterious organisation.

As I considered the offer, my mind raced with possibilities. The idea of having a mentor, someone to confide in and guide me, was like a shining beacon of hope in this uncertain situation. His words were like a tantalising lifeline, promising a way out of the dark cave I had been trapped in for so long. But could he truly be trusted? Lyn clearly trusted him, but I couldn't help the nagging doubts that crept into my mind as I weighed my options.

It was a tough decision, but ultimately, what choice did I have?

"What do you get out of this?" I finally asked, unable to contain my curiosity any longer. "Why help me?" The room fell silent as though my question had caused a great insult, and even Alexander seemed taken aback by my boldness.

After a moment to regain his composure, he replied in a calm, measured tone, "There are a few reasons why I'm offering this. Firstly, my friend asked me to help you and I am more than happy to oblige. Secondly, I have a strong feeling that you will be an invaluable asset to our team. And lastly, I hate seeing potential go to waste, and I can see that you have great potential." He paused before adding, "Does that answer your question?"

Feeling sheepish for questioning his motives, I nodded and said, "Yes, it does. But I do have two more questions - has anyone been able find out what happened to my father? And how long was I held captive by Jeremiah?" My voice trembled slightly as memories of my time in captivity flooded back. But determined to move forward, I waited anxiously for Alexander's response.

The mood in the room shifted as all eyes turned to Alexander. His face became serious as he replied, "We have received reports that there were no survivors at the crash site. Your father's body was found in the wreckage, along with the bodies of two other males. As for how long you were held captive, it was almost five years." He paused before adding, "I have spoken to Lyn, and we understand if you find that hard to believe. But due to Jeremiah's experiments on you, there were periods when you would slip into a coma for days or weeks at a time. This may have skewed your perception of time." A heavy silence fell over the table as I processed this new information. Despite the uncertainty of my future, I felt grateful that they didn't sugarcoat the truth and instead delivered it bluntly.

As I sat there, surrounded by these newfound allies who had already become my support system, I couldn't help but feel a sense of loss and displacement. Even if I tried to rejoin the world and pick up where I had left off, nothing would be the same. I wasn't just a girl anymore; my experiences had forced me to grow up too quickly, and now I was a woman faced with unimaginable challenges.

A stray tear fell down my cheek, and before I knew it, Lyn had enveloped me in her arms. She held onto me tightly, as if afraid that one more shock would break me completely. Maybe she was right, but despite everything, I had made my decision - it was time to move on.

CHAPTER 6

FIDGETED NERVOUSLY, SHIFTING my weight from foot to foot as I looked up at Alexander. His tall stature and commanding presence made me falter, unsure of how to address him. "Excuse me, sir...I mean, Alex," I stuttered, stumbling over my words. He simply grinned, his eyes twinkling with amusement at my obvious discomfort. "No need for formalities," he said casually. "Just call me Alex. Although some of the other recruits have given me...less respectful and more colourful nicknames," he chuckled, causing Minnie's cheeks to flush a bright pink before she quickly looked away.

This interaction reminded me of my past life as a student, with teachers and authority figures who were approachable and friendly. It brought a sense of normality and comfort to the daunting situation we were facing.

My nerves got the best of me as I blurted out my next question. "So when do we leave?" I tried to sound eager, but my voice came out shaky. I turned to Lyn, seeking reassurance from her steady presence. But she seemed lost in her own thoughts.

"You will be leaving shortly," she replied with a hint of sadness in her voice. My heart sank at her words, knowing what was coming next. "Unfortunately, I won't be joining you."

The news hit me like a physical blow to the stomach. I stared up at Lyn with wide eyes, desperately searching for any sign that she was joking. But there was only sorrow in her gaze.

"I have been away from dragon society for too long," she explained softly. "I need to make my presence known before any others get the wrong idea." There was an underlying growl in her tone that sent a shiver down my spine.

As if sensing my distress, she leaned down and pressed a gentle kiss on my forehead. Her cool lips left a lingering warmth on my skin as she whispered, "My little dragon." It was a term of endearment that only she used for me. "I won't be gone for long, and if you ever need me, just let Alex know. Make me proud."

A lump formed in my throat as she spoke, and I couldn't help but feel a sense of loss at the thought of her leaving.

With determination in every step, Lyn strode confidently out of the cabin, her boots crunching against the gravel path. A surge of energy radiated from her, making my heart race in anticipation. As the door closed behind her with a resounding thud, I felt a pang of loneliness wash over me. She was my only companion for the last five years and now she was leaving me behind. I longed to chase after her and plead for her to stay, but I knew deep down that this was the path I had chosen.

Lost in my thoughts, I suddenly noticed Mini's presence beside me. Her knowing look seemed to convey understanding and support. And then it happened - with a swift whisper of power rippling through the air, Lyn transformed into her majestic dragon form. Through the window, I caught a glimpse of the magnificent creature I had come to know so well. But seeing her scales glisten in the sunlight for the first time left me breathless.

I couldn't help but be taken aback by the sight before me. The sheer size and beauty of her dragon form was something that would stay etched in my memory forever. This was a view that no words could fully capture or do justice to.

As I turned away from the window, watching the majestic lynx take flight and disappear into the distant horizon broke my heart. But I couldn't let that hold me back. With determination, I faced the room and asked aloud, "So what happens now?" The commander's voice cut through the silence, "I have arranged for a car to pick us up outside. It will take us to the nearby airport, where a, private jet awaits to transport us to the agency's exclusive training facility." A sense of excitement and unease tingled through me at the thought of what lay ahead. "Make sure you rest on the flight," he continued, "Because once we land, we will hit the ground running with your training." My mind raced with anticipation as I followed him out of the room, ready to embark on this new chapter of my life.

IT HAD ONLY been one week since I arrived at the military training base and met my infamous instructor, Hargreaves, known to all as the drill sergeant from hell. Despite Commander Robinson's warning that I would hit the ground running, I scoffed at the idea - how bad could it be? But as soon as we landed, I was thrust into the clutches of Hargreaves, who tossed a set of pristine gym clothes at me. "Don't just stand there gawking, changing room is over there!" he barked, his harsh tone sending shivers down my spine. In stunned silence, I stood there with my mouth wide open, feeling like a deer caught in the headlights of an oncoming car. Shaking his head in frustration, Hargreaves pointed to a door with a sign that read 'changing room' and let out a deep breath before bellowing, "MOVE YOUR ASS! I WANT YOU CHANGED AND BACK HERE IN FIVE MINUTES. DON'T KEEP ME WAITING!" Without pausing for a response, he began counting down in his aggressive drill sergeant voice. Panic raced through my veins as I sprinted to the changing room, not wanting to anger the strict instructor any further. The adrenaline pumping through my body matched the urgency in Hargreaves' voice, making me realise that this was just a glimpse into the gruelling training that lay ahead.

As I emerged from the changing room, my heart raced with nervousness as I approached him. I was relieved to see that he was still counting, his strong jaw set in determination. "Well, at least you can follow basic instruction," he said with a sneer, his piercing blue eyes scanning over me. Without hesitation, I replied in a loud and confident voice, "Yes." I could feel my nerves causing my volume control to skyrocket.

A small glimmer of a smile crossed his lips before he turned and motioned for me to follow him. "We're going to assess your physical fitness so I know where to focus your training. Do you understand?" he asked in a commanding tone.

I nodded eagerly, eager to prove myself and show that I was ready for whatever challenges lay ahead. As we made our way to the gym, he started conversationally, "I'm assuming you have no combat training?"

I replied in a more normal volume this time, "No, if I'm being honest, I used to be a complete pacifist." Even as the words left my mouth, I surprised myself with how open and honest I was being.

He stopped walking for a moment and looked at me seriously. "I hope all that is in the past because if you think pretty words will be enough to survive in this world, you are sorely mistaken."

My heart sank at his harsh words but deep down, I knew he was right. "I am well aware of that now," I admitted quietly. "And I am determined to move forward and learn how to survive."

With a curt nod, he continued leading the way to the gym. My mind raced with fear and anticipation as I prepared for the gruelling physical assessment that awaited me. But despite my nerves, I felt a spark of determination ignite within me - I was ready to face whatever challenges were thrown my way in this new world.

With a confident push, he swung open the heavy, frosted glass door which let out a soft whoosh as if inviting us into another world. We stepped inside and were immediately greeted by sleek, modern design that seemed to emanate luxury and sophistication. As I followed behind him, I couldn't help but feel like I was entering a state-of-the-art gym - a place I had only seen on TV shows. For someone like me who had never prioritised physical fitness before my abduction, this was a completely new experience.

The gym was unlike any others I had seen before - it was like stepping into the future, leaving all primitive equipment and techniques from the Stone Age behind.

There was an M.M.A cage in one corner, rows of shining treadmills lined up against the wall, various weight machines scattered around, and an array of free weights in another area. As I looked around, impressed and slightly intimidated by the high-tech equipment surrounding me, Hargreaves approached a treadmill and started punching buttons on its control panel.

Carefully, I approached his side, hoping to avoid another outburst. "What is your first command?" I asked anxiously.

"Step up onto the treadmill and begin running," he directed. "I will handle the controls. Simply attach this monitor to your wrist. It will track all of your vital signs. And do not fret - if you collapse, the machine will automatically stop."

Feeling a mixture of anticipation and unease, I climbed onto the sleek, high-tech treadmill and started running as instructed. The floor thrummed beneath my feet as Hargreaves expertly adjusted the speed and incline. With each stride, I could feel my heart pounding faster and my muscles working harder than ever before. Despite my initial hesitation towards physical exertion, there was an undeniable thrill in being in this futuristic gym and pushing myself beyond my limits.

As I settled into a steady rhythm, my heart rate and breathing gradually increased before levelling off. Hargreaves diligently monitored all of my vitals, his sharp eyes scanning the monitors and machines around us. "Keep going for as long as you can," he urged, "just focus on running. This will give me a better understanding of your endurance." My legs burned with fatigue and my chest heaved with each breath, but I was determined to meet Hargreaves' expectations. In between gasps for air, I managed to ask, "What would be considered a good starting score?" But Hargreaves only responded with a stern, "Do not worry about that now. Just keep running." And so I did, my feet pounding against the belt of the treadmill as my body strained to maintain the pace. The room began to blur around me as sweat dripped down my forehead and my muscles screamed in protest, but I refused to give up. This was just a small step towards achieving ultimate physical fitness, and I was determined to see it through until the end.

I lost track of my surroundings as I determinedly put one foot in front of the other. The air was thick and humid, making it hard to breathe. My legs felt heavy and my body ached, but I refused to give up. Suddenly, a wave of dizziness hit me like a ton of bricks.

I stumbled forward, trying to steady myself, but it was no use. My vision blurred and my head spun as if I were on a carnival ride gone wrong. As I struggled to push through the dizziness, my knees buckled beneath me and I fell to the floor with a thud.

I vaguely remember someone placing a cold cloth on my forehead and speaking words of comfort. But all I could focus on was the intense nausea building in my stomach. With every violent heave, my body emptied itself, and I couldn't stop it.

Thankfully, Hargreaves appeared by my side, holding a bucket that caught everything with ease. It seemed like this was a common occurrence for him, as he calmly helped me through the ordeal. Even in my weakened state, I couldn't help but feel grateful for his presence and care in that moment.

My chest felt tight, constricted by the rapid thumping of my heart. My stomach churned and threatened to bring up the rest of my breakfast. I reached for a towel and dabbed at my face, only to find Hargreaves handing me a bottle of water. "You can glare at me all you want," he sneered, "but it's my responsibility to push you until you break, and then push some more." His smug expression made my blood boil. "If you don't like it, then quit." He paused for a moment before adding, "But don't forget, you managed an hour and a half, which is comparable to most professional human athletes." As much as I detested him in this moment, I refused to let him win. Jeremiah never broke me, so this asshole wouldn't either. With fierce determination, I dragged myself up onto my feet and took a swig of water to settle my roiling stomach.

I waited for Hargreaves to continue with the next part of my assessment. My muscles were already burning from the intense physical training, but I refused to show any sign of weakness.

"Alright, if you're ready," Hargreaves said, his voice betraying no emotion. "Next, we will do a flexibility assessment. For this, I need you to copy the poses I perform as accurately as possible. Once in position, you will need to hold still while I inspect how close you come to achieving the pose."

He paused before adding, "If you have ever tried yoga, it is very similar to that." A small burst of relief coursed through me at his words. I remembered doing yoga back in school and it wasn't that difficult.

With a nod of understanding, I kept my mouth shut tightly, not wanting to risk vomiting again.

Hargreaves lead me over to a softly padded floored area, being a tall and muscular man who could easily pass for Arnold Schwarzenegger's twin, he seemed out of place in an area designed for gentle movement

I quickly realised that this was not your typical yoga. The poses were unfamiliar and difficult, and no matter how hard I tried, I couldn't seem to contort my body in the same way Hargreaves effortlessly demonstrated. The contortions seemed impossible for someone of his build. Let alone someone with little to no expense in this discipline

After an hour of trying to mimic his movements, I found myself repeatedly falling on my face in defeat. Hargreaves didn't seem fazed though, and finally called an end to the torture. "Well, that was a disaster," he chuckled. "We'll definitely need to work on your balance and flexibility. Luckily, some of the martial arts you'll be learning will help with that."

just when I thought this fitness assessment couldn't get any stranger, Hargreaves asked me about my experience with dance. "What does dancing have to do with anything?" I snapped in frustration. "Is this some kind of messed up hazing ritual?"

Hargreaves' expression turned serious as he explained, "Dance training can actually help build muscle, increase stamina, improve mobility and flexibility...the list goes on."is words carried a subtle edge of menace, making me realise that I may have crossed a line."I apologise," I quickly interjected. "This is all new to me."

He softened his tone as he explained, "Everything I'm teaching you has a purpose - to prepare you for anything that could happen to you." It was clear that Hargreaves was not just a fitness instructor, but a trainer in every sense of the word.

Hargreaves barked out his instructions with an air of stern authority, his voice cutting through the tense silence of the gym. My heart sunk as I realised that this test was not going to be a walk in the park like I had hoped. "Do you know how to do a push up?" he asked, his eyes boring into mine.

"Yeah," I replied curtly, trying to brush off my sense of disappointment and frustration. He gestured for me to get into position on the mat beside him.

"Good. When I say down, you will lower yourself slowly and with controlled movements. And when I say up, you will push yourself back up to starting position," he explained, his tone leaving no room for questioning. "Just like with the treadmill, we will continue until I say stop or your body gives out." With a deep breath, I got into position, my body already tensing in anticipation of the upcoming challenge.

As I began the first push up, my muscles strained and trembled under the weight of my own body. The room filled with the sound of heavy breathing and the unmistakable scent of sweat. Every fibre in my being screamed at me to give up, but I was determined to push through until the very end. This was not going to be easy, but I was ready to give it everything I had

After another gruelling hour of intense push ups, Hargreaves finally took pity on me and allowed me to stop. My trembling arms gave out as I collapsed onto the gym floor, sweat pouring down my face and my muscles screaming with exhaustion. "You can rest now," Hargreaves said, a hint of amusement in his voice. "I have all the information I need. Go sit on one of the weight benches while I review everything and we can discuss a basic training plan." As I stumbled towards the bench, my body felt like it was made of lead and my breaths came in ragged gasps. The clang and thud of heavy weights being lifted filled the air, accompanied by the unmistakable scent of sweat and determination. But despite the physical toll, I couldn't help but feel a surge of excitement knowing that soon I would be embarking on a journey to better myself both physically and mentally.

However, that excitement was short-lived as I succumbed to exhaustion and decided to lay on the weight bench, thinking it would be a good idea to rest while Hargreaves reviewed my progress. It wasn't long before my eyes grew heavy and slowly began to close. I didn't know how long I had actually managed to sleep - it felt like mere seconds - but suddenly, I was jolted awake by an angry presence towering over me. Hargreaves' face was red with fury, veins pulsing in his forehead and neck as he bellowed at me. If the situation weren't so intimidating,

I might have been slightly impressed by his intensity. "I told you to take a seat, not get comfortable and have a nap!" he thundered, his face turning an alarming shade of purple.

"Join me," he beckoned, leading the way with quick, purposeful strides towards the glass door we had entered through. I hastened to keep up with him, feeling a sense of urgency in his movements. He stopped just a few doors down from the main gym, forcefully pushing the door open and holding it for me to enter.

"Take a seat," he gruffly commanded, pointing to one of the few chairs in the small room. Without hesitation, I sat down and remained silent as he settled into a chair behind a plain wooden table.

The air in the room was tense and charged with anticipation, as if something important was about to happen. The only sound was our steady breathing and the faint hum of equipment from the nearby gym.

As his intense gaze locked onto mine, I could feel the weight of his determination and authority bearing down on me. Every word he spoke carried a heavy presence, settling deep in the pit of my stomach. He began to delve into the details of my training plan, laying out expectations for me going forward. "Firstly," he said, his voice firm and direct, "I want you to know that in the stamina and muscle assessment, you impressed me." His words stirred a sense of pride within me, but I could tell there was more to come. "Considering that you have never done this sort of thing before, your performance was remarkable. However, it should be noted that your comparison is only impressive when compared to humans." He paused, studying me carefully as he continued. "From the information I've been given, you should be able to grow quickly in these areas." His tone shifted then, becoming more serious and stern. "But my biggest concern lies in your flexibility and movement style. Even when compared to humans, your level is severely lacking." I could feel my cheeks flush with embarrassment as I remembered my own clumsiness even in life before all of this. Letting out a soft moan, I hoped he wouldn't probe further into this weakness.

But despite his stern words, I could sense a genuine care behind them. And as he spoke, I couldn't help but feel a wave of determination wash over me. This was where I belonged, and I was ready for whatever challenges lay ahead. "So starting tomorrow," he declared with a commanding tone, "you will be meeting me here at 05:00 for our first run of the day." The thought of such an early start made me groan inwardly. "This will be one hour outside on the base grounds - you are to keep pace with me for the entire run and do not eat breakfast before coming." His instructions were clear, and I could already feel the sweat forming on my brow.

"At 06:00," he continued, "we will go to a secure gym - just the two of us. And I will be pushing your muscles way past breaking point." A sadistic gleam flashed in his eyes as he let this sink in. "This will continue for six hours, followed by a lunch break. But you must be back in the gym by 13:00, where we will spend the next ten hours working on your flexibility." The thought of such rigorous training was daunting, but I knew it was necessary if I wanted to succeed in this new life.

termination and authority bearing down on me. Every word he spoke carried a heavy presence, settling deep in the pit of my stomach. He began to delve into the details of my training plan, laying out expectations for me going forward. "Firstly," he said, his voice firm and direct, "I want you to know that in the stamina and muscle assessment, you impressed me." His words stirred a sense of pride within me, but I could tell there was more to come. "Considering that you have never done this sort of thing before, your performance was remarkable. However, it should be noted that your comparison is only impressive when compared to humans." He paused, studying me carefully as he continued. "From the information I've been given, you should be able to grow quickly in these areas." His tone shifted then, becoming more serious and stern. "But my biggest concern lies in your flexibility and movement style. Even when compared to humans, your level is severely lacking." I could feel my cheeks flush with embarrassment as I remembered my own clumsiness even in life before all of this. Letting out a soft moan, I hoped he wouldn't probe further into this weakness.

But despite his stern words, I could sense a genuine care behind them. And as he spoke, I couldn't help but feel a wave of determination wash over me. This was where I belonged, and I was ready for whatever challenges lay ahead. "So starting tomorrow," he declared with a commanding tone, "you will be meeting me here at 05:00 for our first run of the day." The thought of such an early start made me groan inwardly. "This will be one hour outside on the base grounds - you are to keep pace with me for the entire run and do not eat breakfast before coming." His instructions were clear, and I could already feel the sweat forming on my brow.

"At 06:00," he continued, "we will go to a secure gym - just the two of us. And I will be pushing your muscles way past breaking point." A sadistic gleam flashed in his eyes as he let this sink in. "This will continue for six hours, followed by a lunch break. But you must be back in the gym by 13:00, where we will spend the next ten hours working on your flexibility." The thought of such rigorous training was daunting, but I knew it was necessary if I wanted to succeed in this new life.

For the remainder of the day, we will return to the gym and practice basic hand-to-hand combat techniques. Although you are safe on this base, I feel more comfortable knowing that all recruits have the skills to defend themselves until backup arrives. Let's head to the cage and see how you fare against me.

The fighting cage was like nothing I had ever seen before, a massive circular structure constructed entirely of sturdy metal bars. The floor was covered in a thick mat that showed signs of countless battles and struggles. The air inside was thick with the scent of sweat and adrenaline, sending goosebumps rippling across my skin as I tentatively stepped into the ring.

My stomach churned nervously as Hargreaves led me into the centre of the cage. He began to speak, his tone serious and determined. "These skills are crucial for survival," he explained, sweeping his arm around to indicate our surroundings. "You never know when you may be caught off guard or outnumbered."

He motioned for me to take a fighting stance as we prepared to spar. Hargreaves would be my opponent, training me to defend myself and others from harm. "For the foreseeable future, this will ensure your safety and prevent any unnecessary injuries," he stated firmly.

Despite my nerves, I nodded in understanding and took a breath to steady myself. Hargreaves taught me basic fighting techniques and stances before we began sparring. His movements were lightning-fast and precise, easily deflecting my clumsy attacks. But with each round, I could feel myself improving.

Not only did Hargreaves teach me how to fight effectively, but he also helped me use my newfound strength and agility to my advantage in combat. He showed me how to dodge attacks with my speed and deliver powerful blows with my enhanced strength.

As we trained, I couldn't help but feel grateful for this opportunity to learn from someone as skilled as Hargreaves. Though he could be stern and intimidating at times, it was clear that he genuinely wanted me to succeed and become a formidable fighter.

After what felt like hours of intense training, Hargreaves called for a break. We stepped out of the cage and took a seat on nearby benches, panting and wiping sweat from our brows. "You're a quick learner," he remarked with a small smile, and I couldn't help but feel a sense of pride in my progress.

With a nod and a gesture, he dismissed me to my dorm for the night. As I walked away, my mind was already buzzing with anticipation for our next meeting the next morning. A sense of release and calm settled over me as I made my way through the quiet halls, my footsteps echoing off the polished floors. The perfect lighting and warm temperature of the building created a peaceful atmosphere, like a sanctuary from the chaos outside. I couldn't wait to continue my training tomorrow, eager to learn more from hells drill sergeant .

For 18 gruelling hours each day, my body was pushed to its limits. My feet pounded against the rough terrain of the nature trails, leaving a trail of blood as I ran tirelessly toward my goal. The weights felt heavier each time I lifted them, my muscles screaming in protest as I pushed through one more rep. Even practicing martial arts forms became a battle against my trembling, exhausted body. But beyond the physical challenges, there were also mental ones: yoga and dance classes tested not only my physical endurance but also my focus and discipline. Every night after training, I dragged myself back to my room and collapsed into bed, too tired to even think about anything other than sleep.

The only person I saw besides my intense instructors was Mini – she never failed to offer words of encouragement and support. Her calm presence and soothing voice provided a much-needed respite from the demanding routine. One particularly tough night, when I was on the brink of giving up and calling it quits, she gave me a stern talking-to. As an empathic witch, she could sense my emotions and knew that I was capable of so much more than I believed. With her gentle yet firm guidance, she reminded me of Lyn's belief in my strength and encouraged me to push through. From then on, I gave 100% every single day, determined to become the strong, fierce woman that Lyn knew I could be. Each day presented a new challenge, but with Mini's unwavering support and Lyn's belief in me, I was ready to face them head-on.

The only other soul I encountered aside from the intense instructor Hargreaves was Mini - a beacon of unwavering positivity and encouragement. Her calm demeanour and soothing voice provided a much-needed respite from the gruelling routine. On one particularly brutal night, when my resolve was faltering and my weariness was threatening to consume me, she gave me a stern talking-to. As an empathic witch, she could sense my emotions and knew that I had more strength within me than I believed. With her gentle yet firm guidance, she reminded me of Lyn's unwavering faith in my abilities and urged me to push through the fatigue and doubts. From that moment on, I poured all my energy into each day, determined to rise up as the strong, fearless woman that Lyn knew I could become. Every new day brought its own set of challenges, but with Mini's unyielding support and Lyn's unwavering belief in me, I was ready to face them head-on with courage and determination.

CHAPTER 7

THE SECOND WEEK of training began just like the first, with my hands gripping tightly onto the cold metal of the weight machines. My muscles shook and burned as I pushed through each repetition, sweat trickling down my face and soaking into my clothes, making them cling uncomfortably to my skin. With Hargreaves doubling the weight on the machines, every lift felt like a herculean effort.

I could feel the chill of the metal weights seeping into my skin as I strained against their added heft, my palms slippery with sweat as I fought to maintain my grip on the bar. Despite my body protesting with soreness and fatigue from the previous week's sessions, I pushed on, determined to conquer this new challenge.

Just as I finished my final set, I was called to Alexander's office. My mind raced with thoughts and questions as I quickly made my way there, hoping for some guidance or insight from Lyn. Finally reaching his door, I took a moment to catch my breath before knocking softly and waiting for a response.

The door creaked open as I timidly entered the room. I could feel my heart racing, it was like being called to the principal's office in high school all over again. "Hi Alex, you sent for me?" I said, trying to keep the nerves out of my voice.

"Yes, Jessica, thank you for coming so quickly," Alex replied, gesturing for me to take a seat. As I sat down, my palms started sweating and I tried to steady my breathing.

"I have some things I would like to discuss with you." My mind started racing, had I done something wrong? Am I not performing well enough?

"Of course, have I done something wrong?" I blurted out before he could continue.

"No, you are doing brilliantly, and I need to speak to you about that,"

As I looked at Alex with a mixture of confusion and disbelief, he reached out to reassure me. His expression was one of concern as he continued speaking.

"Your progress has been remarkable, far surpassing our expectations. The intense training you completed in just one week is usually spread out over months for graduating teams. How are you feeling at the end of each day and the start of the next?" His words were a blur to me as my mind struggled to process this new information. Faster than expected? Completing rigorous training in just one week? It all seemed too surreal. And yet, a sense of pride and accomplishment swelled within me as I realised how much I had accomplished.

"Well, the training is definitely challenging, but that's what I expected. By the end of each day, I am completely exhausted. All I can do is eat and pass out from exhaustion. But when I wake up the next day, I feel rejuvenated and ready to tackle whatever comes my way. Although I was hoping to learn more about the paranormal world, so far it has just been intense physical training." I spoke honestly, not wanting to sound ungrateful but also needing to express my concerns.

I spoke honestly, my words carefully chosen to convey both my gratitude and my concerns. As I sat across from Alex, the weight of his expectations settled heavily on my shoulders.

"Yes, there is a good reason for that," he replied in a voice that seemed to hold the wisdom of centuries. "As you can imagine, living in the paranormal world can be physically demanding. Our initial plan was to build up your physical strength before diving into anything else. We expected it would take quite some time for you to reach the required level, but you have exceeded our expectations by a large margin. So now, we'd like to adjust the plan for you." My heart swelled with pride at their praise, but I couldn't help but feel apprehensive about what was to come. They wanted to change the plan for me, and I could sense that it would be no easy feat."We will still focus on physical training first," they continued. "The intensity will increase, but the duration will decrease. This means that your mornings will be dedicated to building your strength and endurance. In the afternoons, after lunch, we will switch gears and give you some time to rest and recover. This part of your day will revolve around learning about our history and culture. Once you have a good grasp on that, we will move on to other subjects such as demonology and other crucial subjects. I will personally oversee this part of your education."

"The next part of your day," He said with a hint of excitement, "will focus on discovering and honing your abilities with Commander Robinson's guidance. Be warned, the workload will be extreme."

I nodded, steeling myself for the challenges ahead. But then they mentioned setting up regular meetings with Him and my instructors to address any issues or concerns. It was comforting to know that they were invested in my well-being.

"Do you find this proposal acceptable?"The words hung in the air between us, like a delicate spiderweb waiting to be shattered. The weight of his question pressed down on me, making my heart race and my palms sweat. His eyes bore into mine, full of intensity and expectation. I took a deep breath and replied, "Yes, that sounds acceptable to me." My voice sounded small and hesitant, but I knew this was a momentous decision. His face relaxed into a smile and he leaned back in his chair, relieved by my answer. But there was still a lingering tension in the air as he asked, "When do we start the new program?" I could feel the gravity of this conversation - it would shape our future together. My mind raced with excitement and nerves as I thought about what lay ahead for us.

"You will start your new training plan tomorrow Jess. For now, take the rest of the day off and enjoy some leisure time. Perhaps you could visit the rec area and unwind, or Mini is available if you desire some company." Alex's warm smile radiated understanding and compassion. "Thank you for all your help and support, Alex. I am grateful for everything you are doing for me." I said my voice was filled with appreciation and gratitude as i slowly made my way out of the room, feeling a sense of relief wash over her like a gentle wave.

Despite the intense physical demands, my time in the gym had become a welcome respite from the chaos of my other daily Classes. The workouts pushed me to my limits, each exercise more challenging than the last. we abandoned traditional cardio and focused more on weight training, for the first part of our morning. Then we incorporated sparing and dance practice into our midmorning , that helped an element of grace and fluidity to my movements. As I settled into this new routine, However, after a few weeks of this new regimen, Hargreaves announced he had a surprise for me during our morning warm-ups My curiosity mixed with trepidation as I wondered what twisted form of torture he had planned for me now.

I was eager to discover his plans. He loved to tease and torture me like this, so after our warm-up, which consisted of a five-mile jog on the treadmill and a 30-minute yoga session, he led me past the regular gym where we usually worked out. We passed several unmarked doors, building up my curiosity and anticipation. Hargreaves always loved surprises and I knew he wouldn't give anything away. Finally, we exited the gym through a door I had never noticed before and entered another building at the other side of the yard. There were guards posted at the entrance, heightening my excitement even more.

The training compound loomed before me, a place I had yet to explore. It held little interest for me in the past; always too exhausted or occupied to spare a thought for it. As we approached, the guards performed practiced motions and waved us through the gates. With each step, I could feel Hargreaves' excitement radiating off of him like heat from a fire. "Are you ready, kid?" he asked with a grin plastered on his face. The nickname irked me, but I let it slide for now. I had no idea what awaited me inside, but my heart was racing with anticipation. I nodded eagerly, and Hargreaves let out a booming laugh.

"Laugh it up, big guy. I'll have my revenge when we spar later." His words only made him laugh even louder, and I couldn't help but chuckle along with him.

My heart fluttered with anticipation as the instructor led me towards a pair of intimidating steel doors. "The surprise is just through that door, and it's also today's lesson," he said with a sly grin. I couldn't help but wonder what was waiting for me on the other side. The doors were colossal, towering over me at nearly twice my height. In the world of the paranormal, I had grown accustomed to such imposing structures, yet these doors seemed almost exaggerated in their size. I could feel the weight of them bearing down on me as we approached. As the instructor gestured for me to open them, I hesitated, feeling a sense of trepidation wash over me. But I pushed aside my fears and placed my hands on the smooth metal surface, pushing with all my strength. To my surprise, they did not give easily - they were much heavier than expected. With a grunt of effort, I gritted my teeth and put more power into my thrust. Finally, with a loud groan, the doors creaked open. Once fully opened, they stayed in place, revealing a short dark and mysterious passage beyond. "Impressive," the instructor said with admiration. "Those are testing gates. If you can't get through them, it's usually straight back to training. Only a select few can do it on their first try, but I knew you had it in you, kid." He playfully ruffled my hair like an uncle would to their favourite niece or nephew. Blushing at this unexpected show of affection, I stepped through the gates into the unknown realm that awaited me

"Now come on, let me show you around," Hargreaves said, beaming with excitement as he led me through a doorway into the weapons testing and training facility. As we stepped through, the darkness lifted and my eyes adjusted to the bright lights that illuminated the room.

I couldn't help but gasp in amazement as I took in the different target setups: a traditional shooting range, what looked like an archery setup, and other weapons target setups. Hargreaves chuckled at my reaction, clearly pleased with himself.

"Wow, what the actual fuck? Why did the room change when we walked in?" I asked in shock.

Hargreaves' smug grin only grew wider as he explained, "There is an illusion spell on the entrance so you can't see anything until you step in. Adds a bit of mystery to the place."

I couldn't help but marvel at the level of magic involved in creating such an illusion. The air was buzzing with energy and anticipation, making it clear that this was a serious training facility for skilled warriors. It was both exhilarating and intimidating all at once.

My excitement was palpable as I eagerly asked, "This is awesome, so where do we start?" I couldn't wait I wanted to get my hands on some weapons and start training.

"Well, let's just go through a few things first," he said with a smile, clearly enjoying my enthusiasm.

"You can use this facility during your downtime to get in some extra practice outside your normal training" His words were like music to my ears. "Second, you will still be required to do physical training. The sort of work we do isn't just about using weapons. We must become weapons if the situation requires it."

As we walked through the sleek halls and past various rooms, he explained the layout of the facility. "This place goes six levels up and six down," he gestured to the elevator doors nearby. "The lower levels are for research and development, so you probably won't need to go there anytime soon. They get a little protective over their projects." He winked playfully before continuing.

"The upper six floors are pure weapons training grounds," he paused dramatically. "The first two floors are dedicated for ranged weapons, the next two are for mid-ranged weapons, and the final two are for close-ranged combat." A thrill ran through me at the thought of testing out various weapons and finding my strengths.

my mentor grinned mischievously. "Today, Your instructors have graciously given you the day off, I have you all to myself." He reached out to squeeze my shoulder encouragingly.

I couldn't believe my luck. A whole day to experiment with different weapons? It was a dream come true. And with my Hargreaves by my side, I knew I would learn so much. "Also, as we explore and try different things, I want you to keep an open mind and give everything a try , I have a feeling I know where your talents are going to lie" he added, his voice filled with excitement. With a grin, I nodded eagerly, ready to dive into this new world of weapons and training.

As Hargreaves spoke, his words were met with my nodding in agreement. But beneath the surface, my excitement was quickly morphing into apprehension. The thought of handling a weapon, any weapon, filled me with terror. "Come on," Hargreaves said, beckoning me to follow him. "Let's go see the quartermaster."

We approached a large weapons cage where a towering man stood guard. He seemed to be expecting us. As we drew closer, the quartermaster warmly greeted Hargreaves with an embrace. From their interaction, it was clear they were old friends.

"I assume you're Jess," the quartermaster said, turning to me with a friendly smile. "Hargreaves has told me about your progress and I've arranged some toys for you to try out." His eyes twinkled mischievously as he gestured towards the array of weapons lining the walls. "Now, am I correct in assuming you had no prior experience with weapons before coming here?" His question hung in the air, causing my nerves to jump even more at the realisation that I was about to handle deadly instruments for the first time.

I nodded my agreement, too nervous to articulate a response. The words hung in the air like a thick fog, heavy and suffocating. "That's good," he said with a slight smile, his tone calm and reassuring. "It means we don't need to train out any bad habits, and we can teach you the most efficient ways to handle your weapons."

My heart raced at the mention of weapons, but I tried to push aside my fear and focus on what he was saying. "I've been told you are fairly strong," he continued, his eyes assessing me. "So we don't need to worry about recoil on firearms."

His words did little to ease my apprehension as he mentioned firearms. But I knew I needed to face my fears if I wanted to learn how to use them properly. "That's what I would like you to start with today," he said, gesturing towards a table covered in various guns. "I have a few sidearms and shotguns. How do you feel about trying them?"

My hands trembled slightly as I stepped closer to the table, eyeing the array of deadly weapons before me. "I can give them a go," I managed to say, though my voice betrayed my apprehension. "But I am apprehensive about them."

"It's good to be apprehensive of them," he replied with a serious tone, his warm demeanour vanishing for a moment. "It will ensure you treat them with the required care and respect." His words carried a weight of importance, and it made me realise that these were not just mere objects. They were weapons designed for one purpose: to kill. And that fact sent chills down my spine.

He then led Hargreaves and me over to a section of a shooting range with a multitude of targets already set up; throughout the entire exchange between the quartermaster, Hargreaves had stayed silent, and it didn't look as though he had any plans of speaking soon, meaning I was purely in the quarter maters hands.

We stopped at a bench that was set up in front of the target area and arranged in front of me where 3 shotguns and 3 handguns were. Seeing them gave my stomach a nervous lurch. This is getting intense fast.

The quartermaster gestured for me to take a seat at the bench, and I did so, my heart pounding in my chest. He picked up one of the shotguns and handed it to me, showing me how to hold it properly and explaining the different parts of the gun.

. The quartermaster's deep, authoritative voice echoed through the shooting range as he introduced each firearm with precision and expertise. "We are going to see how you get on with the shotgun's first lass," he said, his thick accent adding a touch of charm to his words. His weathered hand gestured towards a row of guns displayed on a long table.

"From right to left, we have the Tabor TS-12 gauge rotating tube-fed semi-auto shotgun, which holds 4 shells per tube and has 3 tubes with one shot in the pipe. It requires manual left or right rotation," he explained, my eyes scanning over the details of the weapon before moving on. And passing me the next one in the line up

"Next, we have the DP-12 pump action double barrel rear-loading shotgun with an impressive 16-shell capacity." again we studied every detail before he handed me the next one

And last but not least, the KSG pump action with a maximum capacity of 14 shells."

"Now, before we start shooting, I want to stress the importance of safety," he said sternly. "These are not toys, they are dangerous weapons and must be treated with caution and respect at all times."

I nodded, feeling a sudden wave of anxiety wash over me. I had never held a gun before, let alone fired one.

"First things first, we need to make sure the gun is unloaded," he continued. "Always check the chamber and barrel before handling any firearm."

I followed his lead as he showed me how to check for ammunition and safely unload the gun. Once it was cleared, he demonstrated how to hold it properly for aiming.

"Now, take aim at that target over there," he said, pointing towards a large paper target about 20 feet away.

My hands shook as I raised the shotgun and tried to steady my aim. My heart was racing so fast, I could barely concentrate on what he was saying next.

"When you're ready to shoot, take a deep breath in and slowly let it out as you squeeze the trigger," he instructed.

I followed his directions as best as I could manage, feeling a surge of adrenaline rush through my body when I pulled the trigger. The loud boom of the gunshot echoed through the shooting range and I felt a jolt through my shoulder from recoil.

"Hmm not bad for your first shot," the quartermaster commented with a small smile. "Let's try again."

He helped me adjust my stance and grip until eventually I was able to hit closer and closer to the centre of the target. By my third shot, I was feeling more confident and less anxious.

After practicing with the each of the shotguns for a while,

"right then lass next is the hand guns" said the quartermaster as I fired the last shotgun shell and clearing the chamber to ensure it was safe

The quartermaster pulled out a sleek, black handgun from the case and placed it in my hands. "This is the HK45 tactical," he said, his voice tinged with admiration. "It holds ten rounds per magazine, and one in the chamber. Notice the 3 dot sight system for improved accuracy." I held the gun carefully, taking note of its weight - 27.68 ounces when empty. The powerful .45 caliber rounds it fired promised lethal force.

Next, he handed me a smaller gun, the sig M11-A1 9mm. "This one is designed for concealed carry," he explained. "It has a 3-dot adjustable sight system and can hold up to 15 rounds in the magazine, plus one in the chamber." I took aim at an imaginary target as he continued to describe its features. The weight of this gun was slightly heavier at 32 ounces when empty.

Finally, he revealed the Beretta M9, a classic firearm used by many soldiers. "This one also has a 3 dot sight system, but fires 9mm rounds instead," he stated confidently. Its weight was comparable to the sig - 33.3 ounces when unladen.

After thoroughly familiarising myself with each weapon, the quartermaster led me to a shooting range where I could put my newly acquired knowledge into practice. He showed me how to hold each gun properly, adjust my stance for stability, and fire with precision. Despite his expert guidance, it quickly became clear that guns were not my forte. I struggled to hit even a stationary target with any accuracy.

With a final nod of approval, the quartermaster and I came to a mutual decision that the sig M11-A1 9mm was my best option. As he handed me the weapon, his weathered face took on a serious expression. "Jess," he said in a low voice, "everyone who walks around this facility is armed. Our work is dangerous, and you must always be prepared to defend yourself. I can tell from your brief training that guns are not your forte, but I insist you carry this with you." His words hung in the air, heavy with the weight of responsibility. Reluctantly, I agreed to take on the burden of this new tool.

The quartermaster then equipped me with a sturdy waist harness containing three fully loaded clips of ammo for my chosen weapon. Though I had never been fond of guns, especially after growing up in a society where violence was rare, I felt a sense of empowerment knowing I had a reliable means of protection at my disposal. With a deep breath, I braced myself for the challenges that lay ahead as he sent me off to explore the upper levels of the facility. The gun suddenly felt heavier against my side, and I couldn't shake off the feeling that I was about to enter into a world much darker and more dangerous than anything I had ever known before.

As Hargreaves and I made our way through the sterile, metallic corridors of the facility, I couldn't shake off the unease that clung to me. Each sharp turn and security checkpoint reminded me of the danger that lurked around every corner.

I couldn't help but notice that we bypassed the mid-range weapons section, jumping straight to the higher levels. When I questioned Hargreaves about it, he simply replied with a confident smirk, "No need to waste your time. We can always come back if my intuition is wrong." But his words were tinged with a hint of hesitation, making me wonder what was really going on in his mind.

Pushing aside my doubts, I followed him up the winding staircase that seemed to go on forever. With each step, my nerves grew more frayed. What could possibly be waiting for us on these upper levels? I had a sinking feeling that I was about to find out.

Finally, we reached our destination: the close combat floors. My eyes widened at the sight before me - a traditional dojo setting complete with mats, training equipment, and even bamboo pillars. And in the center of it all sat a stunning woman in athletic wear that could have been mistaken for high fashion. Her dark hair was pulled back into a sleek ponytail and her posture exuded confidence and grace.

She addressed us by name: "You are here earlier than expected, Hargreaves. And you must be Jess," she said with a hint of amusement in her smooth and melodic voice, giving no indication of aggression or hostility despite our sudden appearance.

Hiyori nodded, a small smile playing on her lips. The corners of her mouth turned up in a delicate curve, revealing dimples that added to her charming demeanour. "Yes, I am Hiyori," she said, her voice gentle yet confident. "And as for what's going on, I have been expecting you, Jess. I'm one of the close quarters combat trainers here at the facility. My job is to train recruits like yourself in hand-to-hand combat and other close range techniques."

A surge of excitement mixed with nervousness flooded through me at the thought of learning how to fight using my own body instead of relying on weapons. But I couldn't help but wonder why Hargreaves hadn't brought me here sooner.

"Why didn't Hargreaves bring me here sooner?" I asked, trying to keep my voice steady despite the racing of my heart. "He's been showing me basic self defence, but if that's your specialty, shouldn't you have been teaching me?"

Hiyori's expression turned serious as she answered, "There have been reports of increased threats and attacks against our agency and its agents. We believe it is necessary for all agents to be well-rounded in their training and prepared for any situation that may arise. However, you wouldn't have been able to handle this level of training when you first arrived. That's why we had Hargreaves get you up to speed before I take over."

My determination to prove myself only grew at the mention of danger and being prepared for anything. "So what do you need from me?" I asked, determined to show that I was willing to learn and do whatever it takes to protect myself and others.

"We will assess your current skills and tailor a training regimen specifically for you," Hiyori replied as she motioned for me to step onto the mat.

As we went through various exercises and drills, I could feel myself improving under Hiyori's expert guidance. Her style was fluid yet precise, with each movement having a specific purpose behind it.

After what felt like hours of intense training, Hiyori finally called for a break. As I sipped some water and caught my breath, Hargreaves came over to check up on my progress.

"Well done, Jess," she said with a proud smile. "You have more talent in this area than I was told." There was admiration and surprise in her eyes as she looked at me.

"Thank you, but Hargreaves deserves all the credit," I replied with a grin, feeling a sense of accomplishment. Despite my initial doubts about my abilities, I was starting to believe that maybe I did have what it takes to be an agent for this agency.

"Before we continue, there is something of great importance that we must discuss," Hiyori's words were weighted with meaning as she glanced in Hargreaves' direction. Taking a seat, she motioned for me to join her as she spoke again. "Aside from teaching hand-to-hand combat, I am also responsible for the agency's enchanted armoury."

My confusion must have been evident on my face because Hiyori continued to explain. "Throughout history, there have been countless tales of enchanted weapons - some called magical, or cursed, or blessed. But the truth is, it's often the user who wields these weapons that cause such phenomena. However, there are exceptions, and it is those rare weapons that I am tasked with handling."

As she spoke, her tone grew more serious and her eyes gleamed with knowledge and experience. My mind raced with questions as I struggled to process this new information. "So these weapons are real? And they possess powers?" I asked.

Hiyori nodded solemnly. "Yes, but it's not so simple. These weapons can be unpredictable and even dangerous at times. Some are truly what the legends say - cursed, blessed, imbued with magic, or containing sealed souls within them. These types of magical weapons are well-documented and usually only require a basic understanding of magic to wield. The ones that I am responsible for are much more rare and powerful; they are hardly handled by anyone, not even agency personnel. You see, some weapons are created using magic and anything touched by magic in its creation has something akin to a soul - something that seeks its match. Think of it like a destined weapon. But sometimes, even ordinary weapons used in the paranormal community for extended periods of time can gain sentience due to their exposure to powerful beings."

Anticipating my next question, Hiyori added, "Not everyone can wield one of these weapons. They can be too powerful and can easily overwhelm an individual. However, since Hargreaves has brought you directly to me and he is rarely ever wrong about these things, let us take you to the vault and see what happens."

Her words lingered in the air, leaving me awestruck and filled with wonder at the thought of such powerful and sentient weapons. The once unremarkable armoury now held a mysterious and awe-inspiring presence, as if it was a sacred temple to these ancient tools of war.

With a graceful movement, Hiyori rose to her feet and beckoned us towards a narrow staircase tucked away at the back of the dojo. The wooden steps creaked under our weight as we made our way up, anticipation building with each step.

CHAPTER 8

THE TOP FLOOR of the dojo was reminiscent of a sacred temple, with its traditional setting and soft floor mats that seemed to hug my feet as I walked. The air was thick with the smell of old wood and polished steel, mixed with hints of incense and sweat. As I took in the sight, my sensei, Hiyori, called out to grab my attention.

"Jess," she said, her voice grave and tinged with respect. "This area is reserved for those chosen by a weapon. If you are not deemed worthy, you will never be allowed past this point again." With her warning ringing in my ears, she motioned for me to follow her to a nearby bench.

As we sat down, Hiyori began to explain the significance of the weapons in front of us. She spoke of their ancient history, their immense power, and the great responsibility that came with wielding them. I listened intently, trying to absorb every word as though they were precious gems.

After her brief lesson, Hiyori stood up and placed a hand on my shoulder. "Close your eyes," she instructed, her tone serious yet gentle. "Take a few deep breaths and tell me how you feel." As I followed her instructions, I couldn't help but feel a heavy weight pressing down on me. There was an overwhelming aura in this room, as if thousands of unseen eyes were watching and judging me. My every flaw and insecurity was being exposed under their scrutiny, but I refused to cower to this feeling. I was not the little girl I used to be; nothing would make me feel weak or unworthy.

As I stood in the centre of the weapon room, a feeling of unease washed over me. It was as if thousands of eyes were watching my every move, each pair bearing its own unique voice or emotion. Hiyori's expression softened as she listened to my explanation.

"You have a strong connection with the weapons," she said, her voice calm and soothing. "It is not uncommon for those chosen by a weapon to feel drawn towards it. It is a sign of your potential and compatibility."

I let out a breath I didn't realise I was holding. The weight on my shoulders lifted slightly, knowing that there was some sort of reason behind my unexplainable attraction to these powerful objects.

"But how do I choose?" I asked, looking around at the vast array of weapons in front of me.

"You must listen to your heart," Hiyori replied, gesturing towards my chest. "Close your eyes again and concentrate on which weapon calls out to you the strongest."

With a nod, I closed my eyes and tried to block out the noise and distractions around me. As if on cue, two distinct melodies began to play in my mind - one soft and gentle like a lullaby, the other strong and determined like a battle cry. They seemed to be vying for my attention, neither overpowering the other.

"Which one is it?" Hiyori's voice broke through my thoughts.

"I-I don't know," I admitted, feeling overwhelmed by the conflicting melodies.

"That's okay," Hiyori reassured me. "It takes time to fully connect with a weapon. Just trust your instincts."

Holding onto Hiyori's words, I took a deep breath and opened my eyes once again. My gaze scanned the room, searching for any sign or indication of which weapon was calling out to me. And then suddenly, something caught my eye in the distance -

"There," I said, pointing to a display on the far wall. "It feels like I'm being called in that direction. It's hard to explain, but it's like the way Lyn would speak in my mind, but it's a silent melody."

"Ah, I see," Hiyori nodded, understanding my explanation. She signalled for Hargreaves, who had been standing nearby, to approach us.

"Jessica, tell us what is calling you, and we will bring it to you," she said.

With a newfound sense of determination, I pointed to the display on the far wall. Hargreaves gently picked me up and ran towards the display. My heart raced as we got closer and closer, until finally, we reached the display - full of different types of daggers.

Hiyori followed us with eager steps and opened the case I had been pointing to. Her eyes widened in approval as she nodded at me, giving me the go-ahead. I reached into the case, my fingers trembling with excitement, and caressed the set of traditional Filipino karambits. The curved blades felt smooth and cool against my skin, their sharp edges glinting in the light. As soon as both blades were in my hands, a sense of calm washed over me, like everything in the world was suddenly right again. I ran my fingertips along the razor-sharp edges, feeling a rush of adrenaline and contentment coursing through me. It was almost like they were purring in happiness in my grasp. Glancing up at the two instructors, I could see shock and awe written all over their faces. We sat there in a moment of silence, allowing me to fully bask in this feeling of completeness that only these blades could bring me.

"Jess, we should probably head to one of the training rooms to discuss what's happened and to talk about what happens now," Hargreaves said in a calm and reassuring voice that cut through the chaos that filled my mind. I stood up as if in a trance, my body moving on autopilot as I followed him and Hiyori towards one of the training rooms. My heart was racing with anticipation and fear, but also a sense of pure bliss. With each step, the ground felt unsteady beneath my feet, like I was walking through a dream. We entered one of the training rooms, its walls bear of weapons and equipment, and Hargreaves quickly contacted Alex. Hiyori remained by my side, her presence a comforting weight against my shoulder. Her dark eyes watched me intently, like a predator stalking its prey. As we waited for Alex to arrive, Hargreaves joined us and spoke in a serious tone. "Alex is on his way. We must discuss the ramifications of this and how it might affect the planned training. He's also bringing Killian." His words hung heavy in the air, adding to the already tense atmosphere of the room. "Jess, are you okay? You have been very quiet." Hargreaves' concern was evident in his gentle voice, but I couldn't find the words to respond. My mind was still trying to process everything that had happened.

my voice wavered, uncertain and filled with emotion. "Yeah, I'm.... I don't know. It's hard to describe." I paused, trying to put words to the feelings that swirled within my head. "I feel calm and whole; it's like I didn't even realise a piece of myself was missing until it had been filled. And now I feel more aware, like everything is in sharper definition." As I spoke, I started to noticed the intricate details of the room around him - the fine lines on the furniture, the subtle variations in colour on the walls. "Sounds are clearer, and smells are more pronounced," I continued, my eyes taking in the vibrant colour's and rich scents that filled the space. "Why is everyone so shocked?" i turned to look at my Trainers, seeing their expressions of disbelief and amazement. "I thought you took me there to see if a weapon would choose me...but it feels like something much more profound has happened."

"We will wait for Alex to arrive before giving a full explanation, but I must say, it is quite uncommon for someone to have such an intense reaction. Most individuals do not have any unaided response at all. This only adds to our surprise, as finding candidates with any kind of connection to the weapons is a challenging task for us," Hiyori replied, her voice laced with concern and fascination. She paused, "It's almost as if these blades have been waiting for you specifically." The weight of her words hung in the air, thick with mystery and wonder.

The door to the training room slid open, and Alex entered the room with commander Killian Robinson trailing behind him. The Head Trainer's face was a mixture of curiosity and concern as he looked at me. "Hargreaves contacted me about Jess's reaction," he said, his gaze flickering between Hiyori and I. "I want to see for myself what is going on."

Without any hesitation, I held out my hand towards Hiyori, offering her the Blades that had Claimed me moments earlier. She leaned in to take them took it from my hands, but before her fingerers touched them the blades discharged a spark of energy, shocking hiyori so her hand withdrew like she had just been burned

Alex nodded, his eyes scanning over the Blades then Hiyori's hand before meeting my gaze once again. "We will discuss this further later, but first we must assess if these weapons have impacted your combat ability," he said firmly. "Killian will be your opponent."

My heart skipped a beat at the mention of sparing. I had always been difficulty in martial arts thanks to being so clumsy, but I have been improving thanks to Hargreaves guidance. - but fighting against someone who was wielding a weapon was completely new territory.

As if sensing my unease, Killian gave me an encouraging smile before taking out a blocky looking sword and assuming a defensive stance across from me. I mirrored his movements before bracing myself for his first attack.

The fight was intense and fast-paced, each of us dodging and parrying as we tried to gain the upper hand. Killian was clearly skilled in using his weapon, but I found myself moving almost instinctively - anticipating his next move and countering it effortlessly.

It wasn't long before our sparring session ended with me pinning Killian down on the ground with his own weapon pressed against his throat. As soon as I released him, he stood up with a look of amazement on his face. "You pick up things remarkably fast.

My mind reeled as I stumbled backwards, shock and confusion coursing through every fibre of my being. "Alex, what's going on?" I asked, my voice trembling with nerves. "And how did I do that?" My hands shook as I gestured to the weapons in front of me, still trying to process what had just transpired.

"Did I do something wrong? Was I not supposed to touch these?" The weight of my actions hung heavy in the air, the uncertainty and fear creeping into my words.

"No, Jessica, you did nothing wrong," Alex reassured me, his tone filled with awe and amazement. "According to our records, these weapons have only ever been used by the original warriors who held them. And now, they have responded to your touch." His eyes widened as he spoke, a sense of wonder and reverence colouring his words. "This is truly remarkable."

The sound of gasps and murmurs filled the room as all the instructors looked at each other with wide eyes, their faces stricken with shock. I could feel the weight of their gazes on me, but I didn't quite understand the full ramifications of the situation. "What's going on? Are you all alarmed because of who the blades belonged to? Was it someone evil or dark?" Hiyori's expression was one of surprise and concern. "No, no, nothing like that," she reassured me quickly. "We would never allow something tainted in this facility. But if it will ease your mind, I will investigate and gather all information about the blade's origins for you." Her words brought a small sense of comfort to me and I felt myself relax slightly. It was then that I became aware of a faint humming coming from the blades, almost like a gentle lullaby. But it was a sound only I could hear or feel, like a secret shared between just me and the blades. The soothing hum reminded me of a group of kittens purring contentedly on my lap, a feeling of peacefulness washing over me.

As THE MONTHS passed, I noticed my training becoming easier. Hiyori had spent countless hours researching my weapons and discovered that they were a pair of karambits, forged and wielded by a powerful dragon during the blood wars. These blades were not just ordinary weapons, but tools used to protect the innocent and refugees. They had never called out to another user since their creation. Under the guidance of both Hiyori and Hargreaves, my training was a mixture of workouts in the gym as well as hand-to-hand combat and weapons training. At first, I had to use blunt karambits in order to learn proper form and technique without causing any permanent harm to myself or others. But even with these restrictions, I quickly learned that a blunt weapon could still be deadly in skilled hands. My mentors showed me how to attack pressure points and control my opponents' movements with minimal force.

From the very beginning, I was instructed to always keep myself armed with both my karambits and SIG Sauer. As Hiyori delved further into the history of my blades, she discovered that they were once known as the "Dragon's Claws." The name resonated with me and I decided to adopt it for myself.

Every day brought new challenges and lessons, but I revealed in the opportunity to hone my skills with such unique and powerful weapons at my side. And as I continued on this path of training and self-discovery, I couldn't help but wonder what other secrets these elusive karambits held within them.

My time with Alex was a continuous journey of learning and understanding. He was incredibly patient with me, always willing to spend as much time on a subject as I needed. Through his teachings, I discovered the intricate rules and systems that governed our supernatural society. Each species and subspecies had their own council, overseeing their affairs and decisions. And above them all sat the elders council, made up of leaders from multiple groups, united as equals. But even above this influential body, there was the agency - the enforcers of these rules and protectors of our world. Working with all groups, including humans, they ensured the safety and secrecy of our existence.

But above everyone else, stood the watcher council - the highest authority. Though Alex tried to explain their role to me, I couldn't fully grasp it. He had me poring over materials and information about them, but their purpose seemed to conflict with everything I thought I knew about our world. In the end, we agreed that it wasn't necessary for my education at the moment and we would revisit it later on. Despite my lack of knowledge about them, I couldn't help but feel a sense of intrigue and curiosity surrounding this mysterious group.

Under his tutelage , I have come to learn about the vastness and complexity of our world. He has opened my eyes to the truth behind the legends and fairy tales that have been passed down for generations. From pixies and trolls to mermaids and unicorns, every creature and story holds a glimmer of reality. It was hard to believe at first - such fantastical beings existing in our world - but as I delved deeper into my studies, everything began to make sense. As if by magic, my mind expanded and absorbed all the knowledge imparted onto me.

But there were moments when I questioned my own sanity. Was it possible that I had lost touch with reality and all of this was just a figment of my imagination? Perhaps I was a deranged patient locked away in some asylum, kept away from society for the safety of others. But then, a gruelling session of combat training would bring me back to my senses. Or Mini, my loyal mentor, would sense my troubled state and talk me through it with her words of wisdom. She was truly a remarkable companion - always there to support and guide me through the darkest of times.

As my studies progressed, I found myself encountering a new problem - Commander Killian Robinson. He was my instructor for the practical aspect of magic, and he was a battle mage through and through. From what he had demonstrated during my and lyn's rescue and to me in our lessons, he was an extremely powerful one at that. His presence alone commanded respect and his skills were unparalleled. But despite his expertise, there seemed to be this underlying tension between us.

He was always professional and efficient during our training sessions, but there was something cold about him that made it hard for me to warm up to him. And then it hit me -he had seen me at my most venerable and every time he looked at me I was reminded of the person I was then the dirty broken experiment that needed to be saved. The realisation turn my stomach sour. But I had to get past it. During one of our earlier training sessions he confided in me that he had spoken with the dragon breed about what abilities they expect me to manifest.after what Jeremiah had done. Although they couldn't give any conclusive answers due to the ongoing investigation the where doing in to what the phyla was actually trying to do they did give him a run down on what they believed I might be capable. The list they had given them was long and daunting, and it seemed like a lot of pressure for someone like me who was still trying to grasp the new realities of what had been done to me

Every lesson with Killian seemed to get progressively more difficult. And I soon discovered that being a mage wasn't about leaning frilly words or spells or incantations it was about force of will and mental fortitude. I learned that I had to visualise the outcome I wanted and guide the energy to accomplish my desire. And Lillian's method for teaching me this was to toss lighting, fire balls, ice spears and a host of other magical constructs at me with the intent to kill and see if I survived the barrage. When I confronted him about his barbaric trading methods, . His response surprised me - he believed in pushing people beyond their limits in order for them to reach their full potential. To him, my potential as a mage far exceeded what I thought it was and it was his duty as my instructor to help me realise it.

His words struck a chord within me and I couldn't help but feel grateful for his belief in me. But at the same time, I also felt overwhelmed by the weight of his expectations. It seemed like everyone around me saw something in me that I didn't even know existed.

Killian's training sessions were tough. He pushed me harder than anyone else ever had before but my progress showed little. My control over my abilities hardly improved under his guidance, but I began to develop a deeper understanding of battle tactics and strategy. For dealing with magic users and mages But more than just this, Robinson taught me valuable lessons about humility and determination. He showed me that it was not enough to possess great power and natural ability it was about being Abel to bonce back when you encounter failure

as my training progressed Killian had started quickly establishing that my strength, speed and endurance had increased much more than I could have ever imagined. He said I was about as strong as a young dragon breed in human form,

After enduring a particularly gruelling day, where every aspect of my training seemed to go awry and frustration consumed me, I reached my breaking point. No longer willing to dodge my opponent's attacks or play by the rules, I stormed out to the training field and plopped down on the ground. The sun beat down on my face, adding to my already simmering irritation. "What in all the hells do you think you're doing, Jess?" My trainer's voice boomed above me.

"Simply sitting," I replied, my tone dripping with sarcasm. The look of outrage on his face was almost comical, but my mood was too sour to appreciate it. If circumstances had been different, I might have found it amusing enough to laugh at.

"And how do you think you are going to dodge my assault if you are sitting, or is this you telling me you can now harness your power and Don't need to dodge?"

What a jackass" Nope, *I suck at this, I suck at shooting, and most of what Alex's tries to teach me is now just confusing the fuck out of me, so if you're going to attack, get on with it." I crossed my arms and glared at him. I knew I was acting like a spoilt child, but at that point, I did't care.*

"oh, so you want a pity party, is that it?"

I sat there silently. I wouldn't give him the satisfaction of a reply.

But he didn't stop there. "What is it too hard? Just what I thought, in the end, you are worthless. Can't hit a target at ten paces, can't protect

against magic. I bet you're even failing combat trying. No one wants to tell you because they don't want to upset the poor little experiment."

"What the fuck did you just call me" Before I knew what I was doing, I was up on my feet and moving towards him getting ready to

attack. He raised his hand, and I was flung into the air. It was like I had been hit by a gale-force wind. "What? Are you scared a girl might hit you?" I screamed as I hit the dirt

"Oh dose the experiment think I'm scared of her. That must be a joke. I've seen toddlers with more skill than you have. The only reason you are here is that people feel

sorry for you. You are useless. What would your parents think to see what a joke you've become. You must be happy they can't see you like this. I might ask Alex to forget about training you and let the doctors run their tests on you. At least we might learn something then." He goaded me. Every word that came out of his mouth was a direct hit on my emotional insecurities.

Without thinking I snapped. I don't know how, but electricity burst from my body and shot straight toward Killian. Power was coursing through me, it was like a dame had broken and the power wouldn't stop poring out of me but I didn't care. I would show that prick, Killian, that I wasn't weak or helpless. The wind whipped around me, kicking up dirt and

flinging my hair around wildly. I felt my feet leave the ground. It was like I was in the storm's eye for a moment. I forgot everything around me and just felt the. Power, it was. Beautiful. Nothing else mattered. Then it stopped, and I plummeted to the ground. I landed in a heap tangled up in my clothes,

"Jess, are you okay talk to me" Great, it was Killian the jackass.

"Why do you care? I! 'm just a useless experiment," I said. I could feel tears build this. I knew that's what they all secretly thought of me. I just wasn't prepared for any one to say it. I got to my feet and made a quick retreat to my room. I couldn't stand to have anyone else look at me with pity today.

CHAPTER 9

For the next few days, I locked myself away in my small room, surviving on the meagre supplies from my mini-fridge. The thought of facing the people I once trusted and considered friends was unbearable. Would they see me as a lost puppy, pathetic and useless? Or worse, a failed experiment that needed to be disposed of? My heart raced at the idea, and with each passing moment, I could feel sparks of electric energy coursing through my body, visible arcs dancing between my trembling fingers. It was a constant reminder of what had happened, how it had left me broken and afraid. The fear grew with each passing day, gripping me tight and suffocating any hope of escape. They would surely lock me up for being too dangerous, unable to control this new power that had emerged within me. The walls of my room seemed to close in on me, trapping me in this nightmare.

A rhythmic knocking on the door echoed through the empty room. Mini's voice, muffled and concerned, called out from the other side. "Jess, it's me. We all know what happened so we've been trying to give you space, but I'm getting worried about you." I can feel your emotions, and they're not good. Remember, being alone is never a good idea when you feel like this." Silence followed her words before she continued, "Come on, let me in. I've brought some food for you. You must be sick of surviving on mini fridge snacks." Slowly, I rose from my bed and made my way to the door. feeling like every step was a burden. With a twist of the doorknob I let her in Mini stood there with a concerned expression on her face. And a tray of warm food in her hands. "I brought some real food for once," she said with a small smile before stepping inside and closing the door behind her as I retreated back to my bed, curling up under my blanket as if seeking comfort and protection within its soft folds she made her way forward slowly making her way to wards me , the aroma of home-cooked meals filled the air. It was comforting and overwhelming at the same time.

Mini sat down on the edge of my bed, placing a tray of food on my nightstand. I couldn't bring myself to look at her, afraid of what emotions she might sense from me. But as she started talking, her voice gentle and understanding, I found myself slowly relaxing.

"We're all worried about you, Jess," Mini said softly. "We know it's been tough for you since the incident with Killian. But we're here for you, no matter what."

I didn't respond, still overwhelmed by everything that had happened.

"And I know you must be tired of eating mini fridge snacks," Mini continued, trying to lighten the mood. "So I brought some real food from the cafeteria. Your favourite, pasta Alfredo."

I managed a small smile at her attempt to cheer me up. Mini was always so thoughtful and caring. "Thank you," I whispered.

Mini reached out and squeezed my hand. But I pulled away at her sudden movement. Terrified that the energy that had been pulsing through me would hurt her.

Suddenly realising why I was so scared she pulled her hand away slowly "You don't have to go through this alone, Jess. We're a team."

Tears welled up in my eyes as I finally looked at her. She smiled warmly at me keeping her distance for both our protection.

"I'm sorry," I sobbed into her shoulder. "I've just been so scared."

"It's okay," Mini whispered soothingly. "Let it out."

And for the first time since the incident I let myself cry allowing someone else to see my fear and pain. I was consumed with raw emotion as tears streamed down my face.

When I finally calmed down, Mini handed me a tissue and wiped away my tears with a gentle touch.

"I'm here for you," she said firmly.

I nodded gratefully before digging into the delicious pasta Alfredo she had brought for me.

"would you be able to tell me what Killian told everyone" I said with dread

"okay but only if you think it will help, so he spent some time reviewing how your day had gone and then said that you seemed to have been hitting a wall recently and you where getting frustrated" at the mention of me getting frustrated I couldn't help but snort out a laughter.frustrated was definitely an understatement.

ignoring my outburst she continued.

"he then went into detail about everything that happened when you where training with him and I was there when he explained himself so I assure you he wasn't lying in anything he said to us."

before she said anything else I whispered "I'm sorry I should have known the only reason Alex wanted me here was because of the thing's Jeremiah did to me. He wants to make sure I'm not a threat I see that now" as I spoke electricity crackled over my body, shit I need to calm down I need to breathe. Once I calmed down, Mini smiled at me.

As she spoke, her hand flew up and she lifted a finger, emphasising the importance of what she was about to say. "First thing's first," she declared. "I want you to know that I and the others don't feel that way about you. In fact, we are all extremely pissed at Killian for what he did. He has been incurring the wrath of the entire base for his actions." As she finished her sentence, she held up another finger. "And what he said about you isn't true. No one, including him, feels like that about you," I objected, trying to defend myself. But she spoke over me, determined to get her point across. "Jess, he saw that you had a rough day and thought he would play on your insecurities to see if he could get you to unleash some of your power. And yes, you did show an impressive display of power. But the way he went about it was wrong. I can assure you that he regrets doing it and I will make sure he suffers consequences for his actions." Her words were filled with determination and justice as she stood up for me against Killian's cruel actions.

I nodded, my throat tight and tears threatening to spill over. "I'm sorry I worried you," I said, my voice breaking. "You don't hate me, do you?"

Mini reached out and brushed a tear from my cheek. "No, none of us could ever hate you," she reassured me with a gentle smile She then left my room, telling me to finish eating before resting for tomorrow's training. I did as told, but my mind couldn't rest as I worried about the potential fallout from my mistakes. As I lay in bed, my mind was racing with thoughts about what had happened e. I couldn't believe that Killian would do something like that to me, especially after we had become such good friends. But as Mini had said, he was probably just trying to push me to see how much power I had.

But still, the thought of him hating me for my powers was unsettling. I didn't want anyone on the base to hate me or fear me because of what I could do. I just wanted to be accepted and belong somewhere.

Feeling exhausted from all the emotions and training, I drifted off into a restless sleep.

The next morning, I woke up feeling refreshed and ready to restart my training. As I made my way to the mess hall for breakfast, I noticed that Killian was already there with Mini and the rest of my trainers.

Seeing me Mini immediately waved indicating I should join them. I hesitated for a moment before walking over to them. As soon as I sat down at the table, everyone fell silent. It was obvious that they were all waiting for me to speak first.

"I want to apologise," Killian finally spoke up, breaking the tension. "I shouldn't have done what I did the other day. It wasn't right and you didn't deserve it."

I looked at him with surprise in my eyes. This wasn't the reaction I was expecting from him at all.

"I forgive you," I said softly, feeling relieved that he wasn't angry with me anymore.

"Thank you," he replied sincerely.

From beside me mini gave him a stern look before turning back to her breakfast.

The rest of breakfast was a tense affair, with strained smiles and awkward silences between us. After the plates were cleared and we finished our morning meal, we all scattered to our own activities - me for a training session with Hiyori and Hargreaves, and the rest to whatever tasks they had when not training me. Later in the day, as I attended my training session with Killian, I couldn't help but notice his slight limp. When I asked if he was alright, he brushed it off and said he had just fallen earlier in the day. But his nonchalant attitude raised my suspicions and I began to ask around discreetly. No one would tell me what really happened, only that he had slipped and hurt himself. The knowing looks exchanged between Mini and some of the other members only added to my growing suspicion that she was somehow involved in his accident. It seemed like everyone was looking the other way, protecting her despite her potential involvement in harming one of the trainers.

AFTER MONTHS OF strenuous training, I stood tall and confident, my body finally reflecting the hard work and dedication I had put into mastering my abilities. The world of the paranormal still held many mysteries for me, but I knew that true understanding could only be gained by fully immersing myself in this otherworldly realm. Though Alex's teachings often left me feeling perplexed, I continued to push myself further, eager to unravel the secrets of this supernatural world.

Not only had my mental and physical strength grown, but my skills with a firearm had also undergone a remarkable transformation. While I would never consider myself a sharpshooter, my aim and accuracy had greatly improved from my initial attempts. With determination and perseverance, I could now hit my target 8 times out of ten - an impressive feat considering where I began. As I held the weight of the gun in my hand, it felt familiar and comforting, a symbol of the progress and growth I had achieved on this journey into the unknown.

My hand-to-hand combat skills surpassed all expectations, my karambits becoming extensions of my very being, a lethal instrument that moved with deadly precision and fluidity in the heat of battle. With each strike, I felt the rush of adrenaline coursing through my veins as I sparred fiercely with Hiyori and Hargreaves.

Though they still bested me when they unleashed their full strength, I held my own for several intense minutes before inevitably being thrown to the mat. And even then, I left them with their own injuries from our intense battles, bruises and cuts marking our bodies as badges of honour.

As I honed my physical skills, I also focused on strengthening my mental fortitude. Killian's teachings on self-control and meditation were invaluable in sharpening my mind into a powerful tool. With each breath, I could feel a heightened sense of awareness and clarity wash over me, allowing me to anticipate and react quickly in any situation.

But progress was not always linear. There were moments of frustration where I felt like I was lagging behind the other agents or would never reach their level of expertise. But Killian was always there to remind me that mastery takes time and dedication.

"You are already becoming a formidable agent," he would say with a reassuring smile. "But true greatness comes from patience and perseverance."

And so I pushed on, determined to become the best Agent possible.

Each training session with Killian felt like a test of endurance and willpower. He seemed to take pleasure in watching me struggle, his smug grin never faltering. But I refused to back down, fuelled by the hope that one day I could wipe that smirk off his lips. And after countless gruelling sessions, I finally reached a point where I could hold my own against him. No longer was I just evading his attacks - I had learned to redirect them and even launch counterattacks of my own. But even with all my progress, those damn wind blasts always managed to catch me off guard. Still, I persisted and focused my energy, occasionally catching glimpses of iridescent scales on my skin during moments of intense concentration. But when I tried to examine them closer, they would disappear like a mirage. Perhaps it was just the sweat glistening on my body or my mind playing tricks on me in the heat of our training.

As my training progressed, I were also given opportunities to shadow some of the senior Agents. These experiences were both exhilarating and terrifying - so far they had only been routine assignment like patrolling or guard duties and escort assignments

But each mission taught me valuable lessons in strategy, teamwork, and quick thinking. It was one thing to fight against Hiyori or Hargreaves in controlled training sessions; it was another thing entirely when the chance facing off against real supernatural threats exists. As my training progressed, I was given the opportunity to shadow some of the senior Agents. Each experience was a mix of exhilaration and dread - so far, these had only been routine assignments like patrolling, guard duties, and escort missions. But each mission taught me valuable lessons in strategy, teamwork, and quick thinking. It was one thing to fight against Hiyori and Hargreaves in controlled training sessions; it was an entirely different matter facing real supernatural threats on the field.

As I DRIFTED off into a peaceful slumber, the soft hum of my ceiling fan lulled me into a deep sleep. Suddenly, the loud banging of my door jolted me awake. Groaning in annoyance, I tried to ignore it and rolled over in my bed, pulling the covers up to my chin.

But the insistent pounding continued, growing louder and more urgent by the second. Finally, Mini's high-pitched scream pierced through the quiet and shattered any hope of falling back asleep. With my pillow shoved tightly over my head, I prayed fervently to any higher power that might exist. My desperation and frustration were palpable as I begged for just a few more minutes of rest before facing the day.

But Mini's voice echoed through the walls like an alarm, taunting me with the promise of an exciting adventure. "Jess, I know you're in there. Wake up and open the door, or I'm not taking you with me..." My heart skipped a beat as her words registered. Could it be? Was she really saying what I hoped she was? The possibility of an adventure with my best friend made all the sleepless nights and early mornings worth it. In one swift movement, I threw off my covers and rushed to open the door, ready for whatever awaited us outside.

Standing before me was a very serious-looking Mini, her expression hinting at a thrilling and dangerous mission ahead. "Well, get dressed and meet me at Alexis's office," she commanded sternly. "And do me a favour - try not to look so excited."

My heart raced with eager anticipation as I hastily changed into my mission attire, my fingers trembling with excitement. I meticulously smoothed out any wrinkles in my fitted jacket, adjusting it to ensure a polished appearance. With careful precision, I checked that my trusty gun and knife rig were securely concealed, taking comfort in the weight and familiarity of my weapons. My instructor's words echoed in my mind - never go anywhere without your weapons - and I knew I was prepared for whatever challenges lay ahead.

Taking a deep breath to steady myself, I made my way to our boss's office, the endless possibilities of this mission racing through my mind like wildfire. This could be the moment I had been waiting for, my chance to prove myself and join the esteemed ranks of active agents. As I knocked on the door, my mind whirled with excitement and nerves, unable to believe that I would be embarking on this mission alongside Mini, my best friend and mentor at the agency. A wide grin spread across my face as I envisioned all the thrilling action and danger that awaited us.

I felt a surge of confidence and readiness course through me as I stood outside the door, eagerly anticipating the mission that lay before us. Whatever may come our way, I was determined to face it head on and emerge victorious.

As I stepped into the office, a sense of tension and seriousness hung in the air. My trainers all wore somber expressions as Alex, motioned for me to come closer to his desk. "Jessica," he said gravely, his voice echoing in the quiet room. "Please take a seat, and I will explain your assignment." I sat down in the chair opposite him, my heart racing with anticipation.

Without any preamble, Alex got straight to the point. "I would like you to join Mini on a case in London." My mind raced with excitement and nerves at the thought of being given such a responsibility. I had always dreamed of becoming an agent, but I never expected it to happen so soon.

"I know you have shadowed some of the instructors before," Alex continued, "but this will be different. You will be working this case like any other agent would." He handed me a leather wallet, and inside was a shiny badge and a plastic identification card. I couldn't believe it - they were giving me active agent status for this mission.

"Thank you," I stammered, still trying to process everything. "But are you sure I'm ready?"

"Your instructors think you are ready," Alex reassured me. "And I agree. However, even though you will be actively working this case, I still expect you to continue training." He then mentioned Commander Killian's comments about my powers and how I needed more practice to fully master them.

For a moment, I was speechless. I knew I had been putting in long hours and hard work, but I never realised that my instructors saw such potential in me. "Thank you," I finally said, a mixture of gratitude and determination filling my voice. "I will make all of you proud for taking a chance on me."

I stood nervously in front of my supervisor, Alex, as he delivered the news. "I'm sure you will do your best. I have partnered you with Mini," he said, his voice steady and reassuring. I gave my friend a quick glance, worried that she might see me as a burden, but her beaming smile put me at ease.

"As I was saying, this case isn't ideal for someone's first assignment, but it's also best to get it out of the way. You will be heading to London," Alex continued. My heart raced at the thought of such a high-profile case in such a big city.

"We have received a report of a series of unsolved murders that has been concerning us. And just moments ago, we received word of another victim found. You will head straight to the crime scene and take over the investigation."

My mind whirled with questions and apprehension. "Where in London?" I finally managed to ask.

"Chelsea Park Gardens. You will be met at the site by one of our top crime technicians. The area has already been cordoned off for your arrival. You and Mini will be stationed at one of our field offices in the area." Alex handed us each a thick briefing pack and looked at us expectantly.

"I've assembled all the information we have so far, and I expect you both to read it thoroughly before arriving at the scene," he emphasised. "There is a direct flight to London Stansted waiting for you, along with a driver who will take you directly to Chelsea Park Gardens."

"I have faith that you will both make us proud," Alex concluded, dismissing us with a nod. "And remember, if you run into any difficulties, don't hesitate to ask for assistance." With that, Mini and I left his office and began preparing for our daunting task ahead in the bustling streets of London.

CHAPTER 10

MY HEART RACED as Mini and I hurried to our rooms, frantically packing a bag of essentials while clutching the briefing file in hand. The urgency in my movements was mirrored by the tense set of Mini's jaw as she stood beside me, her eyes darting around the room. We both knew we had to move quickly if we were going to make it to the plane on time.

As we made our way out to the car that would take us to the airport, I took a seat next to Mini and could immediately sense her tension. It radiated off of her in waves, almost tangible in its intensity. "Do you want to talk about what's on your mind?" I asked softly, trying to respect her boundaries.

Mini's fingers tightened on the handle of her suitcase as we climbed into the car. She took a deep breath before turning to me, her eyes searching for the right words. "I'm just worried about this mission," she admitted, her voice laced with nervousness. "It feels like there are so many unknown variables, and I can't shake this feeling that something is going to go wrong."

I nodded in understanding, feeling a knot form in my stomach at her words. "I know what you mean," I said quietly. "But we have to trust in our training and our abilities. I'm sure we will come out on top."

Mini gave me a small smile, but I could see that she was still struggling with her worries. I reached over and placed a hand on hers, offering what little comfort I could.

As we arrived at the airport, our focus shifted to getting through security quickly and making it to our gate on time. My nerves spiked when I was frisked remembering tolerate that I was caring a firearm and set of blades. Before I could panic and cause a scene the guard waved me through. "Have a good flight agent and waved me through. Once onboard the plane, Mini and I settled into our seats and began reviewing the file , making sure we had all of the details memorised

I knew from experience that Mini's empathic abilities could sometimes overwhelm her. She would shut herself off from using them unless absolutely necessary, which meant she often carried a heavy emotional burden with her at all times. If emotions around her ran too high or someone touched her without warning, she would absorb their raw feelings like a sponge, causing her physical pain.

But despite these challenges, Mini never complained or let it hinder her work. She simply found ways to cope and manage, constantly adapting and evolving in an effort to help others. And as we sat on the plane, I couldn't help but feel grateful for having such a strong and resilient partner by my side.

Her voice wavered slightly as she spoke, betraying a hint of worry and exhaustion. "Yeah, I'm okay, Hun," she reassured me. "I just glanced at the file, and it looks like you may have to do much of the heavy lifting in this case." Panic began to rise within me at her words. "What do you mean?" I asked, my heart beating faster. "I need help understanding Mini. You have more experience with these cases than I do. I thought I would only be assisting." The weight of fear and self-doubt settled heavily on my shoulders as the realisation sunk in that I would be taking the lead on this one. But before I could spiral any further into my own thoughts, Mini's calm voice broke through my inner turmoil. "Jess, I have faith in you," she said firmly, her unwavering belief in me shining through her words. "And so does everyone else; otherwise, they wouldn't have chosen you for this case. But I need to warn you about something - as someone with an empathic gift, I can pick up on emotional echoes in any location that has experienced significant emotions. And although those echoes diminish over time, with this being such a fresh and intense case, it might be too much for me to handle without getting emotionally overwhelmed. I don't want that to affect our work or compromise your safety." Her vulnerability and honesty struck a chord within me, reminding me once again of why Mini was not only my partner but also my closest friend in this dangerous line of work.

I took a deep breath and put on my best professional demeanour. "I understand completely, and I'll give it my all," I said, hoping to project a sense of confidence that I didn't actually feel. Mini nodded appreciatively and motioned for us to move on to the briefings. As she smiled at me, I caught a glimpse of the tension behind her eyes. She was trying her best to maintain a brave front as we delved into the work ahead.

The flight felt like an eternity as thoughts raced through my mind about everything that could go wrong on this mission. But as Mini and I landed in on the outskirts of London and made our way to meet up with our our drive, determination set in.

As we pulled up to the dark and desolate crime scene, the ominous feeling in the air was palpable. I glanced over at Mini, who wore a terrified expression on her face. After reading through the file provided by Alex, I understood her fear all too well. "If you're not up for this, I can handle it alone," I offered, picking up on her unease. But she shook her head stubbornly, her complexion growing pale at the thought of what horrors awaited us inside. "No, I'll be fine," she managed to say between clenched teeth.

Our driver stood stoically by the car, his eyes trained ahead as if avoiding looking anywhere else. "I will watch over your belongings here and await your return," he stated in a matter-of-fact tone before resuming his post. His behaviour struck me as odd, but perhaps it was just my inexperience with this line of work. Mini caught my puzzled expression and suddenly burst into laughter.

"I apologise, but seeing your baffled face in this situation is just too priceless." She took a moment to compose herself before leading me towards the police cordon. The sound of sirens and chatter grew louder as we approached, heightening my nerves even more. This was not going to be an easy case As we approached the Corden, Mini's complexion grew increasingly pale and her expression tense. I knew she didn't want to talk about it, so I held my tongue and tried to ignore the heavy atmosphere that seemed to close in around us. The air felt thick and stagnant, like a foul taste lingering at the back of my mouth.

As we reached the police tape, a uniformed officer stepped in front of us, barring our way. "I'm sorry, ladies, this is a secure crime scene. I can't allow you to pass." Mini didn't hesitate, stepping forward with confidence. "I apologise, officer, but could you direct us to the person in charge? We were requested to be here and should be expected."

The officer's stance softened as he looked at Mini, clearly swayed by her charm. "Oh, I see. My apologies, ma'am. Please follow me."

Mini shot me a knowing look. She had used her powers to influence the officer, and it seemed to have worked

The closer we got to the house, the more overwhelming the stench became. It hit me like a punch in the gut - a putrid combination of fear, blood, despair, and pain that assaulted my senses. As much as I wanted to turn back and run away from whatever horrors awaited us inside, I knew I needed to face them head on with Mini by my side.

The air around me was thick and heavy, carrying a putrid stench that seemed to stick to my skin. As I walked closer to the looming building, the smell grew stronger and I could feel it burning in my nose and throat. I tried to hold my breath, but that only made it worse as I had to rely on my mouth for air, filling it with the same rancid odor. Even the uniformed officer beside me covered his nose as we entered the front door. As we stepped inside, the first thing that struck me was the eerie silence. Unlike what I had been taught in training or seen while shadowing others, there was no bustling activity or chatter between colleagues at this crime scene. It was unnervingly quiet, almost as if even the walls were holding their breath in anticipation. The only sound came from our own footsteps, echoing through the empty corridors like a haunting melody. It was a stark contrast to the gruesome scene that lay before us, a contrast of stillness and violence.

A heavy silence hung in the air as we all processed the scene in front of us. The location was even worse than I had imagined, and I could see Mini's expression shift as she took it in. As an Empath, she must have been feeling the intense reactions and last moments of the victim's pain and fear from everyone around her.

"Mini," I whispered, knowing she could still hear me, "do you need to step outside for a moment? This is a lot to handle."

"No, I'll be fine," she replied, shielding herself emotionally. "I just wasn't prepared for that overwhelming wave of emotions. It was difficult to process."

"Okay, let's get this over with," I said, trying to push away my own discomfort and focus on the task at hand.

Ignoring the uniformed officer leading Mini down the hallway, I turned my attention to the crime scene. The front door opened into a small entrance hall, with a staircase on the right leading to the first floor. The officer and Mini went up, but I turned left into what appeared to be a reception room. The air was thick with the scent of blood and fear, and my senses were immediately overwhelmed as I tried to piece together what happened in this seemingly idyllic suburban home. Crime techs buzzed around me, snapping pictures and meticulously cataloguing every detail. Ignoring their activity, I closed my eyes and took a deep breath, centering myself as I had been trained to do. In my mind's eye,

Closing my eyes, I focused on the room, using my heightened senses to piece together a mental image. My fingers twitched as I honed in on the faint scents and emotions that lingered in the space, pushing aside the more recent ones. Slowly, a basic layout emerged in my mind - a starting point for unraveling the chaotic scene of violence and tragedy.

I could sense a woman at the door, letting in two unfamiliar figures. As they made their way back to the reception area, I could feel her nervousness towards them. Meanwhile, three other individuals entered from what seemed like a dining room. The arrival of these visitors had interrupted dinner - I could make out the distinct smells of a man and two children, a boy and a girl. Along with these emotions and scents, I could sense an overwhelming wave of fear that must have nearly driven them mad.

Moving around the room, each step revealing more details, it became clear that the man and children never moved from where they stood - it was as if they were frozen in place. The two visitors were positioned close to the woman, standing over a puddle of blood on the carpet with splatters on the walls and ceiling. It was evident that whatever had happened here was done as a statement to ensure compliance from the others.

Following the droplets of blood that led to the stairs, I realised that all five individuals had gone in the same direction. A decision had to be made: either follow the trail downstairs or head up to find Mini. My curiosity got the better of me, and I followed the bloody path, determined to uncover the truth behind this macabre scene.

The descent down the grand staircase was a slow and treacherous journey, each step bringing me closer to the source of the overpowering stench. The air was thick with the metallic tang of blood and the acrid scent of fear, creating a suffocating atmosphere that made it hard to breathe. My heart raced as I reached the bottom, taking in the scene before me. What had once been a luxurious entertainment area was now a chaotic mess, furniture tossed aside and smeared with blood on every surface - walls, ceiling, floor. The room reeked of violence and desperation. In one corner, the double doors leading to a home office lay broken and splintered, evidence of a frenzied search for something of value. As I tried to piece together what had happened, my senses were overwhelmed and muddled. The overlapping trails of scents made it difficult to discern any useful information. And then there was the blood...so much of it that it was hard to focus on anything else. Even though the main bodies had been removed, remnants of flesh still littered the room in a grotesque display. I could only imagine what horrors the medical examiner would uncover here. Approaching one of the forensic technicians for information, I braced myself for the worst and received confirmation: "The female body is almost unrecognisable...only fragments of her skeletal structure remain." My stomach churned at the thought, but I knew there was more to be discovered among this gruesome scene.

The crime technician's voice trembled as he continued telling me what he knew The boy's body was a ghastly sight, almost as gruesome as that of the woman. Chunks of flesh were missing from all over, revealing raw, bloody muscle beneath. His eyes had been brutally gouged out and lay nearby on the ground and it looks like his tongue was ripped out but we haven't been able to find it yet so are assuming it may have been taken as a trophy. it also appeared as though he had been viciously attacked by a pack of starving dogs before being tossed aside near the shattered office doors." his words hanging heavy in the air like a dark cloud. It was a scene straight out of a horror movie, except this was real life.

The words tumbled out of his mouth, each one weighted with horror and disbelief. "And finally…the male's body was found…sprawled on the ground, in the home offices" he managed to choke out. This was by far the worst of the three. His once strong body was now a battered and broken mess of bones and flesh.

The gruesome sight was almost unbearable to look at. The technician's voice trembled as he struggled to describe what he had seen. "His fingernails were missing, ripped out from their beds, leaving behind bloody stumps. The bones in his hands were shattered, jutting through the torn flesh like broken twigs. His body contorted into a grotesque shape, every joint seemingly dislocated." The forensics tech grew paler with each word and quickly fled the room, likely to find a safe place to vomit. It wasn't until he left that I realised something - we might have a survivor. But the thought alone was enough to make me feel sick myself, and I could only imagine how the tech must have felt witnessing this horrific scene.

With my heart pounding in my chest, I raced back up the stairs of the old Victorian mansion. My sole purpose was to find Mini, my partner in detective work, and get a search started for any clues that could lead us to the missing witness. As I reached the next floor, I could hear Mini's voice echoing from the reception room I had been in just a little while ago. Stepping into the room, I found her locked in a tense standoff with a plain-clothed officer. The man exuded an air of arrogant superiority that immediately put me on edge.

"Look, little girl," he sneered at Mini, "I didn't request your help, and I certainly don't need it to solve this crime scene." Mini bristled like a spiky blowfish, her petite frame seemingly growing in size as she squared off against him. "Check your over-inflated ego at the fucking door," she shot back. "We have been specifically requested to assist here. Obviously, you can't handle this case on your own."

Next to me, I heard a low snigger. Glancing over, I saw a tall man leaning casually against the wall, his dark eyes dancing with amusement. "Dame, she's on fire," he murmured with a wicked grin. "Look at him - he's been struck dumb."

"And who might you be?" I asked, turning my attention back to the man.

"Apologies," he said with a slight bow. "I should have introduced myself earlier. My name is Keith. The London office sent me to assist you both in settling in. Normally I'm just a lab monkey, but it seems they've called all hands on deck for this case before it garners even more publicity.""Okay, Kieth," I said firmly, trying to grab his attention amidst the chaos. "I'm Jess, and we need to break this up before it turns into a full-blown fight." We locked eyes for a moment before turning our attention to the pair in front of us. If I didn't know better, it looked as though the argument was rapidly escalating towards violence. My heart raced as Kith and I bumbled our way through the crowd towards the commotion. Taking a deep breath, I channeled all the authority I had into my voice and bellowed, "ENOUGH!" The sound echoed off the walls and seemed to shake the very foundation of the room. Everyone froze and turned towards me, their expressions ranging from surprise to fear. Even Mini and Keith, who were standing nearby with huge grins on their faces, seemed taken aback by my outburst. Gathering my newfound confidence, I took charge while everyone was still in shock. "Now that you two have quieted down," I continued sternly, "let's focus on what's important: how many bodies have been found?" The room fell silent as they processed my question, some even looking at me like I had grown a third head. But I stood my ground, determined to get to the bottom of the situation.

Do I really have to ask again?" I said, trying to maintain an authoritative presence. The officer, who had been arguing with Mini, turned to me. "And who might you be Little Miss Loudmouth?" he growled.

"You can call me Jessica. I'm Mini's partner on this assignment. Do you have a name, or should I refer to you as 'ass clown'?"The look of shock on his face was priceless, but it quickly morphed into a scowl. "I'm DCI Duncan Lancaster," he replied stiffly. "As I was explaining to your associate, we don't need your help." I cut him off before he could continue. "Look, I'm not in the mood for a pissing contest. Just tell me if you've found the witness yet"

The words flew out of his mouth like shards of broken glass, laced with venom and rage. "What the fuck are you talking about? There was no witness. We got an anonymous call like all the others," he practically spat at me.

I couldn't believe what I was hearing. "How many bodies did you find?" I asked, my voice trembling with disbelief.

"Why is it so important?" he sneered. "They were all found downstairs. If you want to know the cause of death, ask your friend over there. He's already sent them for autopsy at your facility."

I took a deep breath, trying to control my anger, but something inside me snapped. "Look around, you cock womble," I seethed. "How many people live in this house? How many dinner plates have been left at the table? How many bedrooms are there? It doesn't take a genius to see that two children, one boy and one girl, lived here. And two fucking adults, I'm assuming, would be their parents. So where the fuck is the girl if you haven't even found a body?"

I let my words hang in the air, a heavy silence falling over the room. My voice trembles with barely contained anger as I demand, "Why are you all just staring at me? Find her. Now." The house erupts into chaos as everyone scrambles to tear it apart piece by piece, their movements frantic and ruthless. Every nook and cranny is thoroughly searched, each person fuelled by a sense of urgency and determination. We will not stop until we find her, wherever she may be hiding.

CHAPTER 11

As chaos erupted throughout the house and frantic footsteps echoed off the walls, I calmly guided Mini and Kieth down to the entertainment area in the basement. The air was thick with tension and fear, but I couldn't shake the feeling that our missing child was somewhere close by.

I took a deep breath before addressing Mini, my voice filled with urgency. "I know this will be overwhelming, but I need you to tap into your empathic abilities and see if you can sense where she might be." With grave determination in her usually bright eyes, Mini nodded, understanding the gravity of the situation. We descended down the stairs, our footsteps echoing through the dark, debris-filled basement. Mini's brows furrowed in concentration as she probed each room with her empathic senses, searching for any sign of the missing child. The air was thick with fear and distress, a palpable force that seemed to cling onto every object in the room. Every creak and groan of the old house sent shivers down our spines, but we pressed on, driven by our mission to find the child before it was too late.

As we navigated through the dimly lit space, my heart raced with anticipation and dread. I prayed that we would find her unharmed, but deep down I feared the worst. The thought of what she could have already endured made me physically ill.

But then, a glimmer of hope appeared as we stumbled upon a

secure wine cellar tucked away in a corner of the basement. Without hesitation, I opened the door and there she was - our missing child, huddled in a corner and trembling with fear. It was a small miracle that she had managed to escape her attackers and find refuge here.

Relief flooded through me and, tears glistened in my eyes at the sight of her terrified but alive. We may never know how she got away or found her way here, but in that moment, none of that mattered. All that mattered was that she was safe.

With her back pressed against the wall, Mini crouched near the entrance of the small room. Her voice, soft and soothing like a mother's lullaby, filled the air. "Hey there, my name is Mini; I'm here to help. Can you open the door a little for me, sweetheart?" The girl inside seemed hesitant but intrigued by Mini's gentle words laced with magic.

Before DCI Lancaster could enter, I placed myself in his path. His impatience was palpable as he demanded, "Where is she?"

"Keep your voice down," I cautioned, "My partner is trying to coax her out and we don't want to spook her."

"Get out of my way, little miss loud mouth," he snarled, shoving past me in a desperate attempt to reach our young witness.

But it was Mini who had succeeded in convincing the girl to crack open the door just a fraction, showing a glimmer of trust in us and our intentions."

The little girl cowered in the corner, her body huddled and shaking as if she were a wounded animal. Silent tears streamed down her cheeks, leaving glistening trails on her dirt-streaked face. Despite her obvious fear, she held onto a knife with an iron grip, ready to defend herself at all costs. My heart broke at the sight of her, and I couldn't even focus on what Detective Lancaster was doing anymore. He forcefully pushed Mini aside, his gaze intent on the frightened girl. It was a grave mistake. In a split second, the girl lashed out with the knife, slashing and stabbing with all her might. In a moment of pure satisfaction, she scored a brilliant hit to the detective's arm. I couldn't help but giggle at his shocked expression, earning me a death glare from him in return. But it didn't matter to me - all I could think about was how terrified this little girl must be. "What did you expect?" I said firmly. "She's just a scared kid. We need to handle this carefully."

As Mini continued to speak to the girl, her tone remaining soothing and gentle, Keith and I worked to keep everyone else at a safe distance. DCI Lancaster was now nursing a wound on his arm and glaring daggers at us, but we couldn't afford to let him interfere with Mini's progress.

I felt a slight power surge from my partner as she spoke, her words laced with magic that seemed to have an effect on the girl. Her eyes glazed over slightly as if she was entering a daze, but she remained alert and aware of her surroundings.

"I'm sorry about that jerk," Mini said, gesturing towards the wounded detective, "He was in the wrong. He shouldn't have tried to force his way in."

The little girl studied Mini for a moment before relaxing her grip on the knife. She seemed to trust my partner's words, and I couldn't help but feel relieved.

"Now my friends and I are here to help you, sweetheart," Mini continued, taking a small step closer. "Can you let us do that?"

The girl hesitated for a moment before nodding slowly. With Mini's guidance, I knelt down in front of the girl and offered her my hand. Everything about her relaxed. I expected her grip on the weapon to slip, but it was still as firm as when we began. I moved towards Mini and spoke as softly as I could. "Whatever you do, don't take the knife away," she nodded. She understood.the knife was the girls last safety net and we couldn't take it away. Well not yet

"Hi there," I said softly with a friendly smile. "My name is Jess. What's yours?"

The girl looked at me warily before finally answering in a small voice, "Abby."

"It's nice to meet you Abby," I replied warmly. "Do you mind if we sit and talk for a bit? We just want to make sure you're okay."

She hesitated once again before finally nodding slowly. Together we sat against the wall next to Mini, as we sat together Mini continued, talking her voice soft and soothing, "We're here to help you, sweetheart. Let us be there for you." Tears welled up in the girl's eyes as she nodded in understanding, finally allowing us to lend her aid.

Taking in the sight of Mini, who seemed to have everything in hand, and noticing the budding connection between her and the girl, I made my way over to Lancaster to assess his injuries. "That was an eventful encounter," I remarked, examining the wound on his arm. "Do you require stitches, or will antiseptic and a dressing suffice?" He answered with a sneer, clearly still angry from our earlier confrontation. "Well, since civility seems beyond you at the moment, let's just get straight to the point." This statement seemed to shock him, briefly silencing his hostility. "I'm here to complete a job. We didn't intend to cause any trouble, but sometimes things don't go as planned. Your boss requested our assistance. In order for us to effectively help, I need some information on the other. Do you have that information?" My gaze locked with his, determined to get the answers we needed to fulfil our task.

I allowed a moment of silence to pass, giving him time to absorb my words. The tension in the room was palpable, thick like molasses, as the weight of our conversation hung heavily between us.

"I apologise for any added stress i may have caused but this is an incredibly volatile case and it's frustrating to have outside interference." He said his voice was calm, but I could feel his patience wearing thin.

"Let me clarify," I said, "we're not taking over the case from you. We'll work alongside each other and share information. It's in all of our best interests to stop any further harm from coming to innocent people. Can you please tell me what you know about the case, beyond what's written in the file?"

As he looked at me, his expression shifted from guarded to almost surprised, as if he was truly seeing me for the first time. "Wait, you want my help? Usually when other agencies get involved, they just want to take over and claim all the credit."

With a sincere tone, I reassured him, "I couldn't care less about credit. You can take all the glory for solving this case if you'd like. In fact, I'll even write my report in a way that makes you look like a hero. All I want is your insight so we can bring this psycho to justice. and end to this madness." The desperation in my voice couldn't be disguised.

I could see the surprise in their eyes as I requested their input. Their brows furrowed as they hesitated for a moment before responding.

"Yes, me," I confirmed, "I want your thoughts on this case."

Their expression softened into one of curiosity and they leaned in closer, intrigued by my request. Yes, now can you tell me, are there any similarities with the other cases? You were the lead on this from the first case, so what are your impressions?" My words hung heavy in the air, filled with an urgency to uncover the truth. "Leave nothing out," I urged him, "even if you think it's impossible or sounds crazy." His expression turned conflicted at my insistence, but eventually he began to speak, their words painting a vivid picture of their experiences in the case. Every detail was recounted with precision and passion, leaving no doubt in my mind that their insights would be crucial in solving the mystery at hand.

"That's all I can remember at the moment but My mind is currently a jumbled mess, and I must comb through my personal notes to organise my thoughts. But once I have done so, I would be more than willing to share my findings and theories with you and your team."

A chill ran down my spine as I asked the question that had been on my mind since arriving at the crime scene. "Is it possible that this is linked to the other cases? Could it be a copycat killer at work?"

The detective's face grew grim as he responded, his voice low and grave. "I think that the murders are all connected. But that's not all. We have been keeping most of these incidents under wraps, but I can tell you now that we have also had numerous reports of homeless individuals disappearing for weeks or even months before turning up dead. And the number of child abductions has risen drastically in the past 18 months, with many of the missing children eventually being found deceased." He paused, allowing his words to sink in.

My mind raced as I made connections between the seemingly unrelated cases. The victims all had something in common - they were vulnerable, easy prey for someone with sinister intentions. "So these vagrants and kid's...they're ending up like this family?" I gestured to the gruesome scene before us.

He nodded gravely. "Yes, and there are more cases like this that haven't been reported. It took a lot of digging to connect all of these dots."

A heavy weight settled in my chest as the full weight of the situation dawned on me. This wasn't just a few random occurrences caused by a lone creature, as I had naively hoped - it was a sinister thread woven into a larger tapestry of violence and tragedy. Our response needed to be swift and decisive, if we were going to have any chance of mitigating the damage already done. Time was not on our side.

I took a deep breath, bracing myself for the task ahead. "We must finish our work here and return to headquarters," I stated firmly. "The child will accompany my team, and all evidence related to this case must be sent to our facility." Lancaster's expression grew serious as he grasped the gravity of the situation. "Furthermore, I would like for you to develop a working theory of what is occurring here and meet with me tomorrow at noon to discuss it." He nodded in agreement. "Is that enough time for you to gather all necessary information?" I asked, wanting to give him enough time but also aware of the urgency of the situation. He gave another nod. "Excellent. I will assemble my team and the witness, then we will head to our field office. If you come across any new developments, please inform us tomorrow during our meeting. However, if it is urgent and cannot wait, do not hesitate to call me immediately."

I nervously handed him my business card, hoping he would call us if he received any leads. The last thing we needed was for a detective to go missing on our watch. I quickly made my way back to Kieth and Mini, my heart racing with anticipation. To my surprise, they had successfully coaxed the girl out of hiding, although she still clung tightly to a knife in her tiny hands. "Okay, I've left things in the detective's hands and arranged a debrief with him for noon tomorrow at the office," I announced, trying to sound confident. They both nodded in understanding, but before I could say anything else, Mini interrupted me. "Jess, I've explained to Alisha that we are her friends and we are going to take her somewhere safe." As Mini spoke, Alisha timidly poked her head out from behind her human shields. She gave me a hesitant once-over before whispering something to them. I could tell it had amused Mini based on the playful glint in her eye. "

"Oh, Alisha," she said with a warm smile that crinkled the corners of her eyes, "I can assure you that she is quite lovely, despite her intimidating appearance. She may seem stern at first, but all it takes is a plate of cupcakes or cookies to melt her heart. It's as if she transforms into a precious newborn kitten, all soft and cuddly." As soon as the words tumbled out of Mini's mouth, I could feel my cheeks burning with embarrassment. How could she betray me like this? Thrown under the bus with just a mention of sweets.

"First off, let me clarify I may have a love for pastries, cakes, and cookies, but who doesn't? And secondly, am I truly that intimidating?" I can't help but reflect on how I used to be described before – soft and cute. But after rigorous training and exercise, my appearance has certainly changed more than I ever expected it to. Alisha couldn't contain her excitement, at the mention of sweets grinning widely as she glanced at me once again. With a smile of my own, I knelt down to meet her gaze, "Well, since Mini here seems to have a disdain for sweet treats, that just means there will be more for you and me to enjoy together." Alisha giggled slightly,

We gently guided her back to the car, trying our best to shield her from the grim scene that surrounded us. Walking through the house, we urged her to keep her gaze fixed on the floor as we moved past shattered glass and overturned furniture. Despite our efforts, she couldn't block out all of the horrors that lay in front of her. My heart ached as I saw silent tears begin to fall from her eyes; I wished I could join her in crying, but my emotions had to take a backseat for now. This child needed my strength more than ever. We carefully settled Alisha in the backseat, sandwiched between Kieth and Mini like two sturdy protectors. As we drove towards the field office, I made sure everything was in place with DCI Lancaster. The sound of soft snoring caught my attention, and I turned to see Alisha fast asleep with her head resting on Mini's shoulder. In this moment of peace, As I gave her a questioning look, she shrugged nonchalantly. "The poor thing was completely spent, so I simply offered a gentle emotional nudge to help her fall asleep. But even then, she refused to relinquish that bloodied knife," Her words were tinged with sorrow and understanding. The rest of our journey was completed in an almost eerie silence; the shock and horror of what we had witnessed weighing heavily on our minds. Each of us lost in our own thoughts, trying to make sense of the tragedy that had just unfolded before us.

As we arrived at the London field office, I was taken aback. Instead of a typical police station or government building, it was a sleek and modern office tower. The glass exterior gleamed in the sunlight, giving off an air of luxury rather than law enforcement.

the inside was just as impressive as the exterior. The walls were adorned with abstract art pieces, and the floors were polished to a shine. If I didn't know better, I would have thought I had stumbled into a high-end corporate building, not the headquarters of a paranormal defence agency.

A friendly man in a crisp navy blue suit approached me with a warm smile, his teeth gleaming like freshly polished pearls. "Welcome," he said, extending his hand. "I will take care of your things for you." His voice was smooth and professional as he gestured towards the luggage at my feet. "The medical team is on standby to examine the child and ensure she is in good health." He nodded towards a set of elevators at the far end of the lobby, which were adorned with gold etched with intricate designs. "And I was informed that a conference room has been set up for your use."

As we made our way towards the elevator, he continued to fill me in on all the details, his words flowing like honey. "All of this infor-mation has been emailed to Keith," he said, his hand already reaching for the elevator button. "And I've been instructed to let you know that he will be your liaison for the remainder of your visit."

Without a moment to speak or offer my gratitude, he was already out the door, Mini following closely behind me refusing to let anyone else carry the still sleeping Alisha. As we ascended to our designated floor, I couldn't help but be struck by the impressive level of organ-isation and professionalism within this seemingly ordinary office building. Our first stop was the medical wing, and we followed Keith down a pristine white corridor with polished marble floors. The walls were adorned with colourful artwork and large windows allowed natural light to flood in.Finally, we arrived at our destination - a top-of-the-line medical facility that seemed more fitting for a prestigious hospital than an office building.

With gentle efficiency, we laid Alisha on one of the vacant hospital beds. I spoke to one of the nurses, my voice trembling with worry and concern for the young girl.

Mini sat with her nervously watching the sleeping girl chest rise and fall with every breath, always fiercely protective of those she cared about, Mini insisted on staying by Alisha's side so she would have a familiar face there when she woke up. With her innate empathic abilities, Mini could use her powers to soothe and comfort Alisha if needed.

"Jess," Mini said, turning to me with a determined look in her eyes, "I know we had planned for this to be a team assignment, but I can't leave her like this. It wouldn't be right. So I need you to handle it as best you can. Just keep me updated and in the loop. I'll get as much information out of Alisha as possible and coordinate everything that's needed."

As I watched Mini tenderly brush stray strands of hair from Alisha's face, I couldn't argue with her decision. It was clear that Mini's loyalty and love for those around her knew no bounds.

"That's fine," I agreed reluctantly, "but promise me that if things go south, you'll join me in the field to deal with it."

Mini met my gaze steadily and nodded. Her fierce determination gave me confidence that together, we could handle whatever challenges came our way.

"Of course Jess, but I don't think you'll need me. I have faith in you." Mini's words were filled with reassurance and confidence as she looked at me with a supportive smile.

Taking that as Mini dismissing me from the ward, I turned to leave but was stopped by Keith's outstretched hand. "Wait a moment," he said, halting me in her tracks. "If you're planning on staying here with Alisha, I can get a workstation set up for you in this room. You can work on the case and video conference with us in the briefing room. It will save us constantly relaying messages and make communication more efficient." He said to mini surprising us both with his suggestion

My eyes widened with excitement at the idea. "That would be

incredible, Keith. Do you think that would work for you?" I asked Mini

"Absolutely," she replied confidently. "At least that way, I can still give input and support as you need it."

Keiths dedication and willingness to make things easier for me and Mini touched my heart and did a lot to show she could count on him during this difficult time.

Without wasting a single moment, Keith pulled out his phone and began arranging the necessary logistics. Meanwhile, I took a moment to embrace Mini, grateful for her unwavering belief in me. "Thank you," I whispered, holding her close before joining Keith as he finished his call. Together, we made our way out of the ward.

"Let's head to the briefing room first," I said with feigned confidence, eager to distract myself from the gravity of the situation. "Lead the way." Keith gestured for me to follow him and we quickly made our way down the hospital corridors towards an elevator. "We'll be heading to the fifth floor," he informed me. "That's where we keep the armoury and the briefing room's. we are using the conference room next to the facility chief's office. so We might even run into him during your stay here."

As the doors of the elevator closed, I couldn't help but feel a sense of unease wash over me. This would be my new home for the foreseeable future,

"So you're going to be the lead investigator on this?" Keith asked with genuine curiosity, his brows furrowed as he leaned in closer. I nervously shifted in my, feeling the weight of his expectant gaze. "Yep, it looks like it's down to me to keep everything on track," I replied, trying to sound confident but feeling a knot form in my stomach.

Keith flashed me a reassuring smile. "I have complete faith in you, Jess. And the entire agency has your back, so if you need anything, you just need to ask." His words were like a warm embrace, soothing my nerves and giving me a boost of confidence.

"Thank you," I said gratefully, feeling a sense of gratitude wash over me.

"And I'm going to stick with you guys on the case so you won't be alone," Keith added determinedly, his eyes conveying his unwavering support and loyalty.

I smiled gratefully as he showed me into the briefing room. someone had already set up the existing case files that we had available and whiteboards for us to work on. They had also developed a timeline for the case that we knew about. As I looked this over. I realised everything I assumed I would need to do tonight had already been done.

I looked at Keith, giving him an inquisitive look. "We were told that you had a long journey, and with everything you've experienced

today, I thought I would get everything set up so now you can get a few hours rest before DCI Lancaster arrives with his notes and case files, I have also instructed the nurse to ensure Mini gets some rest! Would you like me to take you to your dorm room?" he asked a little sheepishly

I eagerly accepted his offer, but my expectations of a comfortable hotel were shattered

"That would be wonderful, but I was expecting to be staying at a hotel," I replied,

Keith nodded, a small smile playing at his lips. "Actually, we have some living quarters on the top floors for those of us who tend to overwork themselves or for visiting colleagues from other facilities," he explained as we made our way back to the elevator.

entering my designated quarters, I couldn't help but gasp at the room it was surprisingly spacious and well-equipped, complete with a fully stocked kitchen., with floor-to-ceiling windows offering a stunning view of the city skyline. A small seating area and what looked like a criminally comfortable king size beds stood there stunned as Keith handed me a key card and informed me that he would wake me at 7 a.m. so we could have five hours to prepare before the detective's arrival.

Thank you for this accommodation," I said gratefully, but my exhaustion was beginning to catch up with me.

"I'll leave you to rest then. It has been quite a long day," he replied with a nod before exiting the room and leaving me alone with my thoughts. As I closed the door behind him, I couldn't help but feel grateful for this unexpected respite in such a busy and tumultuous time.

CHAPTER 12

As the morning sun rose, casting a warm glow over the land, I checked in on Mini and Alisha before heading to the briefing room. Alisha was fast asleep, her chest rising and falling in a steady rhythm. But Mini was wide awake, her fingers flying across the keyboard of her impressive tech setup. She gave me a quick nod, indicating she was ready to go, and instructed me to make my way to the briefing room while she caught me up on her findings so far.

Following Mini's orders, I turned on my heel and made my way out of the medical ward. The air was crisp and fresh, invigorating my senses as I walked towards the lift that would take me to the briefing room Keith had shown me the previous night. As the doors slid open with a soft whoosh, I stepped inside and pressed the button for my destination. Excitement coursed through me as I thought about what new information awaited us at this meeting.

Being in the briefing room was a little overwhelming, but I had to push on; the tech crew that Keith had mentioned had set up multiple display screens and cameras. Mini's voice sounded from one screen, startling me and making me squeal, "Stop being childish and let's get on with some work." I scolded and She giggled a little at my reaction. "That was so not funny, mini; you nearly gave me a heart attack."

"Please, it will take more than a little fright to kill you off," Mini retorted playfully.

I rolled my eyes at her before focusing back on the screens in front of me. They were showing various bit's of database well as video footage taken at some of the crime scenes footage from different . It was clear that Mini had been hard at work since we last spoke.

The urgency in Mini's voice was palpable as she relayed her findings to me and Keith, who had just entered the conference room. "We have a colossal problem on our hands. After cross-referencing the information and searching through databases of missing persons and any open homicides, I've uncovered a pattern that suggests this has been going on for at least 18 to 24 months. The bodies we've linked to this case have all been discovered in progressively worse condition, with last night's being the worst yet." Her words hung heavy in the air as we all processed the gravity of the situation.

Keith nodded grimly, his expression mirroring my own shock and concern. "I've got the lab techs working on analysing the physical evidence right now. Hopefully, they'll uncover some trace evidence that can give us leads on the identity of this monster we're dealing with." The mention of a monster sent shivers down my spine, knowing that we were dealing with something truly horrific and depraved. The tension in the room was thick as we waited for more updates, unsure of what other horrors may await us in this case.

I gave Keith a scrutinising look, trying to read his expression for any hints of potential insights. "Do you have anything to share with us?" I inquired, my tone laced with curiosity.

With a heavy tone and furrowed brows, Keith's voice overflowed with genuine concern. He gestured towards the row of flat screen monitors lining the wall, each displaying files on the human victims we had uncovered thus far. It was clear that these were not the only casualties. Unofficial whispers had been circulating for months about young paranormals disappearing without a trace or being found brutally slaughtered. Tragically, there had been no acknowledgement or action taken by those tasked with protecting them. The weight of this realisation hung in the air, making it hard to breathe.

A crease formed between my eyebrows, my confusion transforming into disbelief. "Let me get this straight," I said, struggling to wrap my head around the revelation. "Are you saying that these disappearances and deaths are happening within our own community of paranormal beings, and we have been completely unaware?" The realisation sent a chill down my spine - if even those who were supposed to protect and comprehend their kind were now turning against them, what chance did the rest of us stand? The once comforting thought of belonging to a supernatural world now felt like a dangerous and uncertain reality.

The staticky voice of Mini, the agency's communication system, crackled through the speakers. "Jess sweetheart," she began, her tone gentle yet authoritative. "Alex has told you about this before remember, the agencies can only deal with things that are reported," she reminded me, her words carrying both wisdom and weariness. I could picture her sighing as she continued, "But usually, the individual leaders for the community will deal with the problems they have with the use of their enforcers." Her voice grew more serious now, conveying the tensions between authority and autonomy. "And although they acknowledge our authority, they hate appearing weak by relying on us." I could remember the lesson she was talking about. It was one of the many I had difficulty wrapping my head around. Frustration bubbled within me and I sighed in defeat, feeling like a small pawn in a much larger game. Raising my hand in surrender, I knew there was little I could do but follow orders and trust in those who held power over me.

"Okay, I get it, but how do we find out if this is as big a problem as we believe?" Keith's hand shot up into the air, seeking our attention. Mini rolled her eyes playfully and gave him a small smile, trying to ease the tension. "We're not in a classroom, Keith. Just say what you have to say," she said with a hint of amusement in her voice. Despite her words, we all knew that his input was valuable and eagerly awaited his response.

"Well," Keith began, his voice trembling slightly, "I may have arranged a few meetings with representatives from various paranormal factions in the area after your meeting with D.C.I Lancaster."

Mini and I exchanged glances, both of us silently agreeing that this was a potentially good idea. Our investigation needed all the help and information we could gather. My heart raced with anticipation as I asked, "Who did you schedule appointments with?"

"I have secured a meeting with the Mages for later today And for you, there are two scheduled appointments - one with the powerful vampire council and another with the elusive dragon's court, both of which are for tomorrow to give you time to go over any information D.C.I Lancaster may supply" Keith responded nervously.

My mind whirled with excitement at the thought of meeting these ancient and formidable beings. But then Keith added, "They have insisted that they will only meet with you, and no one else from the agency can accompany you." Suddenly, my excitement was tinged with apprehension and doubt. This would be an arduous task alone, without any backup or support from my team. But I knew it was crucial to gain their assistance in solving this looming threat to our world.

"Do you know why it's so crucial for me to go alone?"

"No, but please exercise caution. These two factions hold immense power and wield it recklessly. The mere mention of their names sends a chill down my spine. I suspect this may be some sort of test. Just try your best not to offend them."

The idea of facing two of the most influential players in all of London was enough to make anyone wary, but if they are actively seeking me out, it means they are either afraid or heavily involved in this dangerous game. There's only one way to uncover the truth - I must meet with them.

"Who exactly will be meeting with the sifters? Do they have a ruling alpha who is willing to speak with us?"

"Unfortunately, they have refused to cooperate at this time. It's highly unusual for them to turn down such an invitation, which only adds to my suspicion. Something is definitely amiss, but I cannot seem to pinpoint what it could be. If I receive any new information, you will be the first to know."

With every detail meticulously laid out before us, we pored over each piece of evidence with the utmost care. We didn't want to miss a single clue. It was imperative that I was fully informed before my meeting with D.C.I Lancaster; his opinion held great weight in this investigation and I couldn't afford for him to think I was incompetent or unprepared. As seconds ticked by, my mind raced as I tried desperately to connect the dots between our known victims, but nothing stood out to me.

Lost in thought, I barely registered Keith's throat clearing. He had thoughtfully arranged for us to meet in a quiet room on the ground floor, away from the chaos and clutter of our investigation. I was grateful for his consideration - the last thing I wanted was for DCI Lancaster to see any signs of disorganisation or confusion.

"I'm glad you agree, Jess," Keith said as he gestured towards the multitude of monitors and printouts spread out around the room. The screens displayed a wealth of information and images of potential creatures capable of the sort of carnage we had witnessed just yesterday. Some were grotesque and terrifying, while others seemed almost beautiful in their deadly capabilities. It was a disturbing sight, and one I was sure D.C.I Lancaster was not prepared for.

"Yes, thank you, Keith. I'll be right down," I replied absently, still deep in thought.

Making my way down to the designated meeting room, my mind continued to buzz with different theories and possibilities. When I arrived, DCI Lancaster was already there, carrying multiple file boxes stacked so high that his face was partially obscured.

As expected, Lancaster's notes were a messy jumble of disorganised papers and folders. But as he laid out the details of his investigation, my stomach twisted with a mixture of dread and revulsion. He presented me with multiple thick folders, each one filled to the brim with names, descriptions, and photos of dozens of missing persons. Each name was accompanied by the haunting details of their last known location and statements from anyone who may have had contact with them before they disappeared. These were individuals who had been dismissed and forgotten, deemed unimportant because of their transient lifestyles or labeled as mere vagrants. But it was clear that Lancaster had put in an immense amount of legwork to track down each and every one of them.

"When did you find the time to do all of this?" I asked, wondering if Lancaster's superiors were aware of his secret investigations.

"I've been working on it during my evenings, mornings, any free moment I could spare," he replied calmly. "I've even sacrificed my holiday hours to continue digging."

His dedication and unwavering determination left me truly impressed and humbled. How many others would go to such lengths for those who society has cast aside?

"It gets worse," he said with a heavy sigh, pushing another stack of files across the table towards me. I could see the fatigue in his eyes and the tension in his shoulders, but his determination never wavered as he dove into the next set of documents.

As I began to read through the files, I realised they were all cases of suspicious deaths that had been brushed off as drug overdoses or heart attacks. Lancaster had been right - there was something bigger going on here. But it seemed that no one besides him had bothered to connect the dots and see the true pattern emerging.

With fervour and passion, he walked me through each piece of evidence, pointing out connections and discrepancies that had gone unnoticed by others. Despite the gravity of the situation, I couldn't help but feel a sense of admiration for Lancaster's tireless dedication to solving these seemingly insignificant cases.

Hours passed as we poured over details and cross-referenced information from various agency files. By the time evening arrived, both Lancaster and I were mentally drained and no closer to an answer. We reluctantly decided to call it a night.

Before parting ways, I reassured him that I would keep our lines of communication open and urged him to reach out if he came across any new leads or information. As he left the building, I couldn't shake off the weight of what we were up against - but with Lancaster by my side, I knew we stood a chance at uncovering the truth behind these mysterious deaths.

After his sudden departure, I trudged up to the conference room we were using, my head swirling with all the information we had uncovered. Mini and Keith awaited me there, their expressions eager and expectant. As I launched into my briefing, I could feel the weight of responsibility pressing down on me. It was clear that whatever was happening was much larger and more complex than we had initially anticipated.

The rest of my evening was spent poring over our list of victims, searching for patterns or connections between them. But each lead I followed seemed to lead nowhere, leaving me frustrated and exhausted. As the clock ticked towards midnight, Keith's hand gently rested on my shoulder, his own eyes heavy with weariness. "Jess," he said softly, "you need some rest. You have important meetings tomorrow and you'll need all your wits about you." Reluctantly, I dragged myself to my room, dreading the possibility of a sleepless night ahead.

As I lay in bed, my mind raced through the events of the day and the daunting tasks that lay ahead. The silence of the night was only broken by my racing thoughts and the occasional distant sound of a car passing by outside. Despite my exhaustion, sleep eluded me as I anxiously awaited the challenges that awaited me in the morning.

CHAPTER 13

A FTER A SLEEPLESS night of tossing and turning, I finally dragged myself to the agency's parking structure. As I approached the designated spot, my eyes were drawn to a sleek and polished black 4x4 vehicle. It gleamed under the early morning sun, its curves and edges reflecting the light in a mesmerising dance. Disappointment briefly flickered through me as I realised that for my time at the London office, I would not have access to a chauffeur service. But as I walked closer to the car, excitement surged within me at the thought of being able to drive myself around. Ever since Hargreaves had taken it upon himself to teach me how to operate a car, I had fallen in love with the thrilling sensation of freedom that came with driving. Whenever I needed some time to decompress and relax, I would take long drives around the training base, embracing the rush of wind through open windows and taking in the picturesque scenery. Driving in the bustling city would be a new experience, but one that I eagerly anticipated with curiosity and eagerness. Climbing into the driver's seat, I noticed that the keys were already inserted in the ignition and my destination was pre-programmed into the satnav. A small smile played on my lips as I assumed this was thanks to Keith the guy always seemed to be one step ahead in anticipating my needs.

As I drove towards the Vampire Council estate, a sense of unease crept over me. Everything that Alex had taught me about vampires echoed in my mind - their often volatile nature, their tendency to hold grudges, and their willingness to help only when it benefits them. As the grand gates came into view, I couldn't help but notice the sheer size of the estate. It seemed to stretch on for acres, with not a soul in sight. But I knew better than to think I was alone. The gate swung open effortlessly as I approached, as if welcoming me into its mysterious embrace. I continued up the winding driveway, my heart pounding as I finally came to a stop in front of the looming double doors of the Victorian mansion. This was it - my meeting with the powerful Vampire Council awaited inside those ancient walls.

With a deep breath, I stepped out of my car and made my way up the stone steps to the grand entrance. As I reached for the doorknob, it swung open, revealing a pale figure with a forced smile. It was clear that this vampire was relatively new, no more than a few months old. His red eyes gave away his true nature, still struggling to control the blood lust within him. *"Ah, Jessica from the agency,"* he greeted me smoothly. *"My masters have been expecting you. Please follow me to the library."*

Without another word, he turned and strode confidently into the darkness of the mansion. I followed close behind, steeling myself for what lay ahead in this elegant yet eerie abode of the undead. Every step brought me deeper into their world, filled with secrets and power beyond my wildest imagination. But I was ready for whatever challenges awaited me as a member of the agency appointed to handle supernatural affairs. Let's see what these vampires have in store for me tonight..

The vampire society was notorious for their strict adherence to protocol, so I made sure not to cause any trouble as my escort led me towards the library. With each step, I could feel the palpable pulse of power emanating from the room - it was clear that there were more than a few elders in attendance for our little conversation. This was going to be interesting, to say the least...

Walking into a room filled with some of the most influential and powerful vampires in the area wasn't exactly high on my list of things to do, but I pushed myself forward, hoping to gather enough information to make this journey worthwhile. The sight that greeted me was both intimidating and terrifying - a group of vampires holding seats on the vampire council had gathered here, radiating an aura of danger and dominance.

But I couldn't let my fear show. I took a deep breath and strode confidently into the library, determined to make my presence known. As I scanned the room, I noted the various activities of those present - some were reading books, others smoking cigars, and a select few were engaged in intense conversations. But the moment my escort left and closed the door behind me, all eyes turned towards me.

The weight of their gaze alone was enough to send shivers down my spine, but it was nothing compared to the overwhelming sense of power and bloodlust that emanated from them. It took all of my willpower not to collapse under its weight. This was going to be a difficult conversation, but I squared my shoulders and prepared myself for what lay ahead.

I just had to focus on my breathing, desperately trying to keep my powers in check. I could feel the energy swirling and pulsing within me, eager to be released. But I knew that if I unleashed it now, it would end in disaster. Minutes felt like hours as I stood there, resisting the urge to give in to my rage.Finally, the overwhelming wave of power began to lessen. My body was trembling from the effort it took to control myself now as I relaxed, relief washing over me.

The group scattered, returning to their previous tasks, but one remained. He approached me with a friendly gesture, inviting me to sit at a small coffee table nearby. As he reached for my hand to introduce himself, I instinctively pulled away. "I apologise," I explained, "but I prefer not to be touched." He nodded in understanding before asking, "Am I correct in assuming you are Jesica from the agency?" quickly confirmed his assumption with a simple "yes". But then he posed another question that made my blood run cold. "And am I also correct in my information that you are one of the dragon blood?" His calculating gaze narrowed, and I felt a surge of hatred towards the blood-sucking parasite before me."No," I replied firmly, suppressing the anger in my voice. "You are mistaken. I am not one of the dragon blood and as far as I'm aware, they do not exist." The thought of being associated with the dragon blood from the past was enough to make my skin crawl.

"But that is not why I am here," I continued, ignoring the slight smirk on his face. "As you know, there has been a series of incidents that have caught the attention of the agency. And it seems supernatural in origin, which is why they have sent a team in to investigate." I looked around the room, meeting each vampire's gaze with a cool and confident stare. "And you should all be aware of this because you are all here to put on this little demonstration of power."

The atmosphere in the room shifted at my words. There was a sense of unease and tension. These vampires were used to being in control, but now they were facing a threat that was beyond their understanding.

I could sense their fear and uncertainty, but I refused to let it affect me. Despite being outnumbered and surrounded by creatures who could easily overpower me, I stood my ground with unwavering determination.

"Now cut the crap and let's get on with this meeting," I said firmly, cutting through the silence like a knife.

A ghost of a smile graced the spokesman's face as he leaned back in his chair. "You are as straightforward as your reputation says," he remarked with amusement.

I simply raised an eyebrow in response.

"Very well," he continued, getting straight to business. "We have been aware of these incidents for some time now. But we have no involvement in them."

I carefully studied his face, searching for any subtle changes in expression that could hint at deception or hidden agendas. But his features remained stoic and unreadable, like a mask of polished marble.

"And what about your Local nests?" I pressed, my voice low and cautious. I was referring to the groups of vampires who resided within this city.

"We have our own rules and code of conduct," he replied calmly, his tone smooth and unwavering. "We do not involve ourselves in human affairs unless absolutely necessary."

I nodded slowly, trying to keep my skepticism in check. Vampires were notorious for their opportunistic natures, and it was hard to believe they would not take advantage of any situation that benefited them.

"But as it stands, we fail to see why this concerns anyone from the vampire community." The statement hung heavy in the air, laced with disbelief and ignorance. I couldn't help but be taken aback by their lack of understanding. How could they not see the gravity of the situation? "Are you truly asking me why this concerns you?" I exclaimed, incredulous. "why agree this meeting if that's what you think. And as for why it concerns you...an entire family has been brutally massacred. The gruesome scene suggests that the perpetrator possessed immense strength and control, potentially holding their victims in a trance-like state during the killings. Furthermore, our team suspects that whoever is responsible may be linked to a string of unexplained deaths and disappearances spanning over 18 months."

I paused, letting the weight of my words sink in.

"Surely, with these alarming details, you can understand why I have been called upon to be here."

The spokesman seemed taken aback by my question, but I could see the gears turning in his mind as he tried to come up with a response.

After a moment of tense silence, he cleared his throat and spoke carefully. "We apologize for any confusion or misunderstanding. We were merely trying to confirm that we have no involvement in these incidents."

I nodded, accepting his explanation but still skeptical.

"Fine," I said, not fully convinced. "But you must understand the seriousness of this situation. If whoever is behind these killings is not stopped, it could lead to exposure and possible retaliation against our kind."

The vampires exchanged cautious looks before the spokesman spoke again. "What do you propose we do?"

I took a deep breath before responding. "There are dozens, if not more, vampire sub-species that fit the base profile. Now, we don't know for sure that it is one of these, but I would have assumed that you would want to help us apprehend those responsible to clear yourselves of any suspicion. Do you understand now why this is a concern for the vampire council?"

The council spokesman's voice was firm and unwavering. "No, I don't believe it is in our best interest to aid in your investigation," they stated, his expression stony and unreadable. As to why we requested this meeting with you, let's just say we were intrigued by your presence and this gave us the perfect opportunity for a conversation."

I glanced around the grand library, noticing how the dim light cast shadows on the ornate bookshelves and ancient artefacts lining the walls. A sense of foreboding lingered in the air as I faced him once more. his gaze bore into mine, challenging me to push further.

But before I could respond, he spoke again. "Now, if you don't mind, I believe it's time for you to leave." Without waiting for my response, they stood up and began to make their way towards the exit. "Don't bother showing me out, I can find my own way," I retorted, feeling frustrated and dismissed.

As I made my way out of the library, the remaining council members seemed to converge on the one I had been speaking to. Hushed whispers and exchanged glances followed in my wake, leaving me with a sense of unease about their true intentions.

I'm sure they know more than they are letting on, I thought to myself starting up my car I looked out on to the road ahead I thought if this is how the vampires had reacted may the gods protect me because I had a feeling the dragons would be worse. I put my car in gear and was about to drive off when a sudden knock at my door startled me. Winding down my wind, I was greeted with an annoyingly cheerful grin followed by a very gentle and delicate voice, the type of voice that would be classed as angelic and beautiful, saying, "My name is Abigail, and it is a pleasure to meet you, Jessica If I can be so bold to say that I assume your meeting with the council didn't go as well as you had hoped?"

A shiver ran down my spine as I started up my car and looked out onto the seemingly endless road ahead. The weight of the situation settled on my shoulders as I thought about how much more the vampires must know than they were letting on to, my mind raced with thoughts of the vampires' intense reaction. If this was their response, how would the dragons react? The very thought sent a chill through me. I shifted into gear and was about to pull away when a sudden knock at my door made me jump. . Rolling down my window, I was met with a bright, almost obnoxiously cheerful grin accompanied by a voice so gentle and delicate it could only be described as angelic. "My name is Abigail," she said sweetly, "and it is a pleasure to meet you, Jessica. If I may be so bold to say, I assume your meeting with the council did not go as well as you had hoped?"

My stomach twisted in knots as her words brought back all the disappointment and frustration from that failed encounter. But looking into her kind eyes, I couldn't help but feel a sense of comfort and understanding. Perhaps this new acquaintance would be able to shed some light on the mysterious world of vampires that now consumed my thoughts.

I let out a heavy sigh in response to Abigail's question.

"Unfortunately, the meeting didn't yield the results I had hoped for," I said, the frustration evident in my tone. "But deep down, I knew it was always going to be a long shot." As I spoke, my hand slowly moved towards my firearm, ready to defend myself if needed. It was a reflexive action brought on by years of training with Hargreaves.

Abigail looked at me sympathetically. "I can only imagine how frustrating that must be," she said softly. "But perhaps it's for the best that they didn't give you what you wanted."

I raised an eyebrow at her words. "What do you mean?"

"Let's just say that the council is not known for making decisions that benefit others," she replied cryptically.

I felt a chill run down my spine at her insinuation. Was she suggesting that the council had ulterior motives? And if so, what were they?

Before I could ask any more questions, Abigail continued, "But enough about them. Can we talk about you for a moment?"

I hesitated before answering, unsure if I could trust this stranger with my personal information. But something about her gentle demeanour made me feel safe enough to open up.

"There's not much to tell," I said with a shrug. "I'm just a girl trying to make sense of this new world I find ourselves in."

Abigail nodded understandingly. "And how are you coping with it all?"

I thought back to everything that had happened since the night of my holiday to Ireland and everything that has happened since. and now being thrust into this dangerous political game between different supernatural factions.

A heavy sigh escaped my lips as I admitted, " it's overwhelming." But determination shone in my eyes as I added, "But I am determined to figure it out and do whatever it takes to protect those I care about." A warm smile graced Abigail's face, bringing a glimmer of hope to the somber mood. "That's a good way to turn things around from tragedy," she said before her gaze fell upon my arm where I had begun to reach for my weapons earlier. Flashing me a sly smile, her words dripped with honeyed sweetness. "Now Jessica, that's no way to treat someone who only wants to lend a helping hand." The way her voice carried such empathy reminded me of warm honey drizzled over freshly baked bread.

Her words sent a shiver down my spine.

Abigail stood tall, her shoulders squared and chin held high, exuding a confident aura. But as she spoke, her voice trembled slightly, revealing her fear of being left behind. "Please," she implored, "let me join you in your next meeting with the Dragon representative. They may be more inclined to open up and be honest with me present." Her fingers fidgeted with the hem of her Jacket as she continued, "And who knows, I might even bring some much-needed physical strength to your team." She flashed a charming smile and punctuated her request with a playful wink, adding, "I promise to behave...well, at least I'll try."

Despite my reservations, something about Abigail's sincerity convinced me to give her a chance. My gut told me she wouldn't do anything to deliberately put me in danger. "Fine, get in," I relented, trying to hide the uncertainty in my voice. "But if you try any funny business, I will not hesitate to take you out." Despite my stern warning, Abigail just giggled to herself as though I had said the funniest thing she had ever heard. Nonchalantly, she climbed into the car and buckled up. Her carefree attitude couldn't help but make me wonder what kind of unexpected twists and turns awaited us .

CHAPTER 14

Nervously cleared my throat before asking Abigail, "So, do you have any knowledge about dragons?" I wasn't sure if she was already familiar with them or if I needed to give her a brief explanation. Her response was not very reassuring. "Honestly, vampires tend to steer clear of them. They can be unpredictable and dangerous." Great, just what I needed - someone tagging along who might cause more harm than help.

Feeling a bit irritated, I tried to reassure her that I wasn't an expert either. "I can share what I know. It might come in handy if we encounter any tricky situations." To my surprise, Abigail's cheerful demeanour seemed unaffected by the potential danger.

I took a deep breath, steeling myself for the task ahead. My knowledge of dragons was limited, but I shared what little I knew with Abigail. "They are part of the supernatural community, like many other creatures. And while most can take on human form, they are actually smaller than you might think - except for the ancient ones." My voice trailed off as I recalled my encounter with Lyn, the dragon who had left a lasting impression on me. From what I've heard, dragons can grow to be as large as mountains. But in this realm, they usually stay around the size of one or two double-decker buses. It's only when they need to interact with humans that they will take on a human form. And those who have regular contact with humans often hold positions of power and control in different countries - using their influence for their own gain rather than for the greater good. The legends and stories about dragons may be true in some aspects, but one thing is certain - they are driven by self-interest above all else."

My sat-nav pinged excitedly, signalling that we had reached the destination I had been given. As I pulled into the parking lot, it took me a moment to process what I was seeing. This must be some kind of joke. The building in front of me was an old-style pub called the Dragon's Keep, complete with a mural of a fire-breathing dragon on the side. I couldn't help but let out a small laugh - who knew dragons had a sense of humour?

My companion for the evening, Abigail, joined me as we exited the car and made our way to the entrance of The Dragon's Keep Pub. The old wooden door creaked open, revealing a dimly lit interior and the distinct smell of stale ale and wood smoke that seemed to cling to everything within. As we stepped inside, the chatter and laughter of patrons filled the air, mingling with the sounds of glasses clinking and music playing from a lone jukebox in the corner.

A disheveled waitress, her apron stained and hair askew, looked up from her cleaning duties and asked if it was just a party of two. Before we could respond, a very tall, handsome man appeared behind us, his presence commanding attention. With a smooth voice that sent shivers down my spine, he interrupted, "It's okay, Mona. These lovely ladies will be joining me in the corner booth." "Gudmundur, I didn't see you there," said Mona as she hurried ahead of us. "I'll seat your guests at your usual table, sir." She led us to a secluded corner booth with a wrap-around couch seating arrangement that offered a clear view of the entire venue. From here, I could see all possible exits and escape routes, a detail not lost on me as we were suddenly thrust into this potentially dangerous encounter. As we followed her through the crowded pub, I couldn't help but feel a sense of uneasy brewing in this unexpected meeting place. We passed by tables filled with rowdy groups of friends and couples cozied up in booths sharing hushed conversations. But none of them seemed to compare to the mystery and intrigue that surrounded our new acquaintance who followed in our wake

Gudmundur sat next to Abigail, and with their familiarity and ease around each other, I couldn't help but wonder what kind of history they shared. My curiosity only grew as our conversation with Gudmundur, a member of the elusive dragons , began to unfold.

from what Abigail had said on the drive here I never thought I would see vampires and dragons acting so friendly towards each other. Still, these two seemed like old friends enjoying breakfast at their local greasy spoons. "Okay, you two spill what the fuck is going on.

Abigail chuckled at my bluntness, but Gudmundur simply smiled and motioned for us to order drinks.

My voice was strained as I ground out my words, "I'm not here for drinks. I came for answers." My frustration was palpable as I recounted my assignment to track down and apprehend an individual responsible for a string of murders. These cases were linked to numerous missing persons reports and other suspicious deaths. After being brushed off by the vampire council's representative, who seemed to take pleasure in wasting my time, I had turned to this individual in front of me to see if he had any information or was willing to help. As I took a deep breath, the his smirks only grew wider, clearly finding my increasingly agitated state amusing. "Please," I pleaded, "if you have nothing useful to contribute, just say so now so I can leave." My patience was wearing thin and I couldn't hold back my exasperated sigh.

Abigail's eyes widened in shock and she stared at me as though I had grown a second head, her mouth twisting into a smile before she dissolved into uncontrollable laughter at my outburst. Meanwhile, Gudmundur sat calmly in his chair with a serene smile on his face, as if this were a regular occurrence.

Once Abigail regained control of her emotions, Gudmundur began to speak. "Ladies, welcome to my humble abode. Abigail, it is always a pleasure to see you again and I hope you are well. And Lady Jessica, I don't believe we have had the pleasure of meeting before, but I have no doubt we will get along famously." He paused, fixing his sharp gaze on me. "I understand you have had some negative encounters with the paranormal community, but I assure you, I am not like the others you may have encountered."

His words were comforting and genuine, yet there was an underlying intensity to them that made me wonder what exactly he meant by "not like the others". My mind immediately went to the strange case we were dealing with and how desperate we were for any help we could get. Sensing our need for assistance, Gudmundur asked eagerly, "Now from what you have explained, you have quite a peculiar case on your hands. How may I be of service?" His expression was one of both curiosity and determination, making it clear that he was ready to do whatever it takes to help us.

My doubts boiled over and I couldn't contain them any longer. "Why are you both so eager to assist me?" I demanded, my voice shaking with fear. Memories of the horrific accounts and terrifying histories I had read flooded my mind, making my heart pound uncontrollably. "Everything I've been told about your species has been nothing but dark and sinister." My eyes darted between the two beings in front of me, searching for any signs of deception or malice.

They sat beside each other, their postures stiff and tense as they avoided making eye contact with one another as I spoke. The room was heavy with a palpable tension that seemed to tingle on my skin. I squared my shoulders and spoke firmly, trying to mask the nerves in my voice. "Earlier, Abigail mentioned the longstanding tension between your two factions. It's no secret that vampires and dragons are notoriously secretive and rarely offer assistance unless it directly benefits them. So please, enlighten me. What exactly is going on?" The silence that followed felt electric, like the calm before a storm. I couldn't help but feel like there were hidden agendas at play, and I scanned their faces for any signs of deception or ulterior motives.

This time, Abigail spoke up with a calm authority, her voice cutting through the tense silence. "Jessica," she began, "being what you are means you possess some unique and extraordinary abilities beyond our understanding. We have only scratched the surface of your gifts: heightened senses that allow you to see, hear, and feel things others cannot, superhuman strength and stamina, and accelerated healing powers that surpass human limitations. Am I right so far?"

I shifted uncomfortably in my seat, not wanting to reveal more than necessary. But Abigail seemed to sense my hesitation and pressed on. "We also know that you have stopped aging or at least slowed it significantly," she continued, her eyes never leaving mine. "And there are various other abilities that we may not yet know about. However, there is one particular gift that will be crucial for you in this moment. You possess the ability to discern who to trust and when to trust them. It's like a sixth sense, a nagging feeling at the back of your mind that guides your decisions. What has this intuition been telling you about us?"

My instincts were screaming at me, begging me to ignore the wariness I felt towards these strangers. My gut was telling me that they were good people with genuine intentions, despite my initial reservations. A small part of me resisted admitting it, but my sixth sense had never failed me before and I trusted it now more than ever. As I clenched my fists, my mind echoed with their words - "You can trust us" - and I knew it to be true. With a grudging admission, I replied, "My gut is telling me that you are both trustworthy." The air felt thick with tension and uncertainty, but my senses remained resolute in their conviction.

I forced myself to stand tall and face the two powerful beings in front of me. I spoke with a shaky confidence, trying to hide my fear. "Fine, I will give you both the benefit of the doubt," I said through gritted teeth, "but I warn you now, don't cross me!" My threat hung in the air like a thick fog, but I couldn't back down now. "If you plan to betray me," my voice dropped to a dangerous whisper, "I will hunt you down and destroy you." As soon as the words left my mouth, I second-guessed myself. What had possessed me to challenge two supernatural powerhouses? But it was too late now.

To my surprise, Gudmundur grandly declared, "We understand, Lady Jessica." His deep voice rumbled like distant thunder. "On my honour, I will do you no harm and will lay my life down in your service." Despite his intimidating appearance, there was a hint of respect and loyalty in his words. A small part of me felt relieved that they seemed to accept my warning, but another part couldn't shake off the feeling that I had just entered into a dangerous game with these two mysterious creatures.

"That's a little extreme," I exclaimed, trying to temper my tone. "But I appreciate your enthusiasm." My eyes darted between the pair, searching for any glimmer of hope in their expressions. "Please, just tell me what we know about this case." I pleaded, hoping that they had some tangible information that could lead us to the culprit behind these heinous acts. "Do either of you have any actionable intel that we can use to put an end to whoever or whatever is responsible for this?" My voice quivered with emotion as I hung on their every word, willing them to have something, anything, that could help us solve the case before it was too

"Um, no, we don't have anything, but I would love to have a rundown on the information you have so far and maybe visit the crime scene if that would be at all possible. Wouldn't you agree on Abigail?" Gudmundur said with genuine interest

Abigail tapped her foot impatiently as she glanced at me, eager to see the crime scene. "I agree, seeing the site would help," she said. "Should we head there now?"

I sighed and shook my head. "No, we need to go back to the agency first. I need updates from the team and to check on Alisha, our only witness so far. If she's awake, she might have valuable information."

Abigail and Gudmundur exchanged knowing looks, clearly disappointed that they couldn't break into the crime scene immediately.

"Before you say anything," I continued, "you don't have clearance. And I can't deal with the headache of you getting caught breaking in. You have a choice: stay here and wait for me to contact you later at the scene, or join me while I take care of business."

They quickly agreed to stay by my side.

"In that case," I said with a slight smile, "can we grab some food before heading back? I have a feeling it's going to be a long day." I rubbed my eyes tiredly. "And I definitely need some coffee before I get grumpy."

Abigail let out a giggle and turned to Gudmundur. "You heard her, we need to get this woman some coffee stat!" Her sarcastic comment earned her a playful shove from me.

"If it weren't for needing to cooperate with these idiots," I thought to myself, "I would kick them both right now."

CHAPTER 15

As I DROVE back to the agency, I couldn't help but feel like a babysitter. The vampire and dragon in my backseat were chatting away like old friends, with gudmundur's booming laugh occasionally breaking through. I tried to maintain my tough exterior, but their antics kept making me crack a smile. It was almost enough to make me forget the danger we were facing.

As we pulled up to the agency, flashing lights and a row of police cars greeted us. The neon colours from the sirens cast a sickly glow on the building, amplifying the sense of chaos and urgency. I quickly parked my car next to the cruisers and raced up the front steps, following the sound of raised voices. The air was thick with tension and anger, making it hard to breathe. "What in the world is going on?" I thought to myself as I burst into the building. My eyes immediately landed on Mini, who was screaming profanities at the top of her lungs. Her face was flushed red with anger, her hands balled into fists at her sides. I could practically see a vein throbbing on her temple as she unleashed her rage. But what could have caused such an intense reaction from her? As I scanned the room, my gaze fell upon Detective Duncan Lancaster and two stiff-looking bureaucrats. One of them had a tight grip on Alisha's hand, and the girl looked like she had been crying for hours. Tears streaked down her cheeks, leaving trails of moister in there wake. A surge of fury coursed through me as I let out a low growl, my muscles tensing in preparation for a fight. Without hesitation, I lunged forward and landed a hard punch on Lancaster's jaw, sending him crashing to the ground with a satisfying thud.

With a fiery rage burning inside of me, I lunged towards the person who had made a child cry, intent on continuing to unleash my fury upon them. But before I could reach them, Gudmundur and Abigail swooped in like guardian angels, their strong hands gripping my arms tightly as they dragged me away. My feet stumbled and kicked in protest, but it was no use against their combined strength. We ended up in an empty office, the silence only punctuated by their calm but firm voices as they attempted to reason with me. My anger boiled over, and I let out a guttural roar that echoed through the room. Eventually, I was led to the head of the London office, while my colleagues scrambled to contain and clean up the chaos I had caused in my blind rage. The walls of the office seemed to close in on me as I stood before the imposing figure of authority, my heart racing and chest heaving with emotion.

The imposing figure sat behind his desk, his broad shoulders squared and his hands steepled in front of him. His stern expression was accented by a deep furrow between his brows, giving off an air of authority. "You must be the young lady who caused quite a stir in the lobby," he said, leaning forward with interest. "May I ask what prompted you to take such drastic action? The man you struck was a police officer, after all." His voice held a hint of disapproval, but also curiosity at the my bold actions.

I had heard rumours that you struggled to control your temper, and sometimes reacted impulsively. However, in that particular situation, I couldn't fathom what could have triggered such a strong response from you.

Taking a deep breath, I began to explain my actions. "First of all, it was Mini - she was visibly agitated by whatever was happening. And then when I saw Alisha's tear-streaked face, it ignited something inside me. Earlier, I had a confrontation with the detective and he quickly became the target of my pent-up anger. But what exactly was going on there? When we arrived, Mini looked like the world was ending and everyone seemed to be shouting simultaneously." My voice trailed off as I remembered the chaotic scene that had unfolded before me. It was as if all hell had broken loose in that room.

The large man leaned back in his seat, his fingers tapping on the armrest as he let out a deep sigh. "Unfortunately, the situation is not so simple," he said. He explained that Child Services wanted to take the young girl into protective custody until they could locate a family member. However, the detective that you punched argued that she could be a crucial witness and should remain under their guardianship. He also pointed out the potential harm of removing her from familiar surroundings and trusted adults after what she had been through. My mind raced as I realised the implications for Alisha and the progress of the investigation. The shock must have shown on my face because my boss reassured me, "Don't worry, Jessica. The child will stay with Mini while you work on the case. and we will re-assess the situation once the case is resolved. Then, relief flooded my muscles as they relaxed, and I physically slumped in the chair.

"The detective wasn't here to discuss the girl. It was a happy coincidence that he arrived at the same time as child services.

"I didn't just want to talk to you about the incident in the lobby," he stated, his voice laced with concern. "I also wanted an update on how you're progressing on the case." He leaned back in his chair, waiting for my response.

I took a deep breath before answering, trying to hide my disappointment at not having made much progress. "I haven't had any new developments on the case," I admitted, keeping my tone as professional as possible. "However, both the vampires and the dragons have shown interest in helping us. I brought representatives from both species to see if they could provide any useful leads."

My boss nodded, his expression softening slightly. "I see. And have you debriefed with your team yet?"

I shook my head, feeling guilty for not keeping them in the loop. "Not yet, but I plan to gather everyone in the conference room now and see if anyone has made any progress."

He let out a sigh, his gaze lingering on me for a moment longer before dismissing me with a wave of his hand. "In that case, I won't keep you any longer. But please Jessica, try to remain in control of that temper of yours and keep me appraised of your progress."

At his words, I couldn't help but feel a pang of guilt for losing my cool earlier. With a deep breath, I rushed out of his office like my hair was on fire and quickly made my way to the conference room where my team was waiting for me with eager expressions.

The detective sat slumped in a chair, nursing an ice pack against his already bruised jaw. I could see the frustration etched into his features as he recounted the events that had led us to this moment. Alisha stood by my side, her small hand gripping mine tightly as we made our way into the hallway. She was escorted by two child welfare agents, their stern expressions belying their true intentions.

"Alisha," I said softly, crouching down to meet her gaze. "Do you remember me?" She nodded, a glimmer of recognition in her eyes.

"I will be speaking to everyone about what happened," I explained gently. "We need to catch whoever was responsible for hurting you." I hesitated before continuing. "I would prefer if you waited across the hall with these two kind agents. Would that be okay?"

Alisha nodded again, but this time she gave me a quick smile. As she walked away with the agents, I leaned in and whispered to her that there was a vending machine in the room that she was free to use. The agents might even let her have some treats if she asked nicely and shared with them. A look of pure delight lit up her face before she disappeared into the waiting area.

I turned back to the agents, giving them an apologetic smile. That vending machine was every sugar addict's dream, but Alisha deserved a small indulgence after everything she had been through.

"Excuse me," I said to the agents, rising from my seat. "If you wouldn't mind waiting here with Alisha for just a little longer, I would be happy to discuss her welfare situation with you after my meeting."

They agreed without hesitation and followed Alisha into the waiting area. As I made my way back into the room, I couldn't help but feel grateful for their understanding and compassion towards Alisha's well-being.

As I made my way back to the conference room, I could feel a sense of tension and unease hanging in the air. It was clear that I needed to smooth things over and get everyone back on track. Taking my seat at the head of the table, I cleared my throat and all eyes turned to me, expectant and wary.

"First of all," I said turning to detective Lancaster "I want to apologise for my actions earlier. It was completely out of line for me to strike anyone. I know you're here for an update on our investigation, but unfortunately, we don't have any new leads at this time. However, rest assured that as soon as we do, I will contact you."

Detective Lancaster winced as he removed an ice pack from the side of his jaw. "I don't have any new information on the case, but during my time back at the station, I heard that child protective services were notified about the situation. I thought it was important to let your team know."

Feeling embarrassed and remorseful for my previous outburst, I offered a sincere apology. "I'm truly sorry for my behaviour earlier. It was uncalled for and unprofessional. I hope you can forgive me."

Detective Lancaster's voice cut through the heavy air like a knife. He remained calm and composed, his words measured and deliberate. "It seems like you have quite the workload on your hands," he stated, his tone even and professional. "I too have other cases that demand my attention, but I will keep an eye out for any relevant information and share it with you. Please do the same." As he spoke, the atmosphere seemed to lighten slightly, the weight of our previous conflicts dissipating as we all focused on moving forward with the investigation. We were united in our desire to find justice for the victim. With a final nod, Detective Lancaster bid farewell to those gathered before exiting the room, leaving us to continue our work together.

"Okay, now that's all dealt with," i began, my voice tinged with a sense of defeat. "I feel like I need to apologize to everyone here as well." Each word felt heavy and burdensome as they spilled from my lips. "What I did out there was unprofessional. Nothing I can say will justify my actions," my gaze flickering around the room, unsure of where to look. "But when I saw Mini upset and the tears in Alisha's eyes, it triggered flashbacks to the cave." i took a deep breath, trying to steady myself. "I promise I will try to control my emotions better going forward." my apology hung in the air, echoing through the tense silence of the room. "Now my apology is done," i finished, almost as an afterthought. "Does anyone have any updates?" my tone was hopeful, yet tinged with a hint of trepidation, still unsure if my apology had been accepted by those i had wronged.

Keith's voice cut through room as he stood with determination. "I have made some shocking discoveries about Mr. Silver, Alishas father was not just an innocent bystander. He was a lawyer who defended some of the worst scumbags around town. And we believe that his murder was a message, a statement from someone he crossed paths with in his profession." His words hung heavily in the air, sending shivers down the spines of those listening.

"We have reason to suspect that at least half-dozen men who Mr. Silver defended are now missing," Keith continued, his jaw clenched with anger and frustration. "We also have another body, found mutilated just weeks ago, but we have yet to identify them. I've requested the M.E report and will get it to you as soon as it arrives. But for now, I'm going to start shaking down some of our informants and see if I can uncover any leads." The determined look in his eyes showed that he would stop at nothing to find out what're he could.

"Okay, that gives us something to go on. This could be a turf war. We need to know more about these missing people and the

other bodies. Keith, can you continue looking into that? Also, the detective informed me that they have had a series of vagrants disappear and a lot of mysterious deaths in the last 18 months. I will forward all the details you and mini, but they might be connected" pausing for a moment I took in the room seeing everyone tense at the implications before continuing

"Did you gather any valuable information from the mage's council?" Regrettably, they refuse to acknowledge any reports of missing individuals and only mentioned the common occurrences of fights. However, they did mention noticing peculiar traces of magic throughout the city. I have requested for them to provide us with a detailed list of these occurrences, including the specific dates and times, which they should send to us via email soon. Of course, they will only offer assistance if the situation becomes dire. But that is to be expected. I will gather all the data and collaborate with the laboratory technicians and Mini to detect any possible patterns."

"Do you have any updates from the silver residents? When I was there, I wasn't able to fully investigate the scene. Has anyone else been able to shed light on what transpired?"

Keith launched into his report, his voice steady and composed despite the disturbing details he revealed. "The autopsy on Mr. Silver is still underway, but we have completed the examinations for the other two victims. Based on our initial findings, it seems likely that all three were conscious and aware of their surroundings during the attack. Some kind of paralytic was administered in the Silver's home, rendering them immobile while they watched each other being brutally torn apart and devoured alive. From our preliminary analysis, it appears that the perpetrator was interrupted mid-attack as evidenced by the fact that Mr. Silver's heart remained intact, unlike the others. Additionally, our medical examiner has discovered traces of non-human hair on the victims' bodies. We are currently running a thorough database search to see if we can identify its source. It's possible that Alisha may have witnessed more than we initially thought and retreated to her hiding spot when the attacker left. I advise extreme caution when questioning her."

As we delved deeper into the details of this horrific crime, my head began to throb with a dull ache. The weight of responsibility hung heavy on my shoulders as we worked to piece together this gruesome puzzle.

As Keith's words sunk in, our unexpected vampire guest broke the silence. Her voice was smooth and confident, betraying her centuries of existence. "I assume the Shifter Council is unwilling to acknowledge any issues and refuses to communicate with you?" she questioned, not waiting for a response before continuing. "Their paranoia prevents them from appearing weak, but I have credible information that several pack members have gone missing in recent weeks. Normally, this would not be cause for alarm as shifters often roam into the nearby woods or mountains to give in to their inner beasts for days on end without realising it. However, according to my source, a young couple, expecting a child, has gone missing. They have missed two crucial appointments with a pack doctor, causing concern among the senior members. They are hesitant to cooperate with your investigation out of fear of drawing attention to themselves and potentially becoming targets." The atmosphere grew tense as the gravity of the situation became more evident.

Great, just what we need paranoid and panicked shifters.

"Mini, have you had a chance to speak to Alisha yet?" Mini shook her head, her expression grave as she replied, "Not really. We've managed to get her cleaned up, and she's had a little breakfast, but she is still very wary of everyone. I can feel so much fear and terror radiating from the poor child, it's heartbreaking." She paused for a moment before adding, "I will admit that the two of us losing our collective temper probably didn't help."

I let out a sigh, feeling guilty for losing control in front of the traumatised girl. But then Mini continued with a slight hint of amusement in her voice, "Still, I did sense a spark of amusement from her when you hit the detective!" I couldn't help but cringe at the memory and knew I wouldn't live it down for a while.

Changing the subject, I asked, "Can you tell if Keith is on the right track with his theory that Alisha witnessed everything?"

Mini closed her eyes and focused, her brow furrowed in concentration. After a few moments, she opened them again and replied, "From the general feel I'm getting from her, he's spot on. But I will require some time alone with her to be sure."

Relieved that we finally seemed to be making progress, I nodded and said, "It's probably best if she stays within the confines of the agency until all this is resolved."

"That's fine by me," Mini agreed with a nod. "I will take care of her."

feeling guilty I I spoke up " just to forewarn you, I may have mentioned the free vending machine filled with sugary snacks to entice her." Mini chuckled at my cunning trick and left to retrieve Alisha from child services .

As I focused my gaze on Abigail and Gudmundur, the tension in the room seemed to thicken. The air felt heavy with unspoken words and hidden motives. Both of their factions were known for their reluctance to cooperate with law enforcement, often making it difficult to obtain any useful information from them. And yet, here they sat, seemingly at ease with each other, like old friends catching up. My knowledge of dragons and vampires warned me that this was a rare occurrence and usually ended in violence or threats. So what was really going on? I couldn't believe they were simply playing nice and offering their help without expecting anything in return. It just didn't add up.

Gudmundur straightened his posture and cleared his throat before speaking: "Please accept our apologies for causing any misunderstandings, Lady Jessica. While we may not have much relevant information on your current case, we are more than willing to assist you in any way possible." His words sounded polite enough, but there was a hint of something else beneath the surface. Was it sincerity or something more sinister? As the silence stretched between us, I couldn't shake off the feeling that there was more to this offer than meets the eye.

"Once it is complete," he continued, the low rumble of his voice sending shivers down my spine. "We respectfully request some of your precious time to aid us in a delicate situation. As you mentioned before, Abigail and I have a unique friendship that spans centuries, but we will divulge more information later. For now, I can offer insight into what could have possibly led to the tragic deaths of the Child's family. However, this entity must be under someone's control because if not, its thirst for blood would have left a trail of corpses in its wake." My mind raced with questions as I turned to Gudmundur. "okay what exactly are we searching for?"

"I believe it is a Wendigo, and unless I'm incorrect, it is a freshly made one. You see, a Wendigo isn't summoned in the traditional way a normal spirit would, and it isn't a natural-born demon or monster like, say, a dragon is. A wendigo chooses to descend into

darkness and evil. It starts by eating human flesh. The act of cannibalism is enough to draw the attention of an evil spirit that will whisper encouragement to the cannibal, and the more human flesh it consumes, the hungrier it becomes. The Wendigo is seen as the embodiment of gluttony, greed, and excess: they are never satisfied after killing and consuming one person. They are constantly searching for new victims.

Wendigos are portrayed as simultaneously gluttonous and extremely thin due to starvation. Whenever a wendigo eats its victim, it will grow proportionately to the meal it has eaten, so it can never be full. This is why a Wendigo will be gaunt to the point of emaciation. Its desiccated skin will be pulled tightly over its bones. With its bones pushing out against its skin, its complexion the ash-grey of death, and its eyes pushed back deep into its sockets, the Wendigo will look like a gaunt skeleton recently disinterred from the grave. It will give off a strange and eerie odour of decay, decomposition, death, and corruption."

My jaw hit the floor. "You sat through this whole meeting when you knew what we were facing, and this is the first time you thought to mention it."

"Well, you didn't ask."

damn, he had a point

"Okay, well, at least we now know what's doing The killing. All we need to know now is why and who the hell is controlling it. I will head back to the crime scene and see if I can find anything new. I'm guessing you two still want to check out the scene with me" at this

they both nodded.Everyone got up and began heading off to follow their leads.

I politely asked Gudmundur and Abigail to remain in the conference room while I met with Mini and the child welfare representative. As I made my way across the hall to the designated room, I couldn't help but feel a sense of anxiousness in my stomach. The last time I had seen Mini, she was sitting quietly in a corner, her eyes filled with fear and uncertainty. But as I entered the room this time, I was greeted by a much different scene - Mini and Abigail were happily snacking on treats from the vending machine, their faces alight with joy. It brought a smile to my face, seeing how far Alisha had come since our first meeting. And yet, there was still a sense of unease, knowing that difficult conversations awaited us. But for now, I would savour this moment of calm before facing whatever challenges lay ahead.

Mini and I stepped away from Alisha, leaving alone for a moment. I leaned in close to Mini, my heart racing with anticipation. "What do you sense from our guests? Are they dangerous?" I whispered.

Mini's eyes flickered as she read their emotions. "They're guarded, but I sense a hint of curiosity towards you. They find you amusing and seem intrigued by your reactions," she said, glancing back at them. "I don't think they mean any harm. In fact, it feels like they want to protect you."

"What, why would they want to protect me?" I was reasonably sure the dragon would celebrate if I died, and I had no idea why the vampires would care what happened to me. Well, that was going to have to be a mystery for another day, "Mini, I need you to work with Alisha and try to get me any details you can as to why anyone would want to do this to her family and if she can give us any details on the attack," Mini went back to sit with Alisha. They both began to talk to Ernest. I went to the conference room to collect my two new friends, and as I entered, they became eerily silent. I looked at them and said, "I know you two are up to something. I don't know what it is, and if I'm honest, I don't care. Just give me your word that you will do nothing to impede this investigation, and if you can, then Assist me so that no more die. That would be great, too." Again, they glance at each other for the briefest moments. Abigail responds, "We will assist you on the

condition that once this case is solved, you will sit with us; we have much to discuss with you!!! Great, another headache I didn't need. "Okay, fine, case first, then I'll deal with you two; I'm heading back to the Silver's home. There has to be something that we are missing.

CHAPTER 16

M Y HEART SANK as I pulled up to Silver's house and saw the yellow police tape fluttering in the breeze. The patrol car parked in the driveway seemed to mock me, a reminder that something terrible had happened here. As I approached the officer guarding the entrance, I reached for my credentials, but he waved me off with an exhausted look. Gudmundur and Abigail joined me, their faces grim with anticipation. A heavy, stale stench of blood and fear hit us as we opened the door. Every step we took into the living area felt like walking through a thick cloud of terror that permeated our every sense. The air was thick with it, like a tangible force trying to strangle us. My skin prickled with unease and I had to fight back a shiver as we surveyed the scene before us.

Gudmundur and Abigail slowly circled the home behind me, their eyes scanning every inch of the scene before them. I could tell they were being cautious not to disturb any potential evidence, but they were alert and taking in every detail as they went. I spoke up, breaking the eerie silence that had settled over us.

"Call out anything you see as you see it," I said, turning to face my them both. "I assume you have both done this sort of thing before."

Both Gudmundur and Abigail grunted in confirmation, their trained eyes already picking up on clues and possible leads. Suddenly, Abigail's voice rang out in a sharp shout.

"Where was Alisha found?" she asked urgently.

I was taken aback by her question - I was sure I had already told them that Alisha had been found in the wine cellar, cowering and swinging a knife in fear.

"In the wine cellar," I repeated. "Why do you ask?"

Abigail's response caught me off guard once again.

"I'm picking up her scent," she explained calmly. "From what I'm smelling, she ran to the cellar when she heard sirens from the police."

My thoughts scattered like a deck of cards as I struggled to make sense of her words. Yes, I had a sinking feeling that something was off about this whole situation. Things just weren't adding up.

"Alright, let's keep digging," I replied, my mind racing with possibilities. "Mr. Silver must have stumbled upon something during his work that made his boss turn on him like this." My eyes scanned the room for any clues or evidence that could connect the dots. "He has an office downstairs, so I'm going to head there and search for any files or papers that might shed some light on the situation."

"I'll join you," she said, determination in her voice as we both headed towards the stairs. "And see if you can find any computers or laptops that we can search for more information." The tension in the room was palpable as we set out to uncover the truth behind Mr. Silver's sudden betrayal by his boss.

With a sense of urgency, we combed through every nook and cranny of the house, garden, and garage. The task took us hours, but our diligence paid off as we found documents that seemed promising. They mentioned containers bound for a nearby warehouse, and upon further examination, they were littered with falsified reports and documents. It was clear that another container was on its way to this location - this must be what we have been searching for all along.

I turned to Gudmundur and Abigail who had been reading over my shoulder. "Do you think it's worth checking out the warehouse and seeing if it's connected to our case?" I asked.

Abigail flashed me a toothy smile. "Well, we all know the police force is overworked, so why don't we take matters into our own hands? Let's stake out the warehouse ourselves." She paused before adding, "But first, I have two important questions."

first is to you Gudmundur do you sell blood at the dragon's keep" I gasped in horror surely she didn't think the place we

meet him at would serve Blood, Gudmundur replied good naturally " I have only had the establishment for a very short time as you know sweetest Abigail but I have ensured that we have a few bottles of types A, B, AB, and O one of the witches that I employee is working on a process to flavour the blood as well so you will have that to look forward to if you become one of my regular client!s" "what the hell

please don't tell me you go out and bleed people so you can bottle blood and sell it for a profit" I could feel the heat rising as I got

angrier and the air began to crackle like it had gained an electrical charge, shit I need to get my temper under control I started to take deep calming breaths and I heard Gudmundur explain "we do not condone anyone using humans that way but vampires do need human blood to live, however we have found that Humans will give blood freely if they are given money in exchange for it, so to say it simply we pay humans to donate blood and we never take to much and we ensure that they have a meal before they leave our supervision, I believe the vampier council enforce something similar and those who chose to kill humans for blood are classed as renegades hunted and put down" hearing this managed to calm me down I looked at them both and was about to apologise for my overreaction when the little blood sucker burst out in uncontrollable laughter "wow you really are amazing everything I've heard about you is true. you punch first

and ask questions later, but really you need to control that temper especially if you don't understand the supernatural world more fully"

i grumbled under my breath " yeah I guess I just kinda freaked out a little when you said you sold blood I apologise"

" okay now we have that cleared up do you have all the surveillance equipment you think we will need at the agency?" Yes, we have all the latest tech and a fully stocked armoury I can drop you both at the dragon's keep then get what we need at the agency and meet you when you're done!"

"no, you will come to the dragon keep you will eat and don't worry about any supplies just tell me of anything you specifically require

and I will have it" Gudmundur stated this like it was nothing of consequence, these two might be bigger deals than I originally thought, they carry themselves with a confidence that I have only seen in the Alex and lyn, I think I may have a few questions for these two while we prepare for what is to come.

THE GRAVEL CRUNCHED under my tires as I pulled up to the entrance of the Dragon Keep. The sun was setting, casting a golden glow over the bustling scene in front of me. We entered and were greeted by the same waitress from this morning, her cheery smile and familiar face welcoming us back. She led us to the same table we had used earlier, and Gudmundur wasted no time in placing a grand order: two bottles of 2009 Chateau Petrus, a warm bottle from the top shelf special, and three glasses. The waitress scurried off to fulfil his request, leaving Abigail to raise an eyebrow at him and jest, "Pulling out all the stops with that, weren't you? That stuff isn't cheap even for your high-class clientele. I doubt their pockets run that deep." Gudmundur simply smiled and casually replied, "It's actually from my personal collection. I've been told Lady Jessica enjoys a glass of red wine, and this one happens to be a favourite of mine as well. I've also heard that it pairs nicely with type O blood, and I was hoping you would join us in trying it.while we eat and strategies for our reconnaissance mission, now before we order food I would like to know of any equipment that you believe we may need?"

This is where I jumped in.my mind raced through all the possibilities and scenarios. We needed to be prepared for anything, but also light and agile so we could move quickly. But before I could present my list of necessary equipment, I needed to know the strengths and abilities of my two companions. "Gudmundur, tell me about your experiences and what you can contribute to the operation," I asked eagerly. My eyes scanned his rugged frame and strong features, trying to gauge his capabilities. His response would determine our course of action and what supplies we would bring with us on our journey ahead.

"It is wise of you to inquire," his voice was grave and direct. "In my long years, both as a dragon and a human, I have taken part in numerous wars and battles. However, in our current situation, I have mainly participated in human wars over the last century. I fought in World War I and II, the Korean War, Vietnam War, and the Gulf War. In most of these conflicts, I served in covert operations, proficient in using modern weapons, surveillance equipment, and communication systems. As for my abilities, I am stronger and faster than any human, even surpassing most vampires except for the oldest ones. Being an ice dragon, I also possess a certain control over ice and frost. And while I do have some skill in compulsion, it pales in comparison to Abigail's expertise." His words held a hint of amusement as he turned to her, a small smile playing on his lips. "Isn't that right, my dear?"

Abigail's voice dripped with saccharine sweetness as she flashed her sharp fangs in a toothy smile. The glint of menace in her eyes made me realise that I was dealing with more than just a mere mortal. A shiver ran down my spine as I mentally noted to never get on this vampire's bad side. "Well, he's got me there. I am much better at tinkering with people's minds than the big guy is," Abigail said, her tone dripping with confidence. She exuded an aura of power and control, a predator in the midst of prey. As I focused on her, I couldn't help but feel a sense of unease wash over me. "Okay, Abigail, you're up; what can you bring to the party?" I asked, trying to keep my voice steady despite the fear creeping up inside of me.

my words were met with a small smile and a grateful nod. As she spoke, her eyes glimmered with an otherworldly light, and her posture seemed to shift as if she was ready for anything. "I'm happy you asked," she began, her voice filled with confidence. "Well, all my senses are heightened, so I can usually tell when I'm being lied to just by hearing people's heartbeats or by the fluctuations in their temperature.It also makes me an expert tracker." She grinned mischievously, revealing razor-sharp fangs that glinted under the bars dim lighting. "I can use most firearms available, but I prefer to use blades." With a swift motion, she extended her fingertips into long, deadly claws. "I can also elongate my fingernails into sharper and more durable claws than most blades." Her muscles rippled beneath her clothes as she continued, "And thanks to my enhanced abilities, I possess better than normal strength, speed, and stamina." The listener couldn't help but feel a sense of awe and slight fear at the impressive abilities this woman possessed. "Unfortunately," she added with a slight frown, "I can't use magic or anything like that." The realisation hit me like a ton of bricks - these two were like a walking arsenal. My shopping list could now be significantly reduced, making us lighter and more stealth-like on our journey ahead. A smirk formed on my lips as I realised that having these two by my side might not be such a bad thing after all.

As we discussed our plan, my mind raced with the list of items we would need. Tactical fatigues for all of us, light side arms like the L9A1 Browning or the SA80, a range of tactical blades, a night and thermal vision system, and standard comms in case we got separated. I couldn't help but fidget with my own blades, knowing I had requested others but still finding comfort in my trusty karambits. "Do you think you can acquire all of this?" I asked, eagerly awaiting an answer. But before anyone could respond, our waitress appeared out of nowhere, her footsteps silent despite the clinking bottles she carried on a tray. She placed three glasses in front of us and set the bottles in the centre of the table. With a professional smile, she pulled out a digital tablet and asked if we would like to order something.

A low rumble emanated from my stomach, a clear indication of the hunger pangs that had been plaguing me all day. My eyes scanned the menu with eager anticipation, already imagining the delicious flavours that awaited me. "I'll have the 24-ounce sirloin," I declared with enthusiasm, my mouth watering at the thought of sinking my teeth into a perfectly cooked steak. "And please make sure it comes with all the fixings – a fluffy baked potato, crisp vegetables, and a rich peppercorn sauce," I added with a confident smirk. Gudmundur simply shrugged and ordered his usual without even glancing at the menu, and began pouring our drinks as our attentive waitress walked away. Suddenly, he turned to her and asked in a calm yet urgent tone, "Mona, if Max is available, could you please send him over? It's quite urgent." Without hesitation, Mona hurried away towards the back of the restaurant. A few minutes later, a young boy who couldn't have been more than 18 appeared at our table, slightly bowing before addressing Gudmundur with respect and deference. "My lord," he said softly, "how may I assist you?" His demeanour exuded servitude and obedience, making it clear that he was well-trained in serving those of higher status.

"Max, I would like to introduce you to Lady Jessica and a good friend of mine, Abigail," Gudmundur said, his voice strong and commanding. As he spoke, I noticed Max's expression change from curiosity to disgust. It was clear that he viewed me as something less than human, something vile and repulsive. But I refused to let his disdain affect me. "I need you to assemble a vehicle loaded with the following items," Gudmundur continued, listing off the necessary supplies for our journey. As Max glared at me, I couldn't help but feel a twinge of pity for him. He was clearly afraid of me, afraid of what I represented. "Max, is there something you wish to say?" Gudmundur asked, his tone still calm and collected despite the tension in the air. Max's gaze shifted from me to Gudmundur, and I could see the fear in his eyes grow even stronger. "My lord," Max stammered out, his voice trembling. "I mean no offence, but it is an abomination. It should not be allowed to live, and you should not be forced to be in its company." Despite his words, I could sense the underlying panic in Max's voice as he spoke about me - a creature deemed monstrous by society simply because of my what Jeremiah did to me. But I refused to let his narrow-minded views affect me or my mission with Gudmundur and Lady Jessica.

In a blink of an eye, with such fluidity and silence that the other patrons in the pub were unaware, Max was suddenly hunched over, exchanging words with Gudmundur. From my vantage point, it was clear that Max wore a look of terror as Gudmundur grabbed him by the collar, revealing his right arm covered in shimmering scales and claws where his hand once was. He brandished his transformed fist in front of Max's face and with a deep growl, warned, "If you ever dare to disrespect Lady Jessica again and I catch wind of it, I will end you. Do we have an understanding?" Max nodded slowly, visibly shaking with fear and his eyes widened to the size of dinner plates. "Good. Now get out of my sight and complete your task." As Max scurried away, I couldn't help but notice the faint smell of urine, as if he had truly been scared out of his wits by Gudmundur's threat.

The words spat from their mouth, dripping with disdain and

prejudice. "That wasn't necessary," I forced myself to say calmly, though the anger bubbled up inside me. As a member of the paranormal community, I had been warned to expect this kind of behaviour from dragons in particular. But that didn't make it any less infuriating. The comments and looks stung like a thousand needles, each one piercing deeper into my already wounded heart. It wasn't my fault that some deranged individual had decided to tamper with my genetics. I didn't ask for these abilities, and I certainly didn't need a group of pompous, self-important twat waffles giving me grief about it. Yet here I was, once again being judged and ridiculed for something beyond my control.

The words spilled from his lips like honey, sweet and soothing. "Lady Jessica, you do not deserve to be treated in such a way. You were dealt a very harsh hand, and your conduct is above reproach." His voice was filled with sincerity and empathy, a stark contrast to the harshness she had experienced from others in the dragon community. He continued, "I apologise for how they have treated you. Please know that their behaviour and thoughts do not represent the majority." As he finished speaking, our food arrived, and my stomach growled in anticipation. The dishes presented before us were a feast for the senses. The vibrant colours of the vegetables and spices danced on my plate, tempting me with their aroma. Abigail giggled as she noticed the hunger in my eyes and quipped, "Are you going to devour that delectable meal or simply make love to it with your eyes?" Her playful remark lightened the mood and brought a smile to my face.

A warm flush rose to my cheeks, making them feel hot and rosy as I tried to hide my embarrassment. Hastily diving into my meal, I savoured the rich flavours of the food and the smooth taste of the wine. The cozy atmosphere of the restaurant made me feel relaxed and content.

As we finished our last bites of the delicious meal, I couldn't help but make a mental note to come back here again. Our plans for the night had been discussed over dinner, and now we were preparing to leave. But just as we were about to gather our belongings, my phone began to ring. Glancing at the caller ID, I saw it was Mini calling. Excusing myself from the table, I answered the call while the others started to pack up their gear.

"What's up, Mini?" I asked as I followed them out of the bustling pub and towards the back staff area .

CHAPTER 17

THE OMINOUS WAREHOUSE loomed in the distance, its towering walls and fortified perimeter guarded by biometric scanners and armed patrols. For hours, we had been undercover, observing the site in silence while waiting for the opportune moment to strike. My mind was torn between focusing on the mission at hand and worrying about Alisha, whose shocking news from Mini earlier still weighed heavily on my heart. The thought of her having to deal with it if the results were accurate filled me with sorrow.

As the time approached for our plan to be put into action, my heart raced with a mix of excitement and dread. We had been planning this for the past few hours, but now that it was actually happening, I couldn't help but feel a wave of fear wash over me. The thought of facing heavily armed guards made me shiver, despite knowing that they were only human. But we had a plan, and with subtle manipulations and stealth on our side, we should be able to pull this off without being caught.

Each step towards the looming warehouse felt like walking towards the unknown - danger and uncertainty loomed ahead, but we had to take this risk for the sake of our mission. As I took a deep breath to calm my nerves, I focused on executing our meticulously crafted strategy: infiltration, evidence collection, confirmation of the container's contents, and a quiet escape. It was crucial that we remained undetected, but as we crept closer to our target, doubts started to gnaw at the back of my mind. What if something went wrong? What if we were caught?

Abigail's hand frantically waved in the air, urgently signalling for me to follow her towards the main gate. My heart raced with a mixture of determination and fear as the sound of a rumbling truck grew louder. This was it - there was no turning back now. As we swiftly made our way across the compound, my mind was filled with conflicting emotions - adrenaline mixed with anxiety, determination mixed with doubt. Abigail easily scaled the tall fence surrounding the building, but I hesitated, unsure if I could follow suit. Gudmundur's strong arms scooped me up and carried me over the threshold like a bride being carried into marriage. With one leap, he cleared the 20ft high fence as if it were nothing, but my doubts only intensified as we approached the side entrance of the building. This was it - there was no more time for hesitation or second-guessing. Our fate rested on what awaited us inside that warehouse.

We had to be careful and time our entry between patrols. Abigail went first, skilfully navigating through the shadows to make sure the coast was clear. Within seconds, we were inside undetected. The dimly lit hallway smelled musty and stale, a stark contrast to the bustling outside world.

With each step, our footsteps echoed hollowly against the bare walls of the abandoned building. The quietness was eerie, every sound amplified and magnified in the vast empty space. I could feel the surge of adrenaline coursing through my veins as we moved swiftly, but with careful caution towards our target location. Any misstep or mistake could spell disaster for our mission - an outcome we couldn't afford.

But with Abigail's expert guidance leading us and Gudmundur's strength and agility at our side, I felt a sense of determination and confidence to see this operation through to its end. As we crept further into the building, I braced myself for what we might find inside.But nothing could have prepared me for the sight that greeted us. Instead of the typical military layout I expected, there were rows upon rows of cots set up like a makeshift hospital tent in a war zone. But instead of wounded soldiers, it was children - row after row of them lying unconscious on these cots. Each one had IV leads and oxygen masks attached to them, their tiny forms appearing fragile and vulnerable.

My mind reeled at the bizarre scene before me, but Abigail's steady voice brought me back to focus on our task at hand. She led us towards a staircase that seemed to lead to the next level, where we encountered more of the same unsettling sight - heavily pregnant women and young men who appeared no older than their early twenties.

As we explored further, we stumbled upon what seemed to be an office and a lab area walled off from the rest of the building. The pieces were starting to come together, but questions still raced through my mind - what exactly was going on here?

As soon as we slipped past the threshold, I motioned for my team to move swiftly and discreetly. We had one objective - to search this office and collect any evidence we could find. My heart raced with adrenaline as I watched them work with expert precision, photographing every inch of the room in a matter of minutes. Their experience was evident, and I couldn't help feeling grateful to have them by my side. As they scoured the area, I kept a careful watch on our point of exit, ready to react if anyone caught us in the act. But luck seemed to be on our side - not a soul crossed our path as we made our way towards the lab door. It seemed that all hands were focused on the container, giving us the perfect opportunity to slip in unnoticed.

As we entered the lab, an intense wave of focus and determination washed over us. We moved quickly and silently towards the bank of computers, Gudmundur positioned at the exit while Abigail deftly collected samples. I focused on the networked computers in front of me, my heart pounding with anticipation as I inserted my pen drive and typed in my command code. With skilled precision, I cloned the computer and installed a backdoor for administrative access. The tension was palpable as we waited for the notification that our task was complete. Finally, a green light signalled success and I motioned for us to move out.

We made our way through the building, careful to avoid any wandering guards. As we exited through the same route we came in, we managed to snap some photos of the People laid out on cots, their faces peaceful but their situation concerning.

Our cautious steps carried us towards the loading area, our bodies tense with the knowledge that we were still in enemy territory. Despite our successful infiltration, there was a constant buzz of activity around us, making us acutely aware of the danger we were in. Our goal was to get a closer look at the shipping container and uncover its mysterious cargo.

From our elevated vantage point, we could see the chaotic scene unfolding below. Men clad head-to-toe in hazmat suits were unloading more children from the rusted containers, their small forms huddled together and trembling with fear. The stench of sweat and filth wafted up to us, assaulting our senses and making my stomach churn. But that wasn't the only thing that caught our attention. As the children were led towards a sealed off area, we could make out the glint of plexiglass and hear the faint sound of machinery hissing to life. We crept closer, careful to stay hidden as we witnessed a disturbing scene unfold before us.

It was a giant decontamination chamber, looming over the helpless children like a monstrous beast. They were being forced roughly through one door by the hazmat-suited men, who held what looked like tasers in their gloved hands. The terrified children were then herded to another door, where they were ordered to strip by someone in a hazmat suit wielding a menacing device. Once stripped, they were doused with powerful sprays of water from all angles before being shoved through a third door at the back of the chamber. It was clear that these innocent children were being subjected to harsh treatment against their will, and it made my blood boil with anger and disgust. With our cameras in hand, we captured the unfolding scene with a mix of curiosity and unease. It wasn't just children being unloaded from the container - workers were also carefully unloading secured containers from the back of a large truck. Each one was marked with bright red labels, signalling the presence of hazardous materials within. As we gazed upon the alarming sight, a wave of dread washed over us and settled deep in our chests. The air itself seemed to thicken, making it hard to draw in a full breath. Our hearts sank as we observed the workers handling the containers with extreme caution and precision, their movements betraying the gravity of the situation before us.

Gudmundur and Abigail exchanged worried glances as we took in the disturbing sight before us. We knew we had to get out of there and report back to our agency immediately. This investigation was taking a dangerous turn and we needed to debrief and come up with a plan before it was too late. With a subtle signal, I motioned for them to follow me and we quickly made our way out of the facility before anyone could stop us.

We stealthily made our way out of the heavily guarded facility, careful not to alert any of the guards or cameras. Our hearts were pounding with adrenaline as we quickly loaded our gear into the waiting vehicle. My mind was reeling from what I had just witnessed inside that secretive place, but I knew better than to speak a word of it. The other two members of our team seemed equally shaken, their faces grim and their lips pressed in a tight line. We drove back to the agency in heavy silence, each lost in our own thoughts and trying to process what we had just seen. The tension in the car was palpable, a thick cloud of unspoken words hanging between us as we navigated through the city streets. What secrets were hidden behind those imposing walls? And what would be done with the information we had just gathered? Only time would tell.

CHAPTER 18

Back at the agency, gudmundur and Abigail helped me put together briefings for the entire team. It was tedious office work, but it kept us busy while we waited for everyone to arrive. The bright fluorescent lights and the hum of computers were the soundtrack to our morning, punctuated only by the occasional ring of the phone.

As I focused on putting the finishing touches to everyone's files, gudmundur walked in with a tray full of coffee. The dark aroma of the steaming liquid hit me and I realised how long it had been since I slept. My eyes felt heavy, and my body ached with exhaustion. But there was no rest for the wicked, and with a grateful smile, I accepted the cup from gudmundur.

"Thanks, dragon boy," I said, taking a sip of the hot beverage. "I really needed this."

"Just make sure you keep it coming," I added with a weary grin. Abigail chuckled and continued typing away on her computer.

One by one, the rest of the team trickled into the room. Abigail and Gudmundur took their seats with me, all of us remaining fairly silent while everyone settled in. By the looks people were giving each other, I could only assume that everyone had information for me - and I wasn't going to like it.

"Okay, everyone," I began, feeling a sense of dread build in my stomach. "I will outline what we have so far. Then, you can ask questions or contribute whatever information you have ascertained."

After a quick but tense outline, I turned to Keith and Mini, my heart pounding in my chest. "Do you two have any updates on Alisha's blood?" I asked, trying to mask the fear in my voice.

They both looked at me nervously before Mini finally spoke up. "Sweetie," she said softly, her hand reaching out to touch mine in a gesture of comfort. "We need you to sit down and try not to react. We've also called in a Gudmundur associate for additional information. You're not going to like what he has to say...but we need you to remain calm. Can you do that for us?"

My heart dropped even lower as I looked between them, knowing that this was going to be the worst news yet. But I gathered myself and nodded, giving them my word that I would remain composed despite the inevitable devastation that lay ahead.

My body tensed like a coiled spring, my breaths shallow and ragged as I tried to steady myself. Digging my nails into the cold, unyielding metal of the armrest, I willed myself to stay grounded in the present moment. Mini, with her usual graceful ease, ushered a man into the conference room -

A man who seemed to embody every stereotype of a bookish researcher stood before me. His glasses were slightly askew on his sharp nose, and his unkempt hair fell in wild disarray across his forehead as he hastily pushed it away from his face. The faded jeans and wrinkled shirt hanging loosely over his frame bore witness to the countless hours he must have spent engrossed in research. But when those piercing blue eyes landed on me, I couldn't help but feel utterly exposed. It was as if he could see through every layer of my being with just one glance. This man was an apex predator, exuding an air of danger and power that filled the room. With just one look into his eyes, you could sense the violence simmering just beneath the surface, waiting to be unleashed upon his enemies.

With a commanding voice that resonated through the room, Ogma addressed us all. "Greetings, everyone," he began. "I am Ogma, here at the request of Gudmundur to assess young Miss Alisha and see if she too possesses powers like those of Lady Jessica." We hung onto his every word, our shock evident on our faces.

"I can confirm that the child has indeed been changed, but not in the same way as Lady Jessica," Ogma continued. The air grew thick with tension as we waited for him to reveal more.

"As Lady Jessica knows all too well, the process of changing someone so drastically is excruciatingly painful, and often fatal," Ogma's words sent shivers down our spines. "The reason for this is that we paranormal beings are overflowing with magical energy and power, while humans typically have very little." He paused, letting his words sink in.

"Although there are exceptions, most humans do not have the ability to handle magical energy. And even those who can rarely possess it from birth. So when such power is introduced into their bodies, it overflows and burns them out, ultimately leading to death." The gravity of Ogma's explanation weighed heavy on us, as we tried to comprehend the true extent of what had happened to Alisha.

Before I continue, I must explain a crucial aspect of our paranormal culture: death. When a paranormal being passes away, their body is not simply buried or left to decompose naturally. Instead, it is ceremoniously and carefully burnt, releasing their soul to join their ancestors in the spirit world. This tradition holds true even during times of war or conflict - both our own fallen and those of our enemies are given the same treatment. The reason for this lies in the residual magic that remains within the body and its blood and tissue. Though it may eventually degrade over time, this magic does not decompose as quickly as most other living things. In fact, it can take centuries for the remains and their potent magic to fully deteriorate, which is why we place such importance on burning them properly. Only when the magic has dissipated completely do we consider them worthless remnants of the past.

I nodded along, trying to follow the conversation but still feeling lost. "That is certainly interesting, but I fail to see its relevance in this situation," I spoke up, hoping to gain some clarity. The looks exchanged between the others in the room made it clear that I was the only one struggling to understand Ogma's point.

He let out a deep breath, his expression grave. "Please keep in mind, I can't be certain without examining your blood and tissue, as well as that of the other victims and Alisha herself. But based on my initial findings, I believe that they have been injected with tissue and blood from deceased paranormals." He paused for a moment, allowing his words to sink in. As I processed this information, rage and frustration welled up inside me. I gritted my teeth and clenched down on the metal hand rests of my chair, feeling them twist and bend under my grasp.

With a watchful eye on me, Ogma's voice continued to ring out in the small room. His words were like a weight pressing down on my chest as he revealed the results of Alisha's blood test. "The foreign cells in her body show signs of necrosis, and her magical power is significantly lower than expected."

Nausea swirled in my stomach, and I couldn't help but ask, "What does this mean? Is she like me now, or will her body reject it?"

Ogma's expression was grave as he replied, "It seems her system has already adapted to the blood, irreversible changes have taken place. She may have experienced some mild cold or flu-like symptoms during this process, but nothing compared to the agony you suffered. However, these changes are only beginning. As time goes on, she may experience even more dramatic manifestations of her newfound power." His words hung heavily in the air, and I could only imagine what kind of struggles and challenges lay ahead for Alisha.

"I feel a strong urge to take Alisha under my wing, to guide her and protect her from becoming a threat to herself or others. I understand the need for her to remain here during this investigation, and I am willing to stay by her side to assist in keeping her safe. Furthermore, I am equipped with knowledge about powers and the supernatural world, which I can share with Alisha to help ease her into understanding her abilities without feeling too overwhelmed. And even once the investigation is over, my offer still stands. I will extend the same care and guidance to anyone else affected by this situation," Ogma's words hang in the air as I look around the table, curious if anyone has objections. But it seems that everyone is just as surprised by his proposal as I am. Gathering my thoughts, I finally ask him, "What motivates you to show such kindness towards these children?"

In my experience, the paranormal community very rarely do

something out of the kindness of their hearts? Even gudmundur and Abigail are only helping me in this case because they want to discuss something with me at the end." At the end of my statement, I glared at him with such intensity I would make most grown men cower.

I see the distrust etched into your features, a reflection of the years of mistreatment and hostility our kind has shown you. Even in the presence of my master, you have endured disrespect and even outright aggression. But I want you to know that I hold no ill will towards you. In fact, I would lay down my life to protect these innocent children from any harm, even if it means standing against my own kind. This is not just empty words, but an oath sworn on my magic and witnessed by all gathered at this table," With those final words, I could feel the power emanating from him, a true testament to his sincerity. As he stood, the others around the table followed suit, chanting "on your word we bear witness." The air seemed charged with energy as they all bore witness to his oath, and I was left speechless in awe of the solemnity and weight of the moment.

The atmosphere in the room shifted as Ogma's words hung in the air, heavy with tension and uncertainty. "Shit, things just got real," I thought to myself.

I could see the determination in Ogma's eyes as he spoke, his silver scales glistening in the dim light of the conference room. Despite his fearsome appearance, there was a gentleness to his tone as he offered to protect Alisha . I couldn't help but feel a sense of relief knowing that the children would have someone looking out for them.

Turning to Mini, I saw her expression soften as she listened carefully to Ogma's proposal. She nodded her understanding and turned back to me with a look that said she was ready for whatever was to come. My heart swelled with pride at her bravery.

"Mini, if you have nothing left to report, please accompany Ogma to Alisha and explain that he will be staying with her for a while," I said, trying not to let my voice falter. "Make sure they get along."

As Mini led Ogma out of the room, she shot me a pointed look that told me I would pay for putting her on babysitting duty. But I knew deep down that she was the best person for this job - responsible, level-headed, and fiercely loyal. And with her by their side, I had no doubt that Alisha and Ogma would form an unbreakable bond.

I moved on and asked Keith if he had anything from a forensic standpoint that might help us. He explained at length that he could back everything we had already come to. He would get his team on the recovered information from the warehouse and let me know if they came up with more intel about who might be pulling the strings. The rest of the meeting went on in the same way. The shifter knew something was happening but didn't care as it didn't affect them and refused to get involved, but the mages surprised most. Keith had reached out again asking for any information they might have on wendigo They haven't offered full cooperation. but they have supplied us with information on how we might be able to subdue a wendigo. So, I asked Keith to follow up on that project and gather the equipment and weapons we would need to take the beast down. He rushed out of the office with a gleam in his eyes at the thought of the fight to come.

I was left alone in the conference room, save for my two new companions who seemed intent to stay glued to my side. I wanted to ask for their honest opinions on everything, but before I could speak, the boss of the London office strode in. His presence filled the room, and I found myself drawn to his deep blue eyes that seemed to hold a world of mystery within them. It was like staring into an endless abyss, waiting for something - anything - to stir before becoming completely entranced and lost forever. I shook my head, mentally slapping myself out of it as he approached me with purpose. "Sir, I wasn't expecting you to stop by. How can I help you?" I asked, hoping he was just making a routine visit. He stood there, surveying the room with a calm demeanour, taking note of the monitors and surveillance footage displayed on the walls. Picking up one of the files on the table, he began to leaf through it before fixing his intense gaze solely on me. "I heard your team's briefing and have been receiving updates at regular intervals," he said coolly, as if we were having a chat over drinks. "What are your next steps going to be?"

A sharp jolt of shock ran through my body as I processed the words he had just spoken. With a deep breath, I made the decision to be open and honest, hoping that maybe he could offer some much-needed guidance. "This case is becoming more twisted with every turn," I began, my voice laced with frustration. "We still haven't identified the mastermind behind it all. Gruesome murders, children being subjected to unimaginable experiments using the blood and tissue of deceased paranormals... And then there's the state-of-the-art facility fully equipped with an army of trigger-happy mercenaries guarding it." My mind raced as I weighed our options. "Do we raid the building and rescue the kids? Or do we hold back and gather more intel on the mastermind so we can take them down and shut down the entire operation? Who would have the resources to pull off something like this, and why? What am I missing here, and what should we do?" As I spoke, my own voice sounded pitiful to my ears, betraying the overwhelming feeling of helplessness I was experiencing.

With a gentle yet firm tone, the boss addressed Jessica, "You have many questions and more paths in front of you than even I can see. What I think you should do is irrelevant. This is your case. It is your decision, and I will back your choice." His voice was steady and reassuring, but there was a hint of concern behind his words. "However, at this point, you need rest and sleep. I know that isn't what you want to hear, but with rest comes clarity and whatever road you choose to take, you will need to be at a hundred per cent." He gestured towards the door, indicating for her to leave. "So go back to the dorms and get some rest. I will tell the rest of the team to do the same. You are off the clock until tomorrow morning. At this time, I expect to see you in my office with a plan of action for your next steps in this case."

As the boss finished speaking, his heavy footsteps echoed through the empty hallway as he made his exit. I was left sitting with Abigail and gudmundur, my mind reeling from his words. The weight of my decision hung heavy on my shoulders as I knew it could determine the outcome of their current case.

The dimly lit hallway seemed to stretch on endlessly as we sat in silence, mulling over the boss's orders. But I couldn't sit still any longer. My blood boiled at the thought of innocent children being experimented on while we were told to do nothing. I motioned for Abigail and gudmundur to follow me.

We walked through the quiet halls, our footsteps barely making a sound. When we reached the main hall, I dismissed them with a plan to reconvene tomorrow morning at eight o'clock. We needed time to strategise before meeting with the boss again. With that, I walked away towards the lift, longing for a hot shower and possibly some wine waiting for me in my assigned dorm room.

But as I headed towards the lift, I noticed Abigail following close behind me. Raising an eyebrow, I turned to her questioningly. She just shrugged and said, "I'm not letting you out of my sight. Gudmundur is going to try and extract more information from Ogma while also informing the dragon council about what we have uncovered. He'll be at the agency bright and early tomorrow morning. Hopefully, his findings will affect your decision."

I rolled my eyes and shot a sarcastic question at her, "So, are you going to be my personal bodyguard for the evening?" She let out a hearty laugh in response, her voice light and carefree. "I think I should be the one with a bodyguard to protect me from you," she teased, "but how about we just watch each other's backs while we rest up in your dorm?" Annoyed by her playful banter, I let out an exasperated sigh. "Fine," I conceded, "let's get going." We made our way to the elevator and rode up to my dorm, anticipation building for the evening ahead.

CHAPTER 19

A s I stepped into my assigned dorm room, I quickly shut the door behind me and let out a long exhale, attempting to release the tension that had been building up throughout the day. The walls felt like they were closing in on me, suffocating me with their drab beige paint that seemed to suck all the energy out of the room. "Abigail," I said, trying to keep my voice steady as I turned to face her. "I can call Kieth and arrange for a room to be made available for you." My hand instinctively reached into my pocket for my phone, desperate for any distraction from the claustrophobic atmosphere. As I itched to dial his number, I could practically feel the hot shower waiting for me, ready to wash away the knots of stress in my muscles. Hopefully Keith wouldn't take too long to respond so I could finally relax and regain some sense of calm amidst the chaos of college life.

"No," she said cheerily, her voice ringing out through the small space. "I think I will be quite comfortable in here with you."

Of course she would be comfortable in here with me, I thought bitterly. "Fine, suit yourself," I replied, gesturing towards the cramped seating area in the corner. "Make yourself at home."

Ignoring her presence for a moment, I hurriedly grabbed towels and clothes before disappearing into the small bathroom attached to our room. The scent of bleach clung to everything in there, but at least it was a clean and sterile smell. I rested my forehead against the cool tile wall, feeling its smooth and polished surface against my skin as I took deep breaths to calm myself down. I started the shower, letting the water warm up as I quickly undressed. Stepping under the stream, I hoped that the pressure of the water against my skin would help to soothe my racing mind. But even with the comforting heat of the water, it was hard to keep track of all the conflicting thoughts and emotions swirling inside of me. At least it was helping to release some of the tension in my muscles, as I let out a long groan and arched my back. With each passing minute, I could feel the hot water working its magic on my body, slowly loosening my knotted muscles and allowing me to relax.

Reluctantly pulling myself away from the soothing warmth of the shower, I grabbed a fluffy towel and vigorously dried myself. As I dressed in my comfiest sweatpants and a loose t-shirt, my mind raced with thoughts of what my next course of action would be. Stepping out into the dimly lit bedroom, I found Abigail already perched on the bed, her long legs crossed and her nose buried in her phone. "Did you happen to find anything edible in the kitchen?" I asked hopefully, knowing that Abigail was always prepared for any situation.

To my surprise, my little vampire shadow just smiled mischievously and held up a bottle of red wine and two glasses. "Well, damn, you work fast," I chuckled. "Did you happen to magic up some food too, or are you just trying to get me drunk?" My stomach grumbled at the thought of a delicious meal paired with a glass of wine. The room was filled with warm golden light from the bedside lamp, casting dancing shadows on the walls. I couldn't help but feel grateful for this moment of calm amidst all the chaos and uncertainty in our lives.

"I've taken the liberty of ordering a pizza for you. It should be here shortly, but in the meantime, let's enjoy a glass of wine and get to know each other better," Abigail said with a warm smile, handing me a glass.

My mind raced through my options, wondering if I could use this opportunity to gather more information from her. Ultimately, I decided to take a chance and see what she would reveal.

"Thank you, Abigail. That's incredibly thoughtful of you," I replied graciously, settling onto the bed and savouring the taste of the wine as she sat down next to me. "So, tell me about yourself. What do you enjoy doing in your free time?" I asked, genuinely curious as I leaned back against the pillows with a small smile on my lips. Her response would determine whether or not I could trust her and rely on her help in my current situation.

Abigail took a sip of her wine before answering. "Well, as you know, I'm a vampire. I've been alive for a long time I was born around 500 bc but it's hard to really give you an exact year now," she said with a wistful look in her eyes. "I was turned when I was just 19 years old, and life was very different then."

As she spoke, I couldn't help but marvel at the fact that she had been alive for so long. It was hard to imagine what kind of experiences and changes she must have witnessed over the centuries.

Abigail's voice was filled with a sense of wonder and curiosity as she spoke. "These days, I spend most of my free time learning about and adapting to the modern world," she said, her eyes shining with fascination. It was clear that she was enthralled by the changes that had taken place since her human days.

I sat mesmerised as Abigail shared snippets from her past- tales of adventure and bravery, but also ones of heartache and pain. Despite her immortality, she had lived through so many significant moments in history and had countless stories to tell.

Abigail's eyes were alight with curiosity as she finished another of her thrilling tales and turned to me, asking the inevitable question. "What's your story?"

I hesitated, unsure if I wanted to relive my past in this moment. But then I remembered how Abigail had saved my life and felt compelled to share with her.

"I grew up in a small town in the scenic south east of England, not too far from where we find ourselves now," I began with a chuckle, trying to ease some of the tension building inside me. "But my childhood was cut short when my mother passed away before the abduction and everything that transpired in Ireland. And my father..." My voice faltered for a moment as I remembered his fate. "Well, I'm sure you know what happened to him." I took a deep breath, trying to steady myself. "I was just a young girl then, and even now, after all that has happened, I still feel inexperienced and naive about the world.

But thanks to the help and support I received after being rescued along with Lyn, I haven't been completely alone in figuring out this new reality." A weight lifted off my shoulders as I shared my story with Abigail, grateful for her understanding presence.

Abigail's voice was filled with sympathy as she spoke, her eyes showing genuine concern. "That still must have been a tough ordeal for you," she said gently.

I gave a small shrug in response. "It was challenging, but it also taught me to be strong and independent," I replied, my tone matter-of-fact.

She nodded, looking at me with admiration. "You truly are an impressive young woman," she said sincerely. "And I'm sure your parents would be proud of you."

A bittersweet smile crossed my face. "I'm not too sure about that yet," I admitted with a sigh. "But hopefully someday, I'll live up to their expectations and make them proud."

Abigail's expression softened with understanding before quickly changing the subject. We both knew that some things were still too painful to dwell on for too long.

A sharp knock echoed through the empty room, jolting me out of my thoughts. My stomach grumbled in anticipation as I realised that the food had finally arrived. It was perfect timing, just when I needed something to break the heavy silence that hung between Abigail and I. Her stories from a lifetime of adventures still swirled in my mind, leaving me awestruck. How could she have experienced so much, yet still be here by my side, following my lead? The weight of her experiences threatened to overwhelm me, but I pushed those thoughts aside and focused on the enticing smell of the food wafting through the air. It was a welcome distraction from the overwhelming emotions swirling inside me.

As I opened the door, a delivery guy stood on my doorstep, holding a large stack of boxes filled with irresistible food. The smell of freshly baked garlic bread, topped with melted cheese and spicy sausage from the pizza, along with a side of crispy wings, had my stomach growling in anticipation. I eagerly thanked the delivery guy and handed him a generous tip of £20. It was my usual practice to tip well, in hopes that the delivery guys would remember me and prioritise my orders in the future.

With the delicious aroma swirling around me, I made my way into the lounge and set the boxes down on the coffee table before eagerly digging in. Just as I reached for my wineglass, I noticed that Abigail had already taken care of it and topped it up for me. Perhaps keeping her around wouldn't be such a bad idea after all, if she could continue to keep my glass full.

Shifting gears, I decided to change the subject back to something more relevant to our present situation. Turning to Abigail, I asked, "Please enlighten me about your sudden interest in me during this little slumber party." She returned my gaze with a knowing look, as if what she was about to reveal would shake the very foundation of our world. With an air of mystery, she said, "Perhaps I simply enjoy your company. You are an amusing person to be around and I haven't had this much fun in years."

Shocked by her cryptic response, I raised an eyebrow and asked, "Really? Is that how you're going to play your hand?" I could feel my frustration building, but I tried to keep a cool demeanour. "Fine, be elusive if that's what you want. But once all this is over, I expect some straight answers from you and that giant lizard." With that said, I eagerly dove into the food in front of me, unable to ignore my hunger any longer. The aromas tantalised my nostrils and my stomach growled in anticipation. Settling into a plush cuddle chair, I watched as she lounged on the opposite sofa. I took a sip of wine and savoured the smoothness of it on my tongue. "Well," I said, breaking the silence between us. "If you aren't willing to tell me why you're so interested in me, perhaps you can share your honest thoughts on the case."

As we discussed earlier, the discovery of the warehouse has provided us with crucial data that will undoubtedly aid in your investigation. However, a lingering unease plagues me over the reluctance of the shifter community to assist us. In this world of supernatural beings, information spreads rapidly and their hesitancy raises red flags. Despite the extensive reach of the agency across all factions, as well as Gudmundur's and my personal involvement in this case , they seem unwilling to offer their aid. My suspicion is that whoever is pulling the strings has either coerced or bribed them into silence. While it is not uncommon for packs to take on mercenary work, I highly doubt they would willingly participate in something as sinister as this job appears to be. I think you may want to ask any of the agency shifters to look at the local packs and try to find out what they know"

The tension in the air was palpable as we discussed the possibility of shifter involvement in the case. I couldn't help but feel disappointed and concerned that they were refusing to help, despite their own kind being among the missing. Perhaps they were conducting their own investigations discreetly, or maybe the cases were unrelated and they simply had their hands full. The cheerful demeanour of the little vampire beside me had faded, replaced with a furrowed brow and deep in thought.

In between bites of pizza, I pondered over the situation while Abigail and I sat in silence. As time passed and the food disappeared, our expressions grew increasingly troubled. Abruptly, Abigail broke the silence with a serious tone in her voice. She needed to make some phone calls to verify her suspicions and send a monitoring unit to the warehouse immediately. She urged me to get some rest, promising to fill me in on any new information when I woke up.

Feeling drained and exhausted, I made my way to bed at her swift dismissal. As soon as my head hit the pillow, I succumbed to sleep without a second thought.

CHAPTER 20

A SHARP, RAISED VOICE jolted me awake from my deep slumber. It took me a moment to gather my bearings and realise it was Abigail and Gudmundur engaged in a heated argument with a third voice I couldn't quite place. From the muffled sounds coming from the outer corridor, it was clear that tensions were running high but there seemed to be no immediate threat of violence. With a sense of dread settling in my stomach, I made my way to the en-suite bathroom, shedding my clothes as I went. The hot water cascading down my body helped to ease some of the tension and grogginess from my mind, preparing me for the inevitable chaos that would come crashing down on me today. After mustering as much mental fortitude as I could, I dressed myself in tactical gear - steel-toed boots, lightweight combat pants, an under-armour shirt, and a loose-fit hoodie. To the untrained eye, it may have appeared to be casual attire, but those who knew me understood the true purpose and functionality of each piece of clothing. As I strapped on various weapons and tools, I mentally prepared myself for what would undoubtedly be a long and arduous day ahead. Still lacking a proper dose of caffeine, I stepped out of my dorm room to find the three voices that had awoken me now calmly sipping coffee in the outer hall.

"Why am I being woken up at this ungodly hour by a stranger outside my dorm room, shouting and drinking coffee?" My voice was sharp and unfriendly, causing the stranger and gudmundur to turn towards me, their mouths agape. The stranger's eyes widened in surprise and confusion, while gudmundur's face paled as he realised the consequences of his actions. Abigail, ever the calm one, simply leaned against the wall and spoke in her smooth purr, "I'll get you a coffee and dragon boy will introduce your guest. Please don't injure them." As we made our way back into the dorm, I grumbled to myself about morning people before turning to Abigail and demanding, "I'll take it black with two brown sugars! Now, would either of you care to explain what's going on?" My glare shifted between the two men, but gudmundur was the one to speak first. "My apologies for disturbing you, but this is an envoy from the united packs of London. They have come to seek your help in finding a missing child from one of their prominent pack families. It appears that they believe this case may be connected to your current investigation."

Rage and exasperation boiled in my veins as I recounted the infuriating situation. "After begging for their help in a case where a child has witnessed the slaughter of her entire family, they turn a deaf ear. But suddenly, because some well-connected individual's child goes missing, they feel entitled to barge into my investigation and demand involvement? What is it that you're not telling me?" My voice was sharp and accusatory, fuelled by equal parts disbelief and resentment. "Shifter children are known to disappear frequently, losing themselves in the primal ecstasy of their beast form and losing all sense of time. Is that what this is about? A shifter's selfish desires taking precedence over innocent lives?" My words dripped with scorn and contempt, highlighting my disdain for those who would prioritise their own pleasure over the safety of others.

The man, Milo, cleared his throat nervously before introducing himself. "Allow me to formally introduce myself. My name is Milo and I am deeply sorry for the interruption, but I believe we are both looking for the missing child." His eyes flicked towards the door as if checking for any signs of danger.

"We received a message, a warning really, from the perpetrators themselves. They threatened to harm the boy if anyone dared to interfere with their plans. Our people have been disappearing without a trace and we fear this is just the beginning," he continued, his voice trembling slightly.

"I am here representing the United Packs, though my involvement must remain confidential. I am essentially a lone wolf, unaffiliated with any specific pack, so my actions cannot be used against them. And for all appearances, I work for gudmundur," Milo explained.

I nodded in understanding. "That all seems logical enough. So what information do you have for us? if the packs being coerced into staying away from this investigation?" i asked, hoping to gather any valuable insights or leads.

He slides a thick file over to me

As I sift through the evidence and reports, a sinking realisation hits me - our list of abducted shifters is just the tip of the iceberg. These individuals are not discriminating in their targets; they are taking anyone they can get their hands on, regardless of age or species. It's not just the paranormal community that's at risk; it's everyone. as I let this information sink in milo began tell us what he knew "My investigations have led me to discover that the wear-house your team bravely infiltrated is only one of five total sites controlled by these nefarious figures. While two of the locations appear to be research facilities with no captives, the other two are sinister testing grounds where unspeakable experiments take place. And as for tracing who owns these buildings... it seems they have been purchased under multiple layers of shell and dummy corporations, making it nearly impossible to track down the true masterminds behind this vile operation.

I lock eyes with him, searching for any hint of deceit, but all I find is sincerity. "I am grateful for the assistance you are offering. Has Gudmundur informed you about the current situation and the girl Alisha?" I don't wait for an answer before continuing. "She is currently under the protection of both our agency and a dragon."

He nods, confirming that he has been briefed. Abigail arrives with my coffee, its aroma enveloping me in a warm embrace. I motion for everyone to take a seat. "So Milo, how do you think the silvers fit into this? All we know is that Alisa has been infused with foreign tissue, altering her in ways we still don't fully comprehend. We don't have a clear timeline or method for the procedure, and our lab technicians are still combing through evidence. It seems unlikely that we will get any significant leads from them anytime soon." The others nod in agreement.

"While conducting your own independent investigations, have you come across any mention of a wendigo being involved?" My gaze lingers on Milo's face, hoping to catch any sign of recognition or knowledge.

Milo's jaw clenched and his features hardened into a grim expression as he spoke. The words seemed to stick in his throat, a bitter taste lingering on his tongue."I'm afraid they resorted to unspeakable methods, torturing at least one of the subjects and forcing them to consume raw human flesh." He shuddered at the memory, his eyes haunted by what he had witnessed. "But it's not just about creating more individuals like yourself. They have grander plans - they're trying to build their own army of monsters!" The weight of his words hung heavy in the air, suffocating us with a sense of impending doom. The thought of these experiments not only being cruel but also posing a threat to the world at large was almost too much to bear. But Milo's determination burned bright in his eyes. "I will do whatever it takes to assist you," he vowed, "but as I said before, the united packs cannot publicly get involved." A fire ignited within him as he promised to help us put an end to this madness before it consumed everything in its path.

My jaw hung open as I listened to Milo's speech, my mind reeling with the horrific truth he had just revealed. This was beyond anything I could have imagined, and I knew I had to act fast. These despicable individuals needed to be stopped, no matter the cost. The first step was clear - shut down their facilities and uncover the mastermind behind it all. It had to be someone with immense power, wealth, and influence. Gathering my resolve, I vowed to make my way to the boss's office and rally our team for what was sure to be a long and tumultuous day ahead. A sense of unease settled in my stomach, foretelling the inevitable bloodshed that lay ahead. But I couldn't let fear hold me back - justice had to be served, no matter what sacrifices were necessary.

CHAPTER 21

MY PALMS WERE slick with nervous sweat as I stood before the boss of the London branch, briefing him on our findings. Every word that left my mouth felt like a weight, each one carrying the potential to either impress or disappoint him. After I outlined what we had discovered and presented my plan for synchronised raids on all the confirmed locations, he took a long moment to consider my proposal. His eyes studied me carefully, searching for any trace of hesitation or doubt in my expression.

"I agree with your assessment," he finally spoke, his voice low and commanding. "And I think a synchronised assault is the way forward. With all the information you have gathered, I can confidently conclude that someone with high connections is behind this. We need to move quickly and hit these targets today before they have a chance to destroy evidence or flee." His words sent a chill down my spine, knowing that we were dealing with powerful and influential individuals.

"Before you go and start your preparations," he continued, "I would like you to wait here while I confirm something." I nodded, feeling relieved that he was taking my plan seriously. As he left the room, my mind raced with anticipation and nerves for what was to come. This was a critical moment in our investigation, and the success or failure of our operations relied heavily on this meeting with the boss.

Despite the urgency of the situation, I found myself alone in his office for what felt like an eternity. The ticking of the clock on the wall seemed to mock me, each second passing by with agonising slowness. My impatience grew with each passing minute, feeling like valuable time was slipping away. I desperately wanted to be doing something productive, whether it be planning, strategising, or even kicking down doors. Anything would have been better than sitting here like a scolded school kid. Unable to sit still any longer, I began to pace around the room, trying to release some of my nervous energy through movement.

As Aldrich returned, a tall, dark stranger materialised at his side. My jaw dropped in awe as the man stood at least seven feet tall, with skin the colour of smooth milk chocolate. His eyes gleamed like silver in the sunlight, drawing me in with their piercing gaze. Long dreadlocks cascaded down his back, adding to his already striking appearance. He was dressed in a sleek silver-grey suit that hugged every contour of his muscular frame. It was clear that this man didn't rely on the gym for his impressive physique - every movement exuded an aura of strength and control. His body spoke of years spent honing it for survival, like a seasoned martial artist or soldier. Our eyes met for a brief moment and he flashed me a knowing smirk before sauntering over to the boss's sofa, where he reclined as if he owned the place. Confidence radiated off of him, making it seem like he didn't have a care in the world.

The sudden, stern voice of Aldrich practically screamed, jolting me out of my daydreams about the strikingly beautiful man in front of me. "Jess," he said sharply, "I would like to introduce you to Enlil, a representative of the watcher's council. They have expressed concerns about your recent findings, and Lord Enlil has offered to be our point of contact with the council."

As I tried to compose myself and pay attention to the conversation at hand, I couldn't help but feel intimidated by the imposing figure of Lord Enlil. His piercing gaze seemed to see right through me, and his presence exuded power and authority.

"Don't worry yourself over my presence, child," he spoke in a calm yet commanding tone. "I will only interfere as a last resort. There are many reasons for my visit, and while your case may have played a small part in it, it is not my main focus."

Despite his reassuring words, I couldn't shake off the feeling that he was closely watching every move we made. But I had no time to dwell on it as Aldrich continued to explain our situation to Lord Enlil. With a curt nod, the lord spoke again, "I am confident that you will handle this case successfully, and I look forward to hearing more updates as it progresses." His words held both a sense of assurance and an underlying warning, leaving me wondering what exactly brought him here and what other motives he may have.

As I struggled to make sense of his sudden presence, I turned my attention to Aldrich, doing my best to ignore the shock that Enlil's appearance had brought. "Aldrich," I said, my voice trembling slightly, "if there is nothing else pressing, I would like to gather the team and begin executing our plan to shut down these facilities and uncover the truth behind what's happening here."

A chill ran down my spine as I met Aldrich's steely gaze. His demeanour was cool and collected, but the subtle tension in his jaw betrayed his emotions. "That is an acceptable plan," he stated, his words laced with authority. "However, I expect to be kept in constant communication. In fact, I will establish a backup command centre within these walls to monitor all communications." My heart pounded in my chest as I realised the gravity of the situation. Enlil's presence here meant that our mission was more dire than I had initially thought. We needed to act quickly and efficiently to resolve this case before it caused any more harm. My mind raced with potential scenarios and outcomes as I prepared to brief the team for this crucial operation. Every minute counted now, and the weight of responsibility pressed heavily on my shoulders as we embarked on this dangerous mission.

With my heart pounding in my chest, I quickly made my way out of the Aldrich's office, the weight of our mission heavy on my shoulders. As I turned the corner and reached the conference room, I could hear the muffled sounds of intense discussion from within. With a forceful push, I swung open the door, causing it to creak loudly as it hit the wall. The atmosphere inside was charged with tension, and every member of our team was fully engaged in the task at hand. Gudmundur and Abigail stood at the head of the table, their voices low yet urgent as they shared new information. The once quiet and organised room was now a frenzy of activity as we raced against time to develop a plan that would ensure our success during the upcoming operation.

CHAPTER 22

A s I made my way to the conference room, a sense of unease settled in my stomach. The sudden appearance of Enlil and the mysterious interest of the watcher's council had me on edge. Perhaps I should have reached out to Alex for guidance, but there was no time for that now. My focus needed to be on completing this mission successfully. Afterward, I could seek answers and shed light on the strange occurrences. Stepping into the conference room, I was met with a larger group than I had anticipated. The air was thick with tension and anticipation as we prepared to embark on our dangerous journey. Hopefully, by day's end, we would have more information to work with and bring us closer to our ultimate goal.

As I stepped into the room, every head turned towards me, their eyes filled with a mix of curiosity and tension. The large monitor on the back wall displayed a live video feed from the office I had just left. Enlil, with his impeccable posture and intense gaze, sat confidently in front of the camera while Aldrich, fidgeting restlessly in his chair, refused to meet his eyes. My arrival seemed to bring an uneasy weight into the air, suffocating it like thick molasses. With a polite clearing of my throat, I made my way to the head of the table and settled into my seat, acutely aware of all eyes still fixed on me. The atmosphere was charged with unspoken tension and anticipation.

My presence was known to some, but unknown to others. As

the leader of this mission, it was my duty to inform everyone about the purpose of our gathering. "I have been tasked with setting up 5 raids on facilities that are responsible for heinous crimes - kidnapping, murder, and experimentation on innocent people," I explained to my team as we gathered around the table, maps and schematics spread out in front of us.

"As for introductions, Keith, I believe you are familiar with everyone here. Would you kindly introduce each member for those who may not know?"

Keith's voice boomed with confidence and authority as he addressed the team. "Sure, it would be my pleasure," he said, a warm smile spreading across his face. "Allow me to introduce everyone. First up is Mini," Keith continued, his tone shifting slightly as he introduced the each member. "she is an emphatic healer and water mage, she has proven to be an invaluable asset to our team." A young woman with bright blue eyes and a gentle aura stepped forward, nodding in greeting to the rest of the group.

"As for gudmundur and Abigail," Keith said, motioning towards two imposing figures standing at attention. "They are enforcers for the dragon and vampire councils respectively. They also serve as representatives for their respective councils in matters such as these." The air around them seemed to crackle with power as they acknowledged their role.

"Milo, a shifter affiliated with Gudmundur," Keith continued, his gaze sweeping over the group. "And then there's Osaki," he said, inclining his head towards a striking figure with six tails fanning out behind her. "A six-tailed kitsune and leader of one of our strike teams from the London office." Beside her stood Danielle, another formidable leader from the same office.

"And last but certainly not least," Keith finished, turning towards himself with a grin. "I am a mage myself. While my specialty lies in defensive magic, I do have some offensive spells in my repertoire when needed." The team nodded in understanding, each member radiating strength and determination in their own unique way.

"Thank you, Kieth," I said gratefully, giving him a small nod. "I truly appreciate the introductions, but there are two important details that were missed. First and foremost, I want to make it clear that I am the girl who was experimented on by Jeremiah. We believe that the facilities we will be raiding are conducting similar experiments, so if anyone has any reservations about this mission, please speak up now so we can arrange for suitable replacements."

As I looked around at my team, their eyes met mine with a mixture of amusement and challenge. It seemed like no one had any objections, which was a relief. "Good. So it seems we're all on board with this operation," I continued after a brief pause. "Now onto the second matter at hand - Danielle." I turned to Keith, directing my attention to him specifically. "You failed to mention what type of 'other' she is. Is she a vampire? A shifter? A mage? Or something else entirely? I mean no offence, but it's crucial information that we need in order to determine which facility your team will be assigned to."

Her piercing gaze swept over me with a calculated precision, like that of a hungry predator stalking its prey. Her breaths were shallow and controlled, revealing an unwavering sense of control. The stillness in the room was fleeting, broken only by the sound of her voice. "I am a descendant of Melusine, the mythical serpentine lady of French folklore," she declared, her words dripping with confidence. As I gave her a blank look, she elaborated, "Think of me as a shape-shifter, blessed with the ability to transform into a reptilian form." My mind raced at this revelation - the idea of someone apart from dragons possessing such abilities to ship into a reptile form had never crossed my mind before. But she wasn't done yet. "And to make things even more interesting," she continued, "I have a few additional abilities, much like our kistsune friend Osaki." My thoughts spun in disbelief as I tried to comprehend the full extent of her powers. This certainly added an unexpected twist to our meeting.

"Okay, thank you. That information will prove helpful." I said while considering which site will be best suited for her and her team.

Surveying the room, I carefully began to assign teams to their designated raid locations. "Osaki," I said, turning to the skilled kitsune, "your expertise in illusions and misdirection will come in handy for this mission. I would like you and your team to target the Millennium Mills, a derelict turn of the 20th-century flour mill located in West

Silvertown on the south side of the Royal Victoria Dock. It sits between the imposing Thames barrier and the ExCel London exhibition centre." My gaze flicked down to the information that Milo had gathered, showing that this location was primarily used for research purposes and unlikely to have any live test subjects. Instead, it was likely to be occupied by medical researchers and a few security personnel. Your skills will certainly come in handy here - we cannot afford to set off alarms or draw attention to ourselves."

"That should be a simple task," Her words were spoken with ease, infused with the natural mischief and illusions that seemed to come easily to her kind. The glint in her eye caught my attention, a playful spark that hinted at a mischievous nature lurking beneath her calm exterior. Despite the seriousness of our mission, I found myself captivated by her unique energy and curious about her mysterious kind. As we continued planning, I made a mental note to spend more time getting to know her once our mission was complete. But for now, we had to remain focused on avoiding unwanted attention from the public and utilising our unusual abilities to take our enemies by surprise.

Nestled beneath the towering Battersea power station lies a covert research facility. Our intel suggests that it is primarily occupied by medical researchers, making this infiltration operation all the more intricate and challenging. The once industrial building has now been transformed into a bustling hub of luxury retail and housing, teeming with unsuspecting bystanders. Our knowledge of the facility is limited, and we only know the location of the main entrance.

"Do I have any volunteers to take this site?"

Danielle's confident voice cut through the tense silence, "I will take on this site." Her confident tone and determined stance showed that she had a plan in mind. Her eyes sparkled with hint of excitement. With her unique skills and abilities, I was sure Danielle could gain access to the site without using the main entrance and avoiding detection. once inside I will be able to take care of the security measures in place and shut down all communications to prevent any alarms from being triggered when my team breach the main entrance and we secure the site.

I couldn't believe she was so eager to take on the task. In surprise,

I simply nodded in response. "Do you feel confident that your team will be able to handle it, or do you need any additional support?" I asked. She paused for a moment, considering her answer carefully before responding confidently, "No, I think we have everything under control." Her determination showed in the set of her jaw and the spark in her eyes, giving me confidence in her abilities.

The next site is a testing ground at Abbey Mills Pumping Station. As they approached, the abandoned building loomed in front of them, imposing and foreboding. Its walls were covered in layers of graffiti, each marking a different passing era. The windows were cracked and shattered, allowing glimpses of the dark interior. But looks can be deceiving. According to their intel, the inside had been retrofitted with cells and medical exam rooms, all equipped with high-tech equipment fit for a top-secret experiment. This wouldn't be an easy mission, we all knew it. "Milo," I said with a serious tone, "this one's yours." I knew that not being a member of the agency Milo didn't have a team to support him, but i also felt that he was more than capable of handling the task of leading a new group without issue. "We'll pull members from other units to support you" i continued, my mind already think of the most suitable person for putting together for a working strike team suitable for this dangerous undertaking.

"Keith," I said. "I want you to take charge of the Springfields asylum location. Kieth, I will also need you to work closely with Milo on assembling a strong and capable team for him while you set up your own infiltration squad. Can you both rise to this challenge and complete these crucial tasks for me?" I said my piercing gaze swept across them, making sure they where fully aware of their responsibilities. The weight of the mission hung heavy in the air, but Keith and Milo were determined to succeed. They exchanged nods of determination before turning back to face me, ready to accept the daunting task ahead.

"Okay, so that leaves me with the abandoned surveils psych hospital, Mini said hesitantly, turning to her companions. "I would appreciate some backup on this, especially from you, Mini."

"Not a problem," Mini replied confidently. "I was kinda hoping you would assign me to this one. I might be able to find something there to help the victims." Her determination shone through in her voice.

"Gudmundur Abigail," I said turning to the two remaining members. "Should I assume that you will be sticking with me, or would you like to lend your strength to one of the other teams?"

"Abigail and I will stay with you," Gudmundur responded without hesitation. "and if it's alright with you, I would like Alisha to stay with Ogma during these strikes." he then paused for a moment before addressing the image of Aldrich on the screen. "I have also directed a team of dragon breed and elves to set up a facility outside London for these victims. They will receive all necessary treatment and care there."

Aldrich's eyebrows furrowed in confusion his image learning at us from the wall monitor as Gudmundur's words hung in the air. The tense silence in the room was almost tangible, everyone on edge as they awaited an answer. Aldrich turned his gaze towards me and then back to Gudmundur, his expression stern.

"And who exactly gave the order for this arrangement?" he asked sharply.

Gudmundur stood his ground, unflinching under Aldrich's scrutiny. "I made a brief report to my Queen last night, and this morning I received word that preparations have already begun. I can stop them if you prefer to make other arrangements."

Aldrich's jaw tightened before he let out a heavy sigh. "No, that won't be necessary. Please pass along my thanks to your Queen for her cooperation." The tension seemed to ease slightly as Aldrich spoke, but it was clear that there were still underlying concerns about these sudden preparations.

A slight tremor of fear crept into the Aldrich's usually confident voice, sending a shiver down my spine. But his expression was in stark contrast to the Cheshire-cat grins on Enlil and Abigail's faces. What had I missed? I made a mental note to find out later.

I checked my watch; it read 10 am. The clock was ticking, time slipping away with each passing minute. We needed to move quickly if we were going to pull this off. "Okay, listen up," I commanded. "We launch at dusk. That gives us roughly ten hours to get everything ready.

Will everyone have their teams assembled, recon done on designated sites, and be prepared for combat by then?"

Each member of the team gave me a resounding "yes" along with a determined nod. They scattered, each one focused on their tasks at hand, preparing for what was to come at dusk. The air was charged with anticipation and nerves as we all worked towards our common goal.

As the heavy door clicked shut, my heart began to race. The pressure of gudmundur's intense gaze, combined with the presence of Abigail and Mini, made me feel small and vulnerable. Even the monitor showing Aldriches office had shut down, adding to the sense of isolation. I slumped back in my chair and started to rub my temples, trying to ease the tension building inside me.

"Jess, hun, I can feel your emotions...they're all over the place," Mini said gently, her tone filled with concern. "What's going on? Talk to us."

I took a deep breath, struggling to find the words to express my unease. "Something feels off. I can't put my finger on it, but something about this whole situation just doesn't sit right with me."

Mini nodded understandingly, while gudmundur and Abigail exchanged worried glances. Then, an idea struck me.

"Gudmundur, Abigail...can we use your people for our infiltration team? I don't know any of the London teams and I would feel more comfortable if at least someone on our team was familiar with the people watching our backs."

There was a moment of tense silence as they processed my request. Finally, gudmundur nodded in agreement and promised to arrange for some of his best operatives to meet us at the dragon's keep. A surge of relief washed over me - at least now I knew we had some trustworthy allies on our side.

MY HEART RACED, pounding against my chest, as I watched five teams emerge from the shadows. Each member was adorned with a myriad of weapons, strapped to their bodies like a deadly armour. They moved with precision and grace, their steps in perfect synchrony like a well-oiled machine. Despite my initial thoughts that they resembled Rambo wannabes, I couldn't deny the aura of professionalism and danger that radiated from each of them. And then my eyes widened in amazement when I noticed something even more extraordinary - each team had one member in their warrior state, a magnificent blend of dragon and human with shimmering scales covering their bodies. The overall group became even more formidable with these fierce creatures among them. As they drew near, my muscles tensed and anticipation filled the air. A tall man with a scar running down his face stepped forward, the leader of the group. With a firm stance and unwavering gaze, he addressed Gudmundur with respect and authority. "Sir, as requested, I have organised the troops." His words were confident and his posture unbreakable, showcasing the strength and determination of this elite team.

Gudmundur's voice was rough and commanding, as he spoke to me from beside me. He had six units of highly trained individuals ready to infiltrate and shut down the psych hospital facility. Each team had a specific side assigned to them, with one unit designated as backup in case of any emergencies. A medical team was also on standby, prepared to assist Mini once we secured the area. I couldn't help but feel both nervous and reassured by the presence of such a skilled and well-prepared team. It was clear that this mission was not going to be an easy one.

"Wow" I was impressed. He had got this together a lot quicker than I had thought possible.

"I want it understood that this is my operation, and if any of your people have a problem with what I am, I don't want them coming along. The stakes are high, and we all need to be working from the same page. Do I make myself clear?"

Without missing a beat, gudmundur turned to his people. "Well, you heard the lady. If you have a problem with whom or what she is, let it be known now, and we can get someone to replace you for this operation?" After a few moments of silence, he continued, "We

have a lot depending on us doing our job right. We know that the location is going to be heavily defended. Our objectives are as follows: 1) subdue all hostile forces with minimal collateral damage, 2) retrieve those being held captive and administer any care required, and 3) ensure they don't get a chance to wipe any of their systems or hard copies of any files. We need to get to the root of what they are doing, why they are doing it, and who is pulling the strings.

The soldiers all stood at attention, rigid and focused as they answered in unison, "SIR, YES, SIR."

"Excellent. Now each of you has been assigned a specific task for this mission. But before we begin, I must warn you all that there may be a windigo present. So remain vigilant and prepared at all times." Gudmundur, Abigail Mini, and I exited the back area of the dragon's keep and navigated our way to the dining hall. As we walked, I couldn't help but feel a sense of anticipation building within me. This was it - the moment we had been working toward.

A colourful array of food and a large, steaming pot of coffee sat at the centre of our table. The smell of freshly brewed coffee filled the air, mixed with the aroma of sizzling bacon and eggs. Mini surveyed the spread, her eyes widening in anticipation as she poured herself a cup and turned to me. "What's bothering you?" she asked in that no-nonsense tone of hers. "I can sense it in your emotions and it's ruining my coffee." Mini had always been an empath, able to pick up on other people's feelings and moods, making her an invaluable member of our team. But sometimes her abilities could be a pain, like now when I couldn't hide anything from her. I could try to lie and blame my erratic emotions on the mission, but I knew she wouldn't buy it. She knew me too well.

I turned to face the three of them, my tone serious and urgent. "Something doesn't add up here. The Watcher's Council is suddenly taking an active interest in our affairs, something that rarely happens. And with all the major players involved, it's baffling that I am still allowed to lead this operation. Then there's Aldrich's reaction when you mentioned your Queen and the elves setting up a recovery site. I need answers. Can any of you shed some light on what's really going on?" My heart raced as I awaited their response, my mind racing with possibilities and suspicions. The air was thick with tension and uncertainty, like a storm brewing on the horizon. Every word spoken felt weighty and laden with hidden meanings. It was clear that there was much more at play than any of us realised, and I couldn't shake off the feeling of being caught in a tangled web of secrets and deceit.

Gudmundur was the first to respond, his voice carrying a note of surprise and intrigue. "The watchers involving themselves isn't as unheard of as you might think," he said, his gaze shifting towards the others in the room. "But I agree it is rare, and you're right," he nodded toward me. "With as many people taking an active interest, I would have thought Aldrich would have inserted himself more in the case." Gudmundur's brows furrowed in thought as he continued, "As for his reaction to my Queen and the elves...well, let's just say that Aldrich was involved in a very public scandal a few centuries ago." His tone hinted at a deeper story behind these words. "My Queen was the one who discovered it and bravely exposed it to the kingdom. Needless to say, Aldrich ended up very humiliated." A faint smirk tugged at Gudmundur's lips. "It has taken a few centuries for him to live down his shame." The weight of this revelation hung heavy in the air as everyone processed the implications of Aldrich's involvement in their current situation.

"Okay, that somewhat clarifies why he reacted that way. But it couldn't have been too severe if he's now in charge of one of the agency branches." I said, my brows furrowed in confusion.

"It wasn't necessarily a terrible offence, nor was it illegal. However, it went against societal norms and ultimately damaged his career. If he hadn't been caught, he could have held Alexander's position on the council and within the agency; losing that influence has haunted him ever since. Even the mere mention of the Queen is enough to ignite his anger." gudmundur explained with a resigned tone, their gaze distant as they reflected on this past indiscretion.

Impatiently, I leaned forward in my chair and reached across the table, unable to resist the rich aroma of coffee any longer. "Are you ever going to tell me who this elusive queen is, or is that another one of your dragon secrets?" I asked, frustrated by the constant veil of secrecy surrounding everything in this world.

The dragon across from me smirked, as if enjoying my frustration. "If my sources are correct, she will be at the recovery site when we arrive. You will have the pleasure of meeting her there."

I rolled my eyes, already dreading the encounter with yet another important figure in this society. It seemed like everyone I encountered was someone I needed to impress or please in some way. But I knew I couldn't back down now - too much was at stake.

As the concerns about Aldrich were pushed to the back of my mind, another worry began to nag at me. My thoughts turned to the upcoming raids and I couldn't shake the feeling that they would need more support than they believed. The weight of responsibility on my shoulders grew heavy as I considered the potential consequences. "Can you or Abigail arrange for non-agency affiliated backup teams to be present at the other raid sites?" I asked urgently. "But we must be discreet. No one can know that we have arranged this additional aid. If a mole were to discover our plans, it could have disastrous repercussions for all of us." The tension in the air was palpable as we discussed the delicate balance between preparedness and secrecy.

Abigail stood up from her seat with a determined expression. "I will take charge of arranging the backup teams. The dragons have already committed a significant amount of manpower to this operation, so it's time for me to put my resources to use. As you said, keeping the information about our backup discreet is crucial, so I propose that I handle all planning and coordination for this aspect of the operation. This way, if the backup teams are not needed, their presence will go unnoticed. And until the operation is complete, I suggest that I am the only one kept in the loop about our plans." Her voice was firm and confident, reflecting her years of experience and leadership within the vampires organisation.

I readily agreed to her request, but made sure to impress upon her the importance of her role in my team for the upcoming assault. After meticulously going over every last detail, both the formidable dragon and formidable vampire departed, leaving me alone with my thoughts and trusty companion, Mini.

I spoke softly, barely audible over the sound of our pounding hearts. "Do you truly believe this plan will succeed, Mini?" She didn't answer with words, but instead wrapped her arms tightly around me, pressing her cheek against mine. We sat there for what felt like hours, drawing on each other's warmth and resolve before finally separating to set our plans into motion.

CHAPTER 23

As our team approached the facility, we immediately noticed a surge of activity. The once quiet and unassuming location was now bustling with movement and energy. The security personnel had clearly increased since our last infiltration attempt, their tense postures and vigilant gazes signalling their readiness to defend their operation at all costs. We knew right away that our initial plan would not work - we needed to come up with a new strategy on the spot. As we watched files and equipment being hastily loaded into unmarked vans, the air was filled with frantic chatter from radios as our team communicated with other raid teams at different sites. However, despite our efforts, it seemed like their comms were dead and all I could do was hope that they were okay while we continued towards our objective. The tension in the air was palpable as we pressed forward, unsure of what obstacles may lie ahead but determined to complete our mission.

With beads of sweat forming on our brows, we made a split-second decision and charged towards the building, our hearts hammering in our chests. There was no time for proper planning as we sprinted towards the compound, determined to stop their operation before it could spread to another site.

As we neared the entrance, we divided into teams. One group quickly set up a blockade to prevent any vehicles from escaping, while others positioned themselves at the sides and back of the building, ready to capture anyone who tried to flee. It was a risky move, but it was now or never if we wanted to put an end to this dangerous operation.

With a tap on Gudmundur's shoulder, I motioned towards the truck convoy ahead. "We need to create a diversion," I whispered, "draw their attention while Abigail and I sneak in." Gudmundur's eyes gleamed with excitement as he nodded, his focus already on the targets ahead.

"Make it big and showy," I added with a grin, "we want all eyes on you."

Abigail chimed in, her voice calm and clear. "And don't forget to secure any evidence from those vehicles. But remember, saving innocent lives is our top priority. We can't risk losing anyone for the sake of evidence."

As we crept closer towards the building, Abigail and I quickly made a plan while keeping our comm channels open. "If you need backup, just request it," I reminded everyone. "We can't afford to lose anyone trying to play the hero."

Gudmundur's smirk grew wider, transforming his face into a terrifying mask of determination. His muscles bulged as he expanded in size before charging towards the trucks at full force, like a war god on a mission. The sound of metal screeching and glass shattering filled the air as he plowed through them, drawing the attention of the guards who scrambled to contain the chaos. My stomach churned with anxiety as I glanced nervously at Abigail, who stood beside me with a mischievous glint in her eyes. The air was heavy and still, almost suffocating us with its tension. The only sounds were our heavy breaths and the soft crunch of gravel underfoot as we waited for Gudmundur's plan to come to fruition. Suddenly, a deafening explosion erupted in the distance, shaking the ground beneath us and sending my heart racing even faster. "I'm not sure if this is a good idea," I stammered, my words drowned out by the roar of the blast. But Abigail just smirked, her eyes glittering with mischief and hidden laughter. "Well, you did tell him to get their attention," she teased, barely able to contain her amusement. And indeed, Gudmundur had certainly achieved that goal as the night sky lit up with flickers of orange and red from another explosion that rocked the area. Adrenaline pumped through our veins as we stood there, triumphantly watching our plan unfold - but deep down, I couldn't help but wonder if this was truly a wise decision

With bated breath, we counted down 30 seconds before launching ourselves to the front of the heavily guarded facility. Abigail moved with swift precision, taking down the few remaining guards as if they were mere obstacles in her way. With adrenaline pumping through our veins, we finally breached the doors and dove for cover, ready for any resistance that may come our way. But to our surprise, the scene inside was chaotic and frenzied, guards scrambling in all directions as if their plans had been foiled. We cautiously scanned the area, making sure it was clear before cautiously agreeing to split up and search for our objective. The air was thick with tension and a sense of danger loomed over us as we worked together to reach our goal.

As I cautiously explored the building, I took note of every detail. The rooms were in disarray, as if they had been ransacked by a whirlwind. The cots that once held patients now stood empty and bare, leaving behind only traces of struggle and chaos. Furniture lay overturned, and dark stains littered the floor and walls - remnants of blood. My senses were on high alert as I moved through the eerie halls, my body tense with fear. As I opened myself up to the environment, I could taste the lingering tang of fear and desperation, mixed with the coppery iron scent of blood that had long since dried. But there was something else too - a fresher scent that made my stomach twist with unease. It was a mixture of primal instincts - hunger, desire, pain, and pleasure. This place was not just an abandoned asylum; it held secrets and horrors that took my mind back to the day's I was imprisoned and used by Jeremiah.

As I walked, a heavy feeling settled in my chest. The energy surrounding me felt dark and twisted, like a malevolent force calling out to me. Despite the unease it caused, I couldn't help but feel drawn towards it like a moth to a flame.

I followed the pull of the wrongness, navigating through the dimly lit corridors until I reached a rusted door that led down into the depths of the facility. Every instinct told me it was a bad idea, but something deep inside urged me on.

Determined to uncover the source of this dark energy, I clicked on my comms unit to get Abigail's attention.

"Abby, do you copy?" I spoke into the device, my voice trembling with uncertainty.

"What's going on, Jess? Are you okay, do you need backup?" came Abby's worried response.

"Not yet, but I'm heading down to a lower level. The energy down here feels all wrong. If you don't hear from me in the next ten minutes, please come looking for me and bring backup if possible." My words were rushed and urgent as I prepared to make my descent into the unknown darkness below.

I paused, waiting with bated breath for Abby's response. "Abby, what's wrong? Do you need backup?" I asked urgently. "Is there a problem at your end?"

She hesitated before answering, her voice strained and slightly muffled through the static of our radio communication. "No, Jess, it's fine," she finally replied. "But I might have some logistical issues if you need backup. I've come across a group of survivors and they're not in great shape. I'll try to get them out and then come back to assist you. Just please, please be safe out there."

Her concern for my safety was palpable, even through the crackling of the radio. I could almost feel her worry seeping through the airwaves as I carefully planned my next move. The eerie silence surrounded me, broken only by the faint sounds of distant screams and gunshots. My heart raced as I prepared myself for whatever dangers lay ahead, determined to make it out alive no matter what.

"Okay, get them out safely and maintain radio contact".

Taking a deep, steadying breath, I begin my descent down the spiral staircase. With each step, a sense of foreboding washes over me, like an invisible force is pulling me further into this mysterious place. The stairs creak and groan beneath my weight, adding to the eerie atmosphere.

After what feels like an eternity, I reach the bottom of the staircase and enter a vast, open area. In its past life as an asylum, this must have served as a storage room. But now, it exudes an aura of darkness and malevolence. My heart races as I take in the unsettling scene before me.

Chained to the walls are grotesque creatures that resemble half-human, half-beasts - wendigos. Their eyes gleam with hunger and malice, their distorted forms contorting in agony or perhaps pleasure at my presence. Tears blur my vision and trail down my cheeks as I struggle to comprehend the horror unfolding before me. How could such monstrous beings exist in our world? And why were they here? Questions swirl in my mind as fear grips me tightly and threatens to consume me whole.

I had been told about them, warned even. But no amount of preparation could have truly readied me for the sight before me. Six pairs of glowing eyes fixed on me, their owners hunched over and feasting on the scattered bodies surrounding them. Each creature was a monstrous amalgamation of yellow claws, dripping fangs, and desiccated flesh pulled tautly over their bones. Their stomachs were distended from the carnage they had wrought.

The stench of blood and saliva filled the air, mingling with the metallic tang of death. It was a scene straight out of my worst nightmares, one that I never could have imagined in all its horrifying detail. Some of the bodies were clearly lifeless, while others still writhed in a futile attempt to escape their gruesome fate. Limbs were missing, others gravely injured, and some lay still with an expression of abject terror etched onto their lifeless faces.

Every instinct in my body screamed at me to run, to flee this nightmarish scene. But I was frozen in place, unable to tear my eyes away from the six creatures that continued to feast upon the living and dead alike. In that moment, I knew that nothing could have prepared me for this terrifying encounter.

"Abigail? gudmundur? Can either of you hear me?" I spoke into my comms set the deafening silence of my comms set was all I heard in reply to my desperate calls for backup. "Abigail? Gudmundur?" I tried again, my voice shaky with fear and desperation. But there was only eerie static in response. With a sinking feeling in my gut, I realised I was on my own.

Faced with the terrifying Wendigo and the helpless survivors depending on me, I quickly weighed my options. Could I take down the monster and then call for help? Or should I abandon them and run for help, hoping to return in time to make a difference? Or, perhaps, I could stay and hold off the creature until reinforcements arrived. But how long would that take?

As if in answer to my thoughts, the sound of laughter and heavy footsteps echoed through the storage hall. My choice was made for me - I would have to protect these survivors with everything I had. Raising my voice as loud and commanding as possible,

My voice rang out, loud and commanding, as I yelled to the group: "All survivors, gather around me! We must band together to defend ourselves!"

I could see the surprise and fear on some of the saviours' faces, but they quickly gathered their strength and began limping and crawling towards me. The chains that bound them were tight and constricting, causing them to struggle even more as they moved away from the approaching enemy. Looking closer, I noticed that the chains were also pulling the wendigos towards the walls, dragging them further away from their intended prey. The whole scene was chaotic and frenzied, with cries of pain and terror filling the air.

A low, menacing voice slithered from the darkness on the other side of the hall, sending shivers down my spine. "So you made it all the way down here, little girl," it hissed. I couldn't place the voice, but its familiarity only added to my unease.

The voice, dripping with a hint of malevolence, continued its taunting. It slithered through the air like a serpent, each word laced with twisted glee. The owner of that voice was clearly revealing in my predicament.

"Can you believe it?" it cackled, drawing closer and closer. "Jeremiah captured and the great Alexander taking you in like a lost little kitten." Its mocking tone seemed to echo off the walls, filling the dimly lit room with a sinister energy.

I searched for the source of the voice, my heart pounding in my chest. As it drew nearer, I could feel its presence looming over me like a dark cloud. "All this work to prepare and set up these experiments," it sneered. "But any progress we may lose will be worth it when we have you under our control."

A chill ran down my spine as I realised just how devoted this individual was to their cause. They saw me as nothing more than a means to an end, a tool to achieve their twisted goals. "You are my golden ticket," they whispered, their eyes gleaming with madness. "My key to success. The organisation will reward me generously and I will be set for life."

A sickening feeling settled in my stomach as I listened to their delusions of grandeur. "And when we finally make our move," they hissed, their voice growing louder and more fervent with each word, "no one will be able to stand in our way. No longer will we hide in the shadows, for we shall rule over the humans as is our right. And the paranormal community will kneel before us and treat us like gods." My mind reeled at the thought of such power-hungry individuals gaining control over innocent lives.

It was clear that this person was truly committed to their twisted beliefs and would stop at nothing to achieve their goals. And as I cowered in fear, I knew that I was just a pawn in their deadly game of power and control.

The voice that echoed through the empty alley was filled with venom and arrogance. The speaker, whoever this idiot was, seemed to have a few screws loose in their head. "Look," i sneered, "I don't care about your master plan. But if you think your life will change just because of some title or position, you are massively mistaken. Power and status aren't something that can be given; you have to earn them. And people like you, with zero backbone, will never earn it. You'll always be an errand boy, a pawn in someone else's game. Always following orders, because you don't have the brains or courage to think for yourself. Now show yourself." The air was thick with tension and disdain as the challenge hung in the air, daring the unknown figure to reveal themselves.

"You stupid bitch I will show you that you're nothing" The words where spat out of his mouth like venom, each one laced with hatred and malice. i recoiled at the sickening sound of his voice. "I'll show you just how worthless you are, a mere failed experiment," he sneered. i tried to back away but found myself surrounded by the saviours, their shadowy figures huddled behind Me Like prey just waiting to be devoured

As the dim light revealed a figure surrounded by armed guards and other prisoners, my heart dropped. It was someone I trusted, a fellow ally in this dangerous mission. "No, it can't be...you were supposed to be on our side," I whispered, feeling betrayal and disappointment wash over me. My entire world seemed to crumble as I realised that everything we had fought for may have been pointless.

CHAPTER 24

ALDRICH EMERGED FROM the shadows, his features twisted into a malicious smile. With a gun trained on me, he stepped forward confidently. "Alexander and that dragon queen bitch never expected this," he chuckled, his voice dripping with malice and superiority. The glint of the barrel caught in the dim light, reflecting off his twisted smile. My heart raced as I braced for whatever he was about to do next.

"But I left you at the office with Enlil," I exclaimed, my voice shaking with confusion and fear. How was he standing before me now? "How did you get here?" My mind raced, trying to make sense of the impossible scenario.

"I had my extraction team take down that blowhard after you and your friends left," he replied nonchalantly, as if discussing the weather. "He didn't stand a chance. By the time he wakes up, all this will be over and you'll be back in one of our labs." His eyes gleamed with a sinister glint. "We're curious about what makes you so different from the rest, and we won't let you escape again."

A heavy silence settled between us as his words sank in, causing a chill to run down my spine. The distant sounds of battle echoed through the air above, a constant reminder of the danger surrounding us. In this moment, the possibility of being saved seemed like a distant hope, unless some unforeseen change occurred. I could sense Aldrich's flawless plan looming over us, casting a foreboding aura of tension and imminent peril. It felt as though one wrong move could trigger a deadly outcome for us both.

Aldrich's hand trembled with anticipation as he tightly gripped the trigger. The deafening silence that followed was only broken by a sharp sting on my neck, where I quickly pulled away a small tranquilliser dart. It was clear that Aldrich was not leaving anything to chance in his desperate attempt to maintain control over the situation. His presence alone seemed to weigh heavily upon the air, and I could feel his power emanating from him as he towered over me, gun still pointed in my direction. The tension in the atmosphere was palpable, and I could sense the danger lurking behind Aldrich's cold, calculating eyes.

"Son of a bitch, what did you just shoot me with" I said as

My eyesight blurred and my body went numb as I stumbled forward, the tranquilliser dart taking effect. My once steady grip on my firearm slipped away, rendering it useless against Aldrich's approaching men. With a desperate reach, I fumbled for my karambit knives, their curved blades glinting in the dim light. I knew Aldrich was too much of a coward to get his own hands dirty, but I refused to go down without a fight. As they closed in, I could feel the adrenaline surging through my veins, giving me the strength to face them head on. Today, they would have to earn their paycheque with every drop of blood I shed, for I was determined to go down fighting with every last breath in me.

The guard's heavy metal-studded boots pounded against the cold, concrete floor as he charged towards me, his eyes narrowed in determination. My head throbbed and my vision swam as I struggled to stand my ground against him. The bitter aftertaste of the drug they had injected me with lingered on my tongue, numbing my senses and slowing my reflexes. But I refused to let it weaken me. With a quick sidestep and a precise slash of my blade, I evaded his grasp and drew first blood. A surge of adrenaline coursed through me, briefly sharpening my focus before it was smothered by the effects of the drug. Taking a moment to catch my breath, I surveyed the chamber and noticed more guards entering, their malicious gazes fixed upon me as they followed Aldrich's orders to capture me alive and leave the prisoners they had dragged in for the ravenous Wendigo to deal with. Panic rose within me as I realised I was outnumbered and outmatched. My mind raced as I searched for a way out, knowing that every second counted before more reinforcements arrived. Suddenly, a heavy iron door slammed shut behind them, trapping us all inside together. The air grew thick with tension as we all prepared for the inevitable battle that lay ahead.

The mere thought of losing consciousness and waking up bound and trapped again sent a surge of fear and rage coursing through my veins. I could feel my blood boiling, pulsating with a frenzied energy. My skin seemed to hum with electricity, as if it were a conductor for some unseen force. Arcs of crackling energy crawled over my body, shooting out sparks between different parts of my form. My nails lengthened and sharpened like talons, while my teeth tingled as they transformed into sharp fangs. All of this was happening while I was already in a state of sheer panic and terror, which only fuelled the raw power surging around me. The guards who had just moments ago been ordered to capture me now stared at me with a mixture of awe and fear. Some even seemed on the brink of wetting themselves in their terror.

The intensity of this sensation is indescribable. It's like staring straight at an oncoming tornado, the swirling winds and ominous clouds threatening to consume everything in their path. And yet, there's a rush of exhilaration and pure joy, like the feeling of kissing your first love and finally understanding what it means to be truly complete. The adrenaline coursing through my veins merges with a sense of contentment and fulfilment, creating a whirlwind of emotions that leaves me both breathless and alive.

Without warning, a guard aimed an MP5 in my direction and fired off a burst of bullets. The deafening sound echoed through the room as I stumbled backwards, my body absorbing the impact of each shot. My legs gave out from under me and I collapsed to the ground, gasping for air.

Aldrich's voice cut through the chaos. "What do you think you're doing?" he bellowed. "We need her alive!" Panic flooded through me as I realised the gravity of the situation. This organisation would stop at nothing to keep me contained.

Aldrich barked orders, his tone cold and demanding. "Go over there," he commanded, pointing to a prone figure on the ground.

"Check her vitals and restrain her, even if she appears deceased. We cannot risk losing her." As the guard approached, I couldn't help but think, what an arrogant jerk. He can't even bring himself to check if I'm alive. But then again, why am I still breathing? I didn't have time to dwell on the miraculous fact that I survived a barrage of mp5 ammo. My priority was stopping Aldrich, getting the victims to safety, and ensuring the safety of my team members.

As one of Aldrich's guards leaned over me, his breath warm and moist against my skin, I could feel the beat of his pulse racing under my fingertips. Without hesitation, I slid the sharp edge of my blade across his throat, watching as a gush of blood spilled out onto the ground. As he fell to the side, I sprang to my feet with fluid grace, ready to face whatever came next.

My eyes scanned the rest of the guards surrounding me, their weapons raised and their faces twisted with anger and fear. But I felt no fear. Only an intense determination to stop this madness before any more innocent lives were lost.

With every movement, I could feel the anger burning within me, pushing me forward with an unbreakable focus. the combat training with Hiyori and Hargreaves flooded my mind, guiding my muscles and joints in a perfect rhythm. I moved like a well-oiled machine, precisely striking down each guard that dared to come near.

Using my opponent's momentum against them, I quickly disarmed and incapacitated them, leaving only a few unlucky ones who wouldn't survive to answer any questions about Aldrich's plans. But in that moment, I didn't care about justice or answers. All that mattered was stopping Aldrich from causing any more destruction and chaos.

The once powerful guards, now either laying lifeless on the ground or writhing in pain, were unable to come to Aldrich's aid. Fear crept into his eyes and I could taste its bitterness on my tongue. A small smile tugged at the corners of my lips as I relished in seeing him so vulnerable.

"So, Aldrich, you want me to meet with this organisation?" I asked, my voice cold and detached. My words sliced through the air like a knife, sending a shiver down Aldrich's spine. "Perhaps you can start by telling me where I can find them. We can all have a nice little chat."

I paused, studying his fearful expression for a moment before adding, "And who knows, maybe you'll get a reduced sentence if your information is valuable enough." My tone was full of mocking sarcasm as I toyed with the idea of using Aldrich's fear to my advantage.

The venom in his voice dripped like acid, spewing hatred and defiance. "You ignorant bitch, do you honestly believe I will go with you willingly? You are nothing but a powerless pawn in this game, and even if you somehow managed to overpower me, I am far too deeply entrenched in my connections to ever be left rotting in Tuataras." A cruel smirk twisted his lips as he continued, "No, I think I will have some entertainment at your expense. Let's see how you compare to my pets. These wendigo were once innocent test subjects, but now they serve as my loyal clean-up crew; glorified garbage disposals for when we no longer have use for our experiments. We simply drop them down here and listen to the screams of their victims." The air around them seemed to grow colder as he enjoyed the terror he instilled in his captive audience.

With a dramatic wave of his arm, Aldrich commanded the chains holding six monstrous creatures to the wall to release, sending them crashing to the floor with a resounding clatter. As they shook off their restraints and lunged towards me, I could see the fire in their eyes and hear the primal growls rumbling deep within their massive chests. My instinct was to follow Aldrich as he made a break for the door, but I knew I had a duty to protect the innocent victims trapped in this room with us. With bared teeth and brawn rippling under their thick, matted fur, the beasts closed in on me and I braced myself for the impending battle.

In a voice that reverberated with authority, I bellowed commands to victims huddled together behind me, "If any of these creatures manage to slip past me, I need you to defend those around you. Reinforcements are on their way, but we must hold our ground until they arrive."

Despite the lingering effects of the tranquilliser coursing through my body, I focused all my energy on the massive beasts charging towards me. With no time for defensive strategies, I abandoned all pretences and launched myself into an aggressive attack. My target: the vulnerable knee joints and ankle tendons. If I could immobilise them, my chances of survival would greatly increase.

I landed several powerful strikes, causing one of the beasts to howl in pain as it crumpled to the ground. Adrenaline coursed through me as I continued to battle against the odds, determined to protect those who stood behind me. The smell of sweat and fear filled the air as we fought for our lives against these relentless creatures.

The other wendigo, having learned from their previous mistake, were now waiting just out of reach. They expertly dodged my attacks, forcing me to hold back my rage and frustration. The Wendigo's hunger was palpable, almost suffocating in its intensity. And the fear radiating from their helpless victims only added fuel to the fire.

But I had been trained for situations like this. Hargreaves had drilled into me the importance of being on a protection detail – always knowing where the next victim would be. But this time, it seemed like there were too many to protect. So instead, I focused on keeping up my own attacks.

"Someone check if the door behind us is open and start evacuating the others," I shouted over the chaos, hoping someone would listen and follow my instructions.

But before I could finish speaking, two of the wendigo took advantage of my divided attention and launched an attack towards me.

With a surge of energy, I Channeled power into my blades, amplifying the force of my attack. The first attacker's head was cleaved from its body, a startling result that briefly jolted me out of focus. But the second attacker wasted no time and landed a blow to my abdomen, sending waves of piercing agony through my body. I quickly refocused and blocked its other arm before it could break my neck. Using its own momentum against it, I pivoted on my right foot and twisted its arm behind its back until I heard the sickening pop of the shoulder dislocating. The beast let out a howl of pain, and for a moment, I couldn't help but feel a pang of sadness at the thought that these creatures were once innocent victims. But there was no time for remorse as I continued my attack, bringing the creature to its knees. With all the strength I could muster, I thrust my blade into the base of its skull, ending its misery once and for all. The sound of its final breaths left a heaviness in my heart, but I knew it had been necessary to protect myself and others from their destructive nature.

As I pulled the wendigo's limp body off my bloodied blade, the stench of death and decay filled my nostrils. The scene before me was chaotic and gruesome - two lifeless bodies laid in pools of blood, one survivor groaning in pain, and three remaining targets snarling and frothing at the mouth with wild, primal hunger. My heart raced as I knew I had to act quickly before they turned their focus on me.

But just as I prepared to strike, a timid voice called out from behind me. "The door won't budge and it looks too heavy to break," the voice quivered with fear and desperation. A sense of urgency washed over me as I realised we were trapped in this confined space with no escape. The sob that escaped the woman's lips only added to the tension and uncertainty of our situation. It was now a race against time as I tried to come up with a plan to survive this relentless attack from the ferocious wendigo.

My heart pounded in my chest as I scanned the surroundings, looking for any sign of our pursuers. "Shit," I muttered under my breath, "well, I'll just have to hold out until they find us then." My voice sounded stronger than I felt, but I pulled more power into myself, feeding off the swirling emotions of rage, anger, and fear that surrounded me. Alex had mentioned before that if I could tap into the dragon part of my powers, there would be no limit to what I could do with the energy around me. With a deep inhale, I focused on channeling that power.My body crackled with electricity once again, the energy coursing through me like a raging river. I could feel its power emanating from my core and radiating outwards, filling the air around me.

Focusing my mind, I commanded the energy to form a protective shield around those behind me. It took shape slowly, imperfect but solid enough to withstand an initial attack. With this barrier in place, I could concentrate on the three enemies before me without worrying about those behind me.

But I knew that this shield wouldn't hold forever. It was just a temporary defence against our attackers, one that required all of my concentration and strength to maintain. Still, I held on tightly to the hope that we would be rescued soon and survive this dangerous ordeal.

With the shield firmly in place, I shifted my focus back to the wendigo. Feeling like a caged animal pushed into a corner, I reached deep inside myself and unlocked the pandora's box of my emotions. With each passing moment, my restraints and shackles fell away as I let go of all the pain and sorrow that weighed on my heart. The anger, sadness, and grief from losing my mother, the guilt over my father's death, and the haunting memories of what was done to me in those caves - I channeled it all into a concentrated wave of power.

But this time, I was more in control. I could feel the strength coursing through me, sharpening my senses and awakening muscles that yearned to be used. Despite the intensity of my emotions, I felt light as a feather and invincible. The wendigo continued their relentless assault, pouncing and lunging at me with ferocity. But with ease and grace, I dodged their attacks, revealing in the thrill of battle.

As I fought without restraint, it dawned on me why paranormals were often arrogant - with this much power at their disposal, no one could stand in their way. A sense of cockiness washed over me as I relished in my newfound abilities. But my momentary lapse in focus allowed the wendigo to herd me towards the opposite end of the room, away from those who relied on me for protection. In a corner now, I had to find a way out before it was too late.

My blades sliced and cut through the air, glinting like two steel serpents with hungry mouths. No matter how much damage I seemed to inflict on them, the wendigo just kept coming. But in the heat of battle, all that mattered was my anger and my survival. I saw nothing but their faces contorted in rage; felt nothing but the adrenaline pumping through my veins and the ferocity of my attacks. The stench of warm blood and sweat filled my nostrils, masking any other scents in the air.

The wendigo wouldn't relent, their twisted forms encircling me with a predatory grace. As if responding to some unspoken command, the fourth one, whom I had injured earlier, rejoined the attack. With chilling coordination, they moved as one, their movements precise and fluid as we danced through the chaotic battleground. Despite my best efforts, their numbers and strategic manoeuvres began to take their toll, each strike testing my endurance and will to survive. Hemmed in on all sides, every blow landed with sickening force, leaving me drenched in blood and struggling to stay standing. My once strong arms now felt numb and useless, unable to raise in defence. But still, I fought on, determined to defy the odds and overcome this relentless onslaught of creatures from nightmare.

My body was a canvas of slashes and stab wounds, painting a story of the brutal attack I had endured. The jagged lines stood out in stark contrast against my pale skin, a cruel reminder of my defeat. In the eyes of my attackers, I could see the triumphant glint of victory. They knew they had won, and I was helpless to stop it. My legs gave out from under me as I dropped to my knees, the weight of my injuries finally catching up to me. With every breath, the pain screamed through my body, but I couldn't find the strength to fight back anymore. It was over. As I began to lose consciousness, a loud BOOM echoed through the air. A burst of light and heat engulfed us, signalling some sort of explosion. Maybe, just maybe, there was a chance that the captives would survive this ordeal. But my Wendigo attacker remained unfazed, still focused on delivering the final blow. And as darkness crept in at the edges of my vision, I welcomed it with open arms, ready to escape the horrors of this world for just a little while longer.

CHAPTER 25

As I slowly regained consciousness, my mind was foggy and disoriented. The first thing I noticed was the unfamiliar bed beneath me, its sheets crisp and cool against my skin. Something sharp and foreign was sticking in my arm, and the unmistakable chemical scent of a hospital filled my nostrils.

My ears were assaulted by the incessant beeping of machinery, and in the distance, I could hear the faint sound of a heated discussion. Slowly, I opened my eyes to find myself in a sterile room, white walls and bright lights blinding me momentarily. Tubes and wires were connected to my body, an IV drip inserted into my arm and monitoring equipment taped all over me.

To top it off, I had an oxygen mask covering my face, making it difficult to speak or even breathe properly. my cheeks flushed with embarrassment as i realised i must have been in worse shape than i thought.

i tried to piece together what had happened and how i ended up in this medical centre. But for now, all i could focus on was the discomfort of being hooked up to so many machines, longing for a sense of normalcy once again.

Defeated and exhausted, I couldn't bear the thought of laying in bed any longer without answers. With a deep breath, I pushed back the heavy blanket that covered my battered body. Surprisingly, I found myself clad in a fresh set of matching bra and panties. A small part of me hoped it wasn't Abigail who had dressed me, imagining her teasing me about it later. As I stood up, I couldn't help but wince at the sight of my reflection - 70% of my body was now adorned with shades of yellow, green, and purple bruising. It would take some time to heal, but I knew it wouldn't kill me. As I examined myself further, I noticed deep lacerations crisscrossing my thighs, chest, and stomach. The thought of counting them made my stomach churn. Steeling myself for the challenge ahead, I swung my legs over the edge of the bed and forced myself to stand. It was time to see if I was strong enough to face the outside world with my wounds still raw and exposed

With trepidation, I gingerly placed my feet onto the cool ground, mindful of any sudden movements that could send me toppling over. After a few tense seconds, I straightened my posture, relieved to find that my body could support itself without collapsing. Taking a deep breath, I peeled off the monitoring tabs that had been tracking my heart rate and blood pressure - all those pointless readings that seemed to dictate my life in this hospital. But just as I thought I was in the clear, chaos erupted around me. Alarms blared and doors flew open as a horde of medical staff rushed into the room, no doubt summoned by the sudden burst of activity on their screens. Startled and disoriented, I instinctively stepped back, only to have my legs give out from under me. As I gazed up at the sea of doctors and nurses hovering above me, their worried faces illuminated by the flashing red lights, I couldn't help but feel like a helpless child once again. Among the concerned voices were those of my closest friends - Lyn, Alexander, Gudmundur, and Abigail - who must have also been summoned by the commotion. Once they realised I was alright, the medical team quickly dispersed, leaving us in an uneasy silence.

Lyn knelt down, her graceful movements like that of a swan gliding on water, and gently lifted me up from the cold, hard floor. She cradled me in her arms as if I were a precious, delicate flower that she was afraid would wilt at any moment. For a few moments, we stayed like that in silence, her warmth and love surrounding me like a protective shield. Eventually, she carefully placed me back onto the soft mattress and pulled the warm blanket up to my chin to shield me from the chill in the air. Her voice, usually gentle and soothing, now held a firmness that sent shivers down my spine.

"My little dragon," she said with a stern tone that betrayed her anger, "would you care to explain how you ended up in this bed?" Out of the corner of my eye, I could see Abigail and gudmundur shifting uncomfortably, clearly feeling guilty for whatever role they played in my injuries.

Collapsing into a chair with a leaden heart, I knew that reliving this nightmare would be excruciating. The horrors of the sub-level replayed in my mind like a never-ending horror film as I recounted them to Gudmundur, Abbey, Alex, and Lyn. Their faces mirrored mine, twisted in shock and disbelief at the unimaginable atrocities we had witnessed. Gudmundur and Abbey filled in the horrifying details that I had missed while fighting for survival against our merciless enemies. Gudmundur's harrowing tales of using magic-enhanced weapons and explosives to fend off wave after wave of attackers made my blood run cold, while Abigail's daring attempts to free trapped prisoners from the upper levels left us all breathless. But even as she fought for their freedom, the enemy closed in on her and Gudmundur like vultures, cutting off communication and trapping them in a deadly game of cat and mouse.

As the last glimmer of hope flickered and faded, we were suddenly rescued by a trio of powerful figures – Alexander, Lyn, and Enlil. Their arrival was like that of avenging angels, descending upon our enemies with terrifying ease and decimating them in a matter of moments. The only reason any of us were still alive was thanks to their swift and ruthless intervention.

Once the dust settled and the opposing forces had been cleared, they turned their attention to finding me. They soon picked up on the immense wave of energy I had sent out to shield the remaining survivors while I battled the wendigo. According to eyewitness accounts, Lyn was the first one to reach the sub level and she wasted no time in using her incredible strength to break down the door. Beyond that, details become hazy as I was unconscious on the floor with the wendigo looming over me. All I was told afterwards was that Lyn flew into a savage rage, unleashing her full power against the monstrous creature until it lay dead at her feet. No one would elaborate further, but I was assured that all of the wendigo were now nothing more than lifeless corpses scattered around us.

As the report echoed through my mind, I was struck with a wave of shock. I never realised how much Lyn cared for me, and I certainly didn't think I was on death's doorstep. "What happened with the other strike teams? Did our backup make it in time? Did we suffer any casualties?" My heart raced as I thought about the possibility that others may have lost their lives because of Aldrich's betrayal.

Suddenly, Alexander's reassuring hand landed on my leg, bringing me back to reality. "Relax," he said calmly, "the other sites were warned ahead of time and were more prepared than we expected. Your quick thinking and sending in backup teams saved us from experiencing any fatalities. Some members did get injured, but they will recover in due time."

He continued, "It seems that once Aldrich realised his plan was falling apart, he shifted his focus from hiding his involvement to trying to capture you. He must have hoped to use you as leverage or maybe even offer you up to his boss. That's what the evidence we have recovered suggests." As he spoke, a sense of dread washed over me at the thought of being used as a pawn in this dangerous game.

I nodded, taking in his explanation with a furrowed brow. "From what he was saying before he left me to die," I began, my voice low and grave, "the organisation that he is a part of was also linked to Jeremiah. And although he didn't come out and say it conclusively, he made it sound as though he, along with others, had been to the caves where Lyn and I were held captive. He claimed to have seen me there and even taken part in some of the brutal tests we were put through. But I can hardly recall anyone other than Jeremiah being present during those torturous moments." I paused, my mind racing with doubt and confusion. "Do you think he was telling me the truth? Or was he purposely trying to rattle me and throw me off course?" My fingers clenched into tight fists as I spoke, my suspicions growing stronger by the second.

Alex and Lyn exchanged a knowing glance, their eyes filled with worry and a hint of fear. "Based on what we've discovered today, it seems that there is something much more sinister at play than any of us had originally thought," Lyn began, her voice trembling slightly. "We will need to discuss this further at a later time, but for now, please be patient with us." Alex added in a firm yet reassuring tone. The weight of the situation hung heavy in the air as they both spoke. "We need you all to stay healthy and strong because I see a difficult and trying path ahead for us all." His words were met with silence, the gravity of their situation sinking in for everyone in the room. This was no longer just a simple mystery to solve, it was something much bigger and more dangerous than they could

My words came out in a nervous, jumbled rush. "Well, about that," I began, my voice trembling. "I made a promise to Gudumdur and Abigail to assist them with an urgent matter once this case was resolved. But with how things stand now, it doesn't seem possible. And by agreeing to help them, I may have unwittingly put myself under the authority of a Dagon queen whom I have yet to meet." The silence that followed was heavy and tense, as if waiting for a verdict. All I could think was shit, I'm in trouble.

Suddenly, the air was filled with the joyful sound of laughter, breaking through the heavy tension that had weighed on the group for days. It was a welcome relief, lifting their spirits and bringing a sense of lightheartedness into the room. Lyn sat down next to me, her smile infectious as she assured me that everything had been dealt with and there was nothing left for me to worry about. But despite her reassurance, I couldn't shake off the feeling of unease, knowing that even Aldrich was afraid of the dragon queen.

As I expressed my concerns, they all dissolved into another round of laughter. Tears streamed down Abigail's face from laughing so hard. Yet, in the midst of this merriment, I couldn't help but wonder if there was more to this situation than they were letting on. The uncertainty only added to my nerves.

As I stood my ground with a stubborn look on my face, it must have been obvious to Lyn that I was not backing down. She took a deep breath, trying to calm the tension between us. "My little dragon," she said softly, "you don't need to fear the dragon queen. She loves you. I can assure you of that." But despite her reassurances, I still didn't understand. So I blurted out, "Most dragons hate me. Why would she love me? Can someone please explain? My head is starting to ache from all this thinking." With a defeated sigh, I gave Lyn the saddest puppy dog eyes I could muster. She scooped me into a warm embrace and said, "I know she loves you because I am the dragon queen and I see you as though you're my own daughter." Her words melted away any remaining doubts in my mind. As much as I wanted to ask more questions, Lyn's voice was firm as she said, "Now no more questions. You need your rest." And with that, she gently guided me to lay down and close my eyes. As if on cue, my exhaustion caught up with me and I drifted off into a dreamless sleep, comforted by the steady rhythm of Lyn's heartbeat beneath my ear.

IN THE AFTERMATH of Aldrich's betrayal, the paranormal world was thrown into chaos. The council representatives were in an uproar, calling for investigations and demanding justice for the victims. Some parties urged for the immediate disposal of those affected, while others proposed to study them in hopes of understanding what had transpired. After heated debate, it was ultimately decided that the victims should not be held accountable for the actions taken against them. It was also agreed upon that the agency would take on the responsibility of training and rehabilitating the victims. This new reality came with its own set of challenges and uncertainties, but I found comfort knowing that Ogma would also play a role in this process. His presence reassured me amidst all the turmoil and uncertainty.

Finally, after what felt like an eternity of waiting for the green light from the onsite nurse, I was released from the tight grip of the medical unit. I stepped out into the crisp air, grateful for the fresh scent of freedom. As I strolled towards the hospital doors, my thoughts were interrupted by the low thrum of a powerful engine pulling up next to me. My eyes widened at the sight of an electric pink Shelby Mustang GT 500, its sleek curves and bold color demanding attention. The window rolled down and revealed a bright-faced vampire with a mischievous glint in her eye.

"Hello Jess," she chirped cheerfully. "What are you doing here?"

I fought to keep my voice and body language neutral as I replied, "Just getting some fresh air."

Intrigued by my curiosity, I leaned forward eagerly to peer inside the car. To my surprise, I caught a glimpse of a grumpy-looking Gudmundur sitting in the back seat. With a slight nod, I offered him a small greeting before turning back to the vampire driver and waiting anxiously for her response.

"Oh well, we were just out and about when we heard you were being discharged today. We thought we would come to pick you up and take you back to the dorms," she explained with a sly smile.

"That sounds good. I need to gather my things and arrange transport back home," I replied, relieved at the unexpected offer of help.

"What do you mean 'transport home'?" Abigail asked with a raised eyebrow.

"I mean going back to HQ. I have some more training to complete and then I'll receive orders for my next assignment," I clarified.

"You mean you won't be staying at the London office?" came Gudmundur's voice from the back seat.

"Well, as far as I'm aware, that's not the plan. Unless you two know something I don't," I said as I climbed into the car. Abigail let out a laugh, "We're far too insignificant to know anything like that. We just wanted to give a friend a ride." The interior of the car was luxurious, with plush leather seats and glossy mahogany panels lining the doors. The faint smell of vanilla and sandalwood lingered in the air, adding to the sense of luxury and mystery surrounding my unexpected chauffeur.

I simply shrugged at her, not falling for the same old tricks again. I knew that both she and her partner held high positions in their respective councils, and were also powerful enforcers. But if they didn't want to share their secrets with me, I wasn't going to push it. As we continued our drive, I closed my eyes and allowed myself to drift off into a light slumber.

The sound of their voices became distant as I dozed off, only barely registering their conversation in the background. Before I knew it, we had arrived at the agency's London office. I slowly opened my eyes and stretched my arms as best I could in the confined space of the car. My two shadows unbuckled their seat belts and followed suit, stepping out of the vehicle and joining me on the sidewalk.

"What are you up to?" I accused, eyeing Gudmundur suspiciously. "Don't try to play innocent with me."

"Well, as you pointed out, we do have official titles," Gudmundur retorted grumpily. "We're just here for a progress update on the state of various investigations. We have no nefarious intentions, I swear!"

"I find that hard to believe, dragon boy," I shot back. But if they were determined to come along, so be it. With a huff, I strode towards the building, the imposing figures of a dragon and vampire following close behind me. The sun beat down on us mercilessly, casting long shadows across the pavement as we approached the entrance. The glass doors gleamed in the sunlight, reflecting the towering buildings around us. My heart raced with anticipation and dread as we stepped inside, unsure of what awaited us within those walls.

As I made my way towards the front desk, I was immediately enveloped in a tight bear hug from Mini and Keith. They had been eagerly waiting to ambush me as soon as I walked into the building. Keith's booming voice filled the air, "Well, if it isn't our fearless saviour. Come on, Alex is waiting for all of us." With a smile, he led us down the hallway to what used to be Aldrich's office. However, it had undergone a complete transformation. The space was now filled with cozy sofas and armchairs, arranged around a large coffee table adorned with an assortment of snacks and laptops. It was clear that this room was now a comfortable gathering place for the team.

As I entered the office, Lyn and Alex stood before me, their faces beaming with genuine joy. They welcomed me with open arms and pulled me into a warm, affectionate hug. "We apologise for not coming to see you sooner, but with everything that has happened, we've been dealing with a lot of chaos," Lyn spoke softly, her words laced with genuine concern. "But please know that you have never been far from our thoughts." As she led me to a comfortable sofa, my heart swelled with gratitude and a tinge of fear. The warmth of their gestures showed how much they cared, but I couldn't help feeling apprehensive about what they were about to say.

Alexander's commanding presence filled the room, his deep voice cutting through the thick air like a knife. The tension and anticipation were palpable as he addressed the gathered group, his words weighty with importance. Every eye in the room was fixed upon him, hanging on every word he spoke. "Thank you all for being here," he began, sweeping his gaze over each person in the room. His eyes held a mix of gratitude and seriousness, conveying the gravity of the situation at hand. Lyn reached over and gave my hand a reassuring squeeze, her touch providing a sense of calm amidst the chaos of emotions swirling around us. As Alexander continued to speak, I couldn't help but feel grateful for her comforting presence by my side.

"Everyone in this room is aware of the investigation that has just set the entire paranormal community on edge. We have managed to keep panic to an absolute minimum. But the fact remains that someone has managed to make the head of the London facility betray his people, conduct forbidden experiments on both the human and paranormal communities, and risk the exposure of the secret existence of the paranormal communities to the world at large.

if we don't get to the bottom of it. we really could destroy the world as we know it.

As of now, I am taking full control of the London branch. Jessica, Mini, I am transferring the both of you to London as well. This is not a punishment, but rather a strategic move on my part. With all that's been happening, I feel more comfortable having you both by my side as we try to unravel the true scope of these events. And in addition, I would like to introduce you to two of the three new hires we have made for this branch. Allow me to present agents Abigail and Gudmundur. They have recently resigned from their positions on the paranormal councils and will now be working with us as both liaisons and active agents. Along with our third new member, they will form a team dedicated solely to uncovering the depths of this mystery and finding out who is responsible for setting it all in motion. Jessica, Mini, and Keith, you will also be assigned to this team" before we could raise any objections

Alex pushed the intercom button, beckoning Ogma to join them. "Please come in, we are ready for you now," he spoke into the speaker. A few minutes passed before the door opened and the two men entered the room. As they took their seats, I turned to Lyn with a confused expression. "Why is a police officer here for this discussion?" I asked her.

Lyn simply smiled knowingly and replied, "Be patient, everything will be explained."

I let out an exasperated sigh and took a seat, curious to see how things would unfold.

Standing to greet the new arrival, Alex addressed DCI Lancaster. "Welcome, Mr. Lancaster. Please come in and make yourself comfortable. I trust your tour with Ogma has been quite enlightening thus far?"

Lancaster nodded, his expression a mix of intrigue and disbelief. "It has certainly been...interesting. But I must admit, all of this information is overwhelming. And from what Ogma has told me normal people like me don't usually get to know about all of this so Why have you brought me here?" His gaze shifted between us as he awaited an answer.

Lancaster's sharp and perceptive observation skills did not go unnoticed by Alex, who leaned forward with a glint of interest in his eye. "You possess a rare talent for this line of work," Alex remarked in a low, confident tone. "I would like to extend an offer – join our agency and become a crucial member of Jessica's team. Together, we will comb through every clue and track down those responsible for the missing persons you have tirelessly searched for." He paused, keenly studying Lancaster's reaction. "Do you have what it takes to see this through to the very end, or will you simply walk away?" The weight of Alex's words hung heavy in the air, challenging Lancaster's dedication and determination to solve the case. I could almost feel the immense responsibility that came with accepting such a proposition. It was no surprise when Lancaster nodded in acceptance, officially joining my newly formed team.